D1291306

THE LETTER

by

Ed Munson

The contents of this work, including, but not limited to, the accuracy of events, people, and places depicted; opinions expressed; permission to use previously published materials included; and any advice given or actions advocated are solely the responsibility of the author, who assumes all liability for said work and indemnifies the publisher against any claims stemming from publication of the work.

All Rights Reserved
Copyright © 2021 by Ed Munson

No part of this book may be reproduced or transmitted, downloaded, distributed, reverse engineered, or stored in or introduced into any information storage and retrieval system, in any form or by any means, including photocopying and recording, whether electronic or mechanical, now known or hereinafter invented without permission in writing from the publisher.

Dorrance Publishing Co
585 Alpha Drive
Pittsburgh, PA 15238
Visit our website at www.dorrancebookstore.com

ISBN: 978-1-6376-4111-8
eISBN: 978-1-6376-4948-0

THE PLAYERS

Family and Friends

Bailey L. Stewart, *associate justice, US Supreme Court*
Zachary W. Longfellow, MD, *world-renowned heart specialist, husband of Justice Stewart*
Mandy Gibbs, *personal aide to Justice Stewart*
Francis Yates, *Secret Service, personal driver and bodyguard for Justice Stewart*
Matthew Arthur Brumfield III, *Harvard President, former dean of the law school*
Spencer Crockett, *former federal judge, deputy attorney general, special prosecutor*

Supreme Court

Walter Gallien, *chief justice, US Supreme Court*
James DeBarrow, *associate justice, US Supreme Court*
Gordon O'Driscoll, *associate justice, US Supreme Court*
Stephanie Yost, *associate justice, US Supreme Court*
Julia France, *solicitor general, US Supreme Court*
Johnson Vold, *marshal, US Supreme Court*

Bailey Stewart Team

Candice Towner, *Justice Stewart's chief of staff*
Alexander Hailwood, *Justice Stewart's executive legal counsel*

White House

John Jefferson McCade, *president of the United States*
James A. Fox, *White House chief of staff*
Gilbert H. Butterfield, *secretary of state*
Neal R. Wendt, *national security advisor*

Congress

John A. Fishel, *speaker of the House of Representatives*
Robert A. French, *Senate majority leader*

Department of Justice

Elizabeth S. Cookson, *attorney general*

FBI

Randall S. Payne, *director, FBI*
Curtis A. Mitchell, *deputy director, Special Investigations Unit, FBI*
Kevin Charles ("Casey") Kincaid, *special agent, FBI*
Jenny Warner, *special agent, FBI*

National Archives

Anita D. Wright, *archivist*
Elaine Meserve, *deputy archivist*

Brumfield Team

Megan Polkinghorne, *dean, Harvard Law School*
Paul Hooper, *deputy dean, Harvard Law School*

Miscellaneous

Dr. Cyril H. Wecht, *world-renowned forensic pathologist*
Dan Paddington, *partner, Dickson, Strong & Paddington law firm*
Charles Wingo, *CNN*
Angela Bonaventur, *owner, Old Ebbitt Grill*
Dr. Stuart Bach, *president and CEO, Orin Pharmaceuticals*

Disclaimer

This is a work of fiction, but it relies on events that actually happened or were presumed to have happened. Names, characters, businesses, organizations, places, events and incidents are either the product of the author's imagination or are used in a fictitious manner, solely for the enjoyment of the reader. Any resemblance to actual persons, either living or dead, or actual events, is purely coincidental.

The author has made attempts to give due credit to people, places and events. The author and publisher do not assume and do hereby disclaim any liability to any party for any loss, damage, or disruption caused by errors or omissions, whether such errors or omissions result from negligence, accident, or any other cause.

—Ed Munson, author of The Letter

DEDICATION

***To all those people who have brought me to this place and time,
some known, some not known, a profound thank you.***

was the first on the winding street gave him a view of beauty as the street dipped down and his route continued.

The house itself was of plantation vintage, rebuilt and reshaped over the years. It sat on approximately five acres of land that included a creek several feet in the front of the house and three tiers of grounds in back that wrapped around a large pond and a thick forest. The sides were well away from neighboring houses. The entire estate was secured by a laser system that, when activated, kept out intruders and unwanted animals. Perhaps just as unique was the old English drawbridge that the good doctor had installed several years ago to complete a childhood fantasy. While he never got the moat he desired, the running creek with a width of nearly eighteen feet served a similar purpose. And although the creek wasn't actually deep enough to be navigable, the drawbridge that lifted in the middle actually worked.

As for the house, it was a two-storied work with a complete built-out basement. The veranda lapped the house, jutting out from time to time to feature sitting areas. During the summertime and other warm days and evenings, the veranda in the back of the house was the place to be, as the setting sun dipped beyond the pond and trees. Refurbishing included as many as four hundred standard windows and several dormer windows which allowed sunlight throughout the nearly ten thousand square-foot house.

There were three master suites along with seven other rooms that could be used as bedrooms. Zach and Bailey each had their own offices, replete with shelving that displayed books and mementos. The walls of each office were adorned with pictures with noteworthy people, along with citations, proclamations, and resolutions from a multitude of people and organizations.

The two offices were separated only by another room, this one complete with a spectacular collection of sports memorabilia. The doctor had collected such memorabilia over the years, most of it gifted to him by noted sports personalities. Bailey allowed her husband this luxury, as she enjoyed sports almost as much as he did and occasionally went with him to events and activities. The walls alone were not enough to display all such items, so the doctor found time to rotate the memorabilia when he felt inclined. She just shook her head when he did so.

On most court days, especially the week after the first Monday in October, there was a flood of materials for her to review, including briefs, addendums, and other case references that were meant to help the nine justices take special notice. That meant using more than daylight time to get to everything. Add

Dedication

To all those people who have brought me to this place and time, some known, some not known, a profound thank you.

CHAPTER 1

Longfellow Estate, Fairfax, Virginia

The letter was delivered to a unique white iron mailbox, conveniently stationed a foot off the road so the carrier could easily make his deliveries to the homes in this unconventional part of what was known as the Fairfax 'commons.' There was nothing common about the area, as the homes were all different from each other on expansive acreage. The neighbors all knew each other, but a walk next door wasn't short.

A lingering and warm autumn breeze traveled with Ronnie Fry, who had been the mail carrier for these parts for more than 20 years. He welcomed the downturn in the hot weather and humidity. Cooler weather certainly was on the way, and then the old saying *Neither snow nor rain nor heat nor gloom of night stays these couriers from the swift completion of their appointed* rounds would seem a harsh consequence for this type of job security.

At least this neighborhood and the others on the route provided some form of viewing pleasure. The streets were generally clean, there was a wide variety of trees that provided relief from the hot summer sun, and people liked keeping their estates or the like in good condition. The houses never looked like they needed to be painted or have landscaping replaced. It just happened when it was time. Even during the harsh winters, the houses in this area looked picturesque.

Fry loved the bend in the road that brought him to a bank of homes on the right and a serene park-like setting on the left. While all the homeowners here had made their mark, the Longfellows were by far the best known, and he enjoyed seeing them from time to time. He liked to refer to the doctor as "Doc" and Justice Stewart as "Your Honor." The fact the Longfellow estate was the first on the winding street gave him a view of beauty as the street dipped down and his route continued.

The house itself was of plantation vintage, rebuilt and reshaped over the years. It sat on approximately five acres of land that included a creek several feet in the front of the house and three tiers of grounds in back that wrapped around a large pond and a thick forest. The sides were well away from neighboring houses. The entire estate was secured by a laser system that, when activated, kept out intruders and unwanted animals. Perhaps just as unique was the old English drawbridge that the good doctor had installed several years ago to complete a childhood fantasy. While he never got the moat he desired, the running creek with a width of nearly eighteen feet served a similar purpose. And although the creek wasn't actually deep enough to be navigable, the drawbridge that lifted in the middle actually worked.

As for the house, it was a two-storied work with a complete built-out basement. The veranda lapped the house, jutting out from time to time to feature sitting areas. During the summertime and other warm days and evenings, the veranda in the back of the house was the place to be, as the setting sun dipped beyond the pond and trees. Refurbishing included as many as four hundred standard windows and several dormer windows which allowed sunlight throughout the nearly ten thousand square-foot house.

There were three master suites along with seven other rooms that could be used as bedrooms. Zach and Bailey each had their own offices, replete with shelving that displayed books and mementos. The walls of each office were adorned with pictures with noteworthy people, along with citations, proclamations, and resolutions from a multitude of people and organizations.

The two offices were separated only by another room, this one complete with a spectacular collection of sports memorabilia. The doctor had collected such memorabilia over the years, most of it gifted to him by noted sports personalities. Bailey allowed her husband this luxury, as she enjoyed sports almost as much as he did and occasionally went with him to events and activities. The walls alone were not enough to display all such items, so the doctor found time to rotate the memorabilia when he felt inclined. She just shook her head when he did so.

On most court days, especially the week after the first Monday in October, there was a flood of materials for her to review, including briefs, addendums, and other case references that were meant to help the nine justices take special notice. That meant using more than daylight time to get to everything. Add on personal time and other family things to consider, and it worked into a fifteen-hour day.

Weekends were a time to draw a breath, assuming there wasn't some meeting or social event that required at least an appearance. With or without spouse, the calendar was full.

This Friday night, following another well-thought-out dinner, Bailey planned to take some personal time and mellow out in her study, replete with soft background music and a glass of Courvoisier. With Zach off to a symposium in Amsterdam for the next few days, there was time to be alone, though she'd be spending the first part of it reviewing her mail.

Among her duties as chief of staff at the house, Amanda Gibbs was the one to make sure the house was kept up, meals were served with efficiency, and above all, that Justice Stewart enjoyed her free time. That included relieving Justice Stewart from having to sift through the mail. Ultimately the judge relied on her to answer personal correspondence, a responsibility Amanda relished. It made her feel important and confident. The judge trusted her judgment as to what things might be somewhat important and what items were of a priority in nature.

Bills, invitations, and requests from a multitude of organizations were handled on a monthly basis. That left three stacks: stack C for the recipient to decide on, stack B for what was termed official business, and stack A for those items marked personal for either the doc or the judge. Of the eighteen to twenty pieces of mail that were received on average every day, devoid of catalogs and flyers, a piece of mail that reached A or B was favored.

Amanda—Mandy, as she preferred to be called—was a sharp one, with a creative and curious mind. She also had a sense of humor that made the judge laugh. Mandy had been a communications major at the University of Southern California. She had been introduced to the judge during a seminar series in Los Angeles, and the two hit it off so well that Mandy accepted a summer internship prior to her senior year. Mandy hadn't planned on going into the political arena, but after graduation the judge asked her to stay on as a full-time aide in charge of the house.

It was as if the two were related, like mother and daughter. They seemed to know what the other was thinking. They agreed. They disagreed. The judge had the final say, of course.

Always being curious when she fetched the contents from the carriage-house mailbox that bordered the street, Mandy did her usual sorting but conveniently left the interesting envelope on top of one of the stacks for the judge's review. She tapped her finger on the envelope and wondered to herself what surprise might be waiting inside. She even turned the envelope every which way to catch a glimpse of anything. No luck there. The envelope, and its contents, would have to wait.

Letters, packages, and all deliveries to the court were scanned and x-rayed before they reached a justice's office. Those sent to a residence were scanned when received at the post office. To prevent someone simply dropping something sinister into a mailbox, the carrier had a key to open the box and insert his delivery, and contents were removed via a separate key on the opposite side. Few people knew the residential addresses of people in politics.

The day's court session had held her hostage, Bailey thought. But that was the usual for the highest court in the land. There were no simple solutions. Attorneys had spent endless hours preparing for a brief moment in judicial time to argue a point. And the Supreme Court was the last bastion of defense for some, offense for others. It was there that nine people, who had earned their seat on the court with their judicial knowledge, with some bias, sat in judgment.

The judge had had enough judgment for one day, so flipping through the mail, her Courvoisier in hand, seemed appropriate. She was most curious about the large envelope. Inside was a six-page single-spaced computer-generated letter.

Ivanhoe Letter—1

Dear Justice Stewart:

It is with the highest regard and confidence that I am writing you this letter to solicit your help. From things that have been written and said about you, I know you are a compassionate and honest person who cares about the ordinary person and the country. I have done additional research into your background, from your upbringing through your schooling through your days on the bench, both on the state and federal levels.

I must admit that you seem to have everything that I would want in a judge because of your search for the truth and your consistent record of fairness to one and all. If what I say here makes as much sense to you as it does to me, then I will know I have gone to the right person.

Recently I received some interesting information—quite by accident, I can assure you. Don't ask me how I came by this information. Let's just say it happened as part of a series of events. The initial information I retrieved startled me, raising my eyebrows because it had a particular interest to me. I continued along the path that was afforded me, and even more interesting facts and figures were staring at me. "My God," I said to myself. "This is wild."

My eyes became fixed to my computer screen. I felt I had been shot with adrenaline. The worries of the day or recent past were put on the back burner, so to speak. I was looking through a window of the past and the visions were crystal clear.

I felt a happiness, as if a burden of uncertainty, doubt, and frustration had been lifted from all around me.

Was this true? Is any of this confirmed or authenticated information? Will people believe what there is here? I needed to know for sure. Not simply because I had wondered about these things all of my life, but because others had spent their lifetimes wondering about them as well.

When I say I found this by accident, I mean that in a literal way. I had been researching a project and was sent an email from an unknown source. Normally I simply delete such correspondence or send to my junk mail. But this one had a cryptic message, one that only I would understand. So I opened it. It was a plain message, stating that I would be receiving a letter soon, for my eyes only.

I did receive an envelope soon thereafter, with the paper inside, neatly folded, bearing the words For Your Eyes Only.

I ask that you read my letter in its entirety and then make your own judgment. It is a roller-coaster ride, so here we go . . .

I learned what happened at Pearl Harbor and why; the why, where, and how of the assassinations of JFK, Robert Kennedy, Martin Luther King, Abraham Lincoln and others; the gasoline crisis; the health problems of AIDS, herpes, Legionnaires' disease . . . even cancer.

Then there's information about extraterrestrials, crewed space flights, biblical artifacts. I mention these because they seem to be more in the public's consciousness than lesser-known pieces of history.

It's all here. All the truths, the half-truths and even the outright falsehoods that have been perpetuated through the years. It's a chronicle of humanity's past, as we know it, well documented and substantiated. Some of the information I did not know about before. Some of it represents the flip side of what I had been taught or led to believe. It is, in a word, overwhelming.

That brings me to you. Because of what I believe you stand for, I honestly believe the public has a right to know some of the information. I can't go so far as to believe the public should know everything, because it may lead to chaos.

So, why you and not someone else? Well, you are part of the government service, to be sure. But unlike any member of the executive or legislative branch, the judiciary—the Supreme Court—is appointed for life. I figure you will be there for a long time and will be able to cross party and political lines without fear of reprisal. Also, you can open doors where the everyday person cannot. You can ask things from a legal point of view, where others might hide.

I ask that you champion the cause. To let the truth be known about some things, for the good of the country and perhaps humankind. I have the information that could and would startle many. The questions are how to present it and how it could be placed in the right hands for the good of all.

I am not asking for personal gain through money, power or whatever. I am an ordinary person who only seeks the truth and wants something to believe in through all of my days. And I would like to think that if history has been written incorrectly, then maybe we have a chance to make it right for those who will follow.

I invite you to let me know what piece of history (like those mentioned earlier) piques your interest the most. I will give you full details on that item, to show I truly have what I say I do.

Because I want to stay in the shadows and avoid any potential conflicts about the information I have, I wish to be known as "Ivanhoe." If you are interested in learning more, please place an ad in the personal section of the Washington Post *any Monday through Thursday. Your initial five-point header should read IVANHOE and the body copy should indicate the subject you are interested in.*

When I see this, I will contact you again by mail. I have made other provisions for the dissemination of information in the event of my demise/incapacitation or yours, should you decide to join the cause. If you decide not to pursue this, I have made arrangements to go elsewhere. I do want you to know that the loss of this information is fail-safe. Subsequent communication with me will be through the newspaper, quite possibly the Post.

Because of this cache of information, I have become an astute follower of the inner and outer workings of all branches of the federal government. I hope this will become a more perfect union.

Thank you for reading this and I hope to see your favorable response.

Respectfully,

IVANHOE

Transfixed by the words in the letter, she put down her snifter and the letter and stared out the windows that showed the darkness with a sliver of the moon in the western sky.

"Oh, my," she thought. "Where is Perry Mason when I need him?"

She never got to the rest of the mail.

CHAPTER 2

The World of Bailey Stewart

The world around Bailey Stewart always seemed to fill her with curiosity. She learned to do for herself at an early age, having to compete with her older sister Karen for the attention of their parents, who were busy with their careers. Her mother was a career Army medical officer and her father was a judge. It left little time for her parents to discuss the working aspects of their jobs.

That meant Bailey and Karen needed to fend for themselves. Both were studious, Bailey anticipating a career in law while Karen was a black-and-white numbers person who would hang a CPA shingle someday. It was through her competition with her sister that Bailey set some high aspirations. Karen's slight about her supposedly higher IQ (it wasn't) set the stage for Bailey's mission in life: to be better than her sister in everything. And so it would be.

Bailey graduated from De la Salle High School in Concord, California, with honors, earning straight A's in her final two years and being chosen class valedictorian. Her commencement speech, "I Am a Figure of Speech," drew high acclaim from not only her school administrators and classmates, but from seemingly everyone in attendance, due to its commonness and insight into everyday life. The speech was picked up by the local media and eventually made it into an editorial in *Time Magazine*.

While she had opportunities to go to many prestigious law schools, she chose Harvard University, mainly on the advice of one of her high school's guest lecturers, Alexander Hailwood. At the time, he was the dean of Stanford University Law School, but he also loved teaching advanced academics to gifted high school students who had a special interest in the law. He himself had graduated from

Harvard and encouraged Stewart to expand her horizons on the opposite coast. She took a road not yet traveled into a different culture and mindset.

Now she was a part of a different parade.

Mandy and the cook, Grace, were gone for the weekend and Francis Yates, assigned as the protection detail for Justice Stewart, was spending some time with some pals in a friendly poker game. He had additional plans for the weekend, but would be on call if the judge needed him. So, Bailey had the house to herself.

As was her routine when she wasn't exhausted, she would find solace in the lap pool that had been built to have a picturesque view of the pond, forest, and western sky, yet assured privacy within an enclosed room with tinted windows, allowing the Longfellows year-round use. She stripped off her clothes and dove in, using her swimming skills to fight off some built-up tension.

A quick shower left her some time for reading before calling it a day. She picked up one of her Clive Cussler novels and was making every attempt to read at least one chapter before dozing, but the contents of the letter had left her anxious. She read the letter again and pondered what to do.

She decided to text Zach, who was six hours ahead of her in Amsterdam. She merely said there was something she needed to discuss with him when he returned from his trip in a couple of days. That couldn't come soon enough for her. Some four hours later he had responded with *what's up?* and she simply stated *talk to you soon*.

Although there was free time on weekends, she had some social engagements to tend to. Saturday morning she attended the Fairfax Women's Club as a keynote speaker. That afternoon she was with the Chamber of Commerce for a new building dedication. The evening was cluttered with a political gathering in DC.

Sunday was supposed to be a day to just relax, but the words of the letter did not allow her to do much of that. She jotted down some notes, cataloguing people to see or contact. It also meant analyzing facts, something at she was good at. She was anxious to talk to Zach.

The Supreme Court

Though not included on any list of the "Wonders of the World," the stately White House, Capitol Building, and Supreme Court Building are viewed as the heart of the government to Americans. The city of Washington,

DC, is commonly referred to as DC, and to many in the world it is the seat of power, as the country seems to be at the center of attention.

Each building that houses one of the three branches of government has a majestic look, all with a Corinthian style. For those who work there or visit on official business, and for tourists, they are unique.

The dawn of the new day came with a golden sun and the judge liked to get to the court grounds by six, so she and her driver Yates were there almost every morning at that time.

To get into the guard-secured underground garage required a special ID badge, a handprint, and a retinal scanner, not to mention the car verification. Each member of SCOTUS also needed to be verified through a sophisticated security system, removing any possibility that someone had hijacked the justice and/or the car.

Among the many secrets that the general public is not aware of is an elaborate tunnel system that connects most of the government buildings. They originally were put in place for security reasons, but over time they have served as a convenient way to get from one place to another when the DC weather and snooping eyes were considered not civilized; at least, that is what President Teddy Roosevelt thought when he added to the maze.

The entrance to the elevator had its own security protocol. The quick ride to the second floor was so seamless that one really could not feel the initial lift or the smooth stop. All but one justice had an office on the third floor, which had its own reception area with offices arranged in a circular fashion.

Each justice had their own idea of how to decorate, and Justice Stewart adorned her walls with pictures and mementos of her days in the legal profession and in politics. The outer office had room for her special executive counsel, three law clerks, and a separate area for her chief of staff. The wood-lined inner sanctum had a mahogany desk, a conference table that seated six people comfortably, a couch, a hidden bar, and a private bathroom with a shower. The plate-glass office window overlooked the grandness of DC, very similar to the view offered by many of the area offices to their powerful inhabitants. She often enjoyed just looking out at the stunning scenery.

With the contents of the letter vividly stuck in her mind, she felt as if she needed to work out a plan to move forward. She was both curious and excited to at least make some contact with Ivanhoe, but to say what, she wasn't sure.

After another day of reviewing petitions and making copious notes, it was time to summon Yates for a ride home.

CHAPTER 3

Francis Yates—Behind the Scenes

Yates was a perceptive man, and that served him well during his travails. He was a marksman when he was thirteen and by the time he was eighteen had more knowledge of firearms than most people who served in the FBI. Among his other skill sets was his ability to act on (and counteract) anything to do with cars. His father and his grandfather were mechanics, so he learned early and thoroughly.

He was recruited by the Secret Service following his graduation from Virginia Tech. He was so astute with weaponry that he was assigned to security details for top political dignitaries, both from the US and from abroad.

His Secret Service days were well documented with commendations for bravery and acuity far beyond his job description. But he stepped back from one offer of assignment after another to be a personal aide to Supreme Court Associate Justice Bailey Stewart. He was more than a personal driver. He was her protector, a confidant who sensed possible danger and seemed to be a step or two ahead of others in his line of work.

Yates had met Justice Stewart when she was a federal judge exchanging questions and answers during the senate confirmation hearings for her nomination to the Supreme Court. He had been with her every day, and after the confirmation she asked him if he was available to join her on a regular basis. His acceptance came with the words, "I would be honored."

Those who knew him didn't mess with him. Those who crossed him in the line of duty paid the price. As an aside, he became a long-distance runner at VT after he figured he wasn't a sprinter and had no inclination to do any of the field events. He had also became interested in boxing, which morphed into the martial arts.

For those who knew him in his younger days, Francis was his name. As he traveled through his adult years, he became known as Yates.

Yates was all in. He would use all of his skills to make sure Justice Stewart was safe at all times. And that meant her husband Dr. Longfellow would be safe as well. Yates was part of the family and even had a well-appointed guest house on the Longfellows' estate in Fairfax.

Stewart had met Yates in the underground garage and the two were on their way to Fairfax. Yates noticed a quietness in the judge.

"Your Honor, something seems to be troubling you. Need to talk?"

"I wish I could get a handle on this but I can't, and there is a sensitivity about this dilemma," she said. "I'd like to share, but I need to filter some things through my mind before I do. I hope you understand."

"Certainly. Feel free to share whatever, whenever. I am here to listen and help in any way."

"I appreciate all that you do—for both us. Believe me, when I have analyzed this, you will be in the picture. I can tell you now, though, this could be something really big."

Zach Longfellow Makes an Appearance

With the light of day turning to dusk, Yates drove the car over the drawbridge and around the semicircular drive to the front door where Zach Longfellow stood tall and waited. The judge had thought about his return all day, with a chance to share her thoughts in the privacy of their home. The quick embrace and welcoming kiss was a good start. They were soulmates and had been so for all of their twenty-eight years of marriage. Although from different backgrounds, they seemed to have a multitude of similar likes and dislikes, including people. There was no hatred of anyone, but they clearly recognized the pompousness of politics, spiced with clear hypocrisy and vile rhetoric. They shared their beliefs behind closed doors, away from prying eyes and ears.

"Doctor Longfellow, I presume," she said.

"At your service, Justice Stewart," Zach responded. "Dinner is waiting. Everyone is gone, so we have the evening to ourselves."

After enjoying Grandma's Company Casserole, they made their way to the family room. Bailey had deferred her conversation about what was troubling her until after dinner in order to catch up on the doc's recent trip. He was more than willing to oblige, as he was winding down from what felt like longer than a week-long series of talks, which although welcomed, sapped his energy. But he was anxious as well to know what Bailey's cryptic message meant.

"So, what's going on?" he asked.

"Zach, am perplexed as to what to do with any of this."

"You, perplexed? That is not like you. Let's have it."

"A few days ago I got a six-page single-spaced letter that outlined some rather startling things. It was from an anonymous source, although the name Ivanhoe was at its end. While I do not think this is classified, there's an implied reference. And I am not sure how to proceed, although I'm going to share it with you anyway."

"Was there any return address or postage with a cancellation?" he responded.

"No, nothing other than the pages inside, which ended with a request to make further contact through the *Post* if I was interested. My curiosity alone led me to be interested. But with whom and for what?"

"Then I'd love to see it."

She handed him the pages then sipped on a Courvoisier while he read the document carefully and nursed his black sambuca. Although his time clock was advanced four hours, he was very alert as he took his time to read the pages. He even read through it all twice.

His first reaction was to ask if this was for real. She countered that it seemed to be, although not corroborated.

"I was thinking of getting in touch with Matt Brumfield at Harvard to see if being involved in any of this would constitute a conflict of interest," she said. "If this was merely hearsay without any corroboration, then the point of continuing to pursue would be moot."

"Don't you think contacting Matt before getting some more corroboration might be the best tack? Maybe this Ivanhoe has something that could be easily verified, although if he says some of this has been suppressed, it might not be that easy to find out if it's true. To say you want proof of a cover-up of the Kennedy assassination, for instance, would require a lot of digging into some pretty deep covers," he said.

"I'm more than curious enough to at least ask Ivanhoe to state what he has and go from there."

"Who says it has to be a man, this Ivanhoe? It could be a woman, too. Secrecy seems to be the word of the day."

"This has all the earmarks of government secrets, although not seemingly of national security jurisdiction. I want to pursue this, but I'll need your help."

"Let's roll," he said.

"Up for a dip?"

They shed their clothes and were all in.

Buoyed by sharing her secret, Bailey slept much better, and the new day would come soon enough.

CHAPTER 4

Washington Post Classified Ad

The "State Your Case" line with the header IVANHOE appeared in the personals advertising section of the *Washington Post* and was one of 117 that day, offering or soliciting for something. To the casual reader, the line was lost and innocuous. To the intended reader, though, it meant everything. There was a connection.

Ivanhoe thought of the appropriate response, knowing that relating information in the newspaper would not be a very realistic way to go. Directions on a minimal level would be fine, but long text would not be practical. This could become another Deep-Throat-type clandestine relationship. It would take some doing to protect more than two people and keep any trails from being followed. Current surveillance techniques left nothing hidden from government sources—known and unknown—as well as hackers.

Because of this, Ivanhoe had to be clever.

After looking through the personals each day for the response to her "State Your Case" ad, Judge Stewart was struck by the words "IVANHOE—I will post my response" in the long list of entries on Sunday, a day when the section expanded greatly. She had almost given up looking after nearly two weeks with no sign of anything from this Ivanhoe person. She questioned the validity of the original letter and the value of the contents. Now she was intrigued again.

But what was "post a response" supposed to mean? *Post* as in newspaper? Post as in public posting? Perhaps an internet posting? But how would this Ivanhoe know her home email address? There was no direct email address to the court. All such messages to the various divisions of the court are filtered, as they are in other government agencies, to protect privacy and prevent hacking. There are many firewalls for those reasons.

The judge was anxious to take up the chase. As a jurist, she was keen to get the facts and then determine what course of action to take. She contemplated the possibility of a complete hoax, that someone out there simply had an active imagination. Secrets, governmental or otherwise, had been talked about, scrutinized, fiercely debated, and even dismissed throughout history.

In modern times, with the age of communication through advanced technologies such as television, satellites, the internet, and cell phones, almost anything could be found, analyzed, reanalyzed. And it was all but certain that not everyone would agree with the same material, given the same facts at the same time—like a jury. That is what made her profession so enlightening to her. In her earlier days as a superior court judge, then a member of the state Supreme Court and then the federal bench, she was amazed at how some cases evolved, based simply on the presentation of the defense.

With the header TARGET, the line "Pick Your Curiosity" appeared in the *Post* classifieds two weeks later. That caught the judge's eye. Ivanhoe was ready for the game to be played.

She responded with KENNEDY as the header, and once again, "State Your Case" followed.

Another letter reached the iron mailbox at the Longfellow estate. The single-spaced letter was direct and to the point.

CHAPTER 5

Ivanhoe Letter—2

Dear Justice Stewart:

Because of the length of the material and the sensitivity as well, I will have to send you information through the postal service (I thought you would get my reference to posting my response). I would think there would be a curiosity as to who I am and where I am coming from, but I ask that you do not try to find me, as it would jeopardize our connection.

I have a great deal of information to share and I would rather share it with you for your review as opposed to dropping it on the Post's doorstep. As I stated in my previous letter, I have a fail-safe backup in the event something happens to me.

For the time being you simply will have to trust my judgment and understand my reasons for sharing this serendipitous information with you. Since I have read all of the information that has come to my attention, I am quite sensitive to what I think should be known, but I am but one person. Still, in my opinion, some of this should be left for public consumption, some should not.

Consider that at various moments in our lives, there are times when you think you could hear a pin drop. Like time stands still. Like Rod Serling had something to do with it. This collection of documents and data simply came together at a moment in time and was captured by an individual who pulled it all together. And then it was given to me and I have chosen to share it with you, because I know you will do what is right.

On to our subject at hand—Kennedy. I assume you want to know about both John and Bobby, but this letter will focus on the death of the president, though some of it is intertwined. The president's assassination certainly was gruesome, and it was planned. As you will see, there are story lines that cross over, but at least one man knew everything that was going on—not that he planned anything, just that he knew specific details and did nothing to stop either murder. We'll get to him later.

Be mindful that history records what happens, but not necessarily why. Conspiracy theorists abound when the "why" isn't known. There are some loose ends with "why" because not everyone or everything is accounted for, and closure is denied for many who simply want to know why something happened.

JFK's assassination is perhaps the most perplexing in recent memory because millions of people around the world were a part of it in some way. As Americans, we felt violated, and many to this day lack closure. But the whole sad story drills down to the essence of what I laid on your doorstep some time ago. Government secrets are entrusted to a few, usually for more than one reason. Even the president doesn't have full access to all information.

Verified records show that CIA assassins and operatives from various other countries were recruited to kill Kennedy. These operatives were not working under the guise of a government agency, but were contract killers, used for scores of hits for numerous reasons. The original plot to kill the president was hatched by the Mafia because Kennedy had reneged on some legal issues. The original hit was to be in Chicago, but when the presidential plans changed, so did the assassination plot. Bobby knew Jack was walking a tightrope with his mob ties. His election in 1960 was rigged with the help of the mob, and that was a favor to be repaid. Any word of Jack's hands-off policy toward suspected mob leaders was suppressed. His sleeping arrangements with mob women was ignored and subsequently used to gain access to the White House.

The coordination of the president's travels was carefully choreographed, right down to the route where the motorcade was going. Documents verify that. Trust me, no one person could have obtained all of that information, planned on being in Dealey Plaza at the right time, taken the only shots, and gotten away cleanly. Lee Oswald may have been a part of the logistics team, but he didn't even pull the trigger.

How far in advance did the local people know the parade route and the timing of the motorcade? How far in advance did Oswald start working at the depository and what were his specific duties? While he was used to guns, Oswald wasn't a sharpshooter like trained assassins of the CIA and terrorist ilk. There weren't any prints other than a partial palm print on the butt of the gun. No gloves ever were found. Add the fact the rifle had a bad scope and tended to misfire from time to time and you are asking even the best sharpshooter to perform an impossible task.

I mention all of these facts because the suppressed documents show that there were four shooters, all set on timers, all with backups. The first shooter was in the School Book Depository and fired the first shot, which hit the president in the back. The second shooter shot almost simultaneously and was positioned on the roof of the Dal-Tex Building, located northeast of the book depository and north of and further behind the target in Dealey Plaza. His shot got John Connolly as he turned to the left after the first shot hit Kennedy. This was the so-called "magic bullet," one that investigators said hit Kennedy then made a right turn and continued through Connolly.

The third shooter was located to the side behind the fence on the grassy knoll and caught Kennedy in the throat as the president's head turned from the stinging pain in his right shoulder. The fourth shooter positioned himself on the railroad bridge, hitting the right side of the president's face as his head turned again, exiting out the right occipital area and spewing brain matter all over the back of the limousine and hitting Secret Service Agent Rufus Youngblood. The laws of physics determine that the president could not have been hit with all of the bullets from the rear and have the back of his head explode. If anything, he would have been propelled forward, not to the side.

Some have argued that witnesses near the grassy knoll fence and the train bridge did not see any gunman or anything out of the ordinary. Ever wonder why extras are used in movies? They simply stand, sit or do what they are told and repeat the exercise as many times as it takes to get the scene right.

In the world of CIA operatives, the Mafia, and other sinister cloak-and-dagger agencies, the doers are not supposed to get caught. And none of these people got caught. Instead of walking away from the fracas, they walked into it and then melted away. One was dressed as a police officer, another had a pin that designated him as a government security person. The fake Oswald hid in the building, waited for the police and others to come rushing in, and then casually left through the front door. Oswald was never on the top floors of the depository, but his job was to make sure the shooter got away.

As for officer J. D. Tippitt . . .

All shooters and their cast of extras made their ways to various roads and outlets. All were paid in advance and they had their own timetables to get out of town. Amid the chaos, no one ever checked the airports, bus companies, car rental agencies, or outlet roads for identification. Just who were they looking for? That would have involved an instant action and intense coordination. The Secret Service has protocols for all possible scenarios, but unforeseen tangents can throw off the best of responses. Connecting the dots in quick fashion simply did not happen in Dallas.

By the way, the president was dead before he got to the hospital. Arrangements had to be made for the succession process, so announcements as well as medical help at the hospital were for show.

This was not a government coup. Lyndon Johnson was told by his secret operatives that something was going to happen. In fact, the question posed to him was, "Do you want to be president? If you do, then do as you are told and duck when you hear commotion." Johnson merely raised an eyebrow . . . and ducked when he heard the firecracker sound of the rifle bullet. Two Secret Service agents quickly fell on him.

So that is what we know from firsthand accounts, including comments by Secret Service personnel, John Connolly, even Jackie Kennedy. If there wasn't something clandestine going on, then why were the autopsy photographs and other x-rays sealed for fifty years? If the truth were to be known, it would startle even the most patriotic.

Yes, there was a reason why no one has come out and said what they knew and/or heard or saw. It's called buy-off and an outright threat to kill everyone in one's family, as far back as someone can go. Even Johnson found out the truth and was never the same. He anticipated the same could happen to him and his family. That is why he ducked the reelection campaign of 1972.

So now comes the question of why.

Aside from Kennedy's snub of the mob, to whom he and his father Joe were indebted, JFK rankled those on both sides of the aisle. He was playing the rich kid with all of the power. It was his intention to back out of Vietnam, champion the cause of civil rights, and unilaterally soap box for a nuclear test-ban treaty with the USSR and other emerging nuclear nations. The Vietnam retreat was potentially damaging from a public relations standpoint, but it was the loss of business in perpetuating the war that was not acceptable.

If you think about it, the United States always seemed to get into some international conflict when the economy was soft or down. World Wars I and II revived the economy, and both brought back national pride. Both were started with a catastrophe, ones we knew would happen. But that's another story.

The Vietnam conflict wasn't strategic, and it served only one purpose—to boost the economy. We were never threatened with a worldwide takeover like Germany sought in the west and Japan sought in the east during WWII. Had Germany won with the help of Japan, Europe would have remained steady for only a few years. Then we would have had World War III and the United States, Russia, and China would have joined forces. Where that would have left Europe is anyone's guess. The United States would have been helpless to restore any semblance of order after the two other powers got into a squabble.

Although the foundation of the military industrial complex has been around for centuries, it was Dwight Eisenhower who first spoke of it openly, asserting that the world is run by big business. As Deep Throat used to say on many an occasion, "Follow the money." As I mentioned, there was one person in the government who had access to everything that happened, before and after. I'll save that for another time.

Respectfully,

IVANHOE

As astonished as she was with the first letter, this one set her back a step or two. She read the letter again and welcomed the time to share it with Zach when he got home, which was any minute now.

Zach had had his own tension-filled day, directing another heart transplant, the fifty-ninth in his distinguished career. The fact he was a master at it gave him great satisfaction. The fact he was able to teach others was a gift he treasured.

No sooner had he entered the door than Bailey handed him the latest letter. "You need to read this. This is some serious stuff and we need to respond."

"Ivanhoe?" he asked.

"Most definitely," she responded.

Without sitting down for what he had hoped would be a quiet dinner, he became immersed in the contents of the letter. His glass of chardonnay was gone by the end of the first reading. Bailey was into her second glass of cabernet.

The look of astonishment on his face said it all.

"This is not for the faint of heart, and there are some folks who wouldn't want this information, if proved to be true, to see the light of day even now," he remarked.

"I think it's time to call Matt," she said.

CHAPTER 6

Matt Brumfield

Matthew A. Brumfield, now Harvard president after serving for the better part of twenty-seven years as dean of the law school, was a traditionalist. A classic. Born and raised in the state of Vermont, he was a lawyer turned judge turned dean who became president of one of the most prestigious universities in the nation's history.

Burlington, Vermont, located on the eastern shore of Lake Champlain, had been his home for his first twenty-two years, culminating with his graduation from the University of Vermont as valedictorian. His father, a well-known and respected attorney in Burlington, had encouraged him to go to Harvard for his law degree.

Matt excelled in all of his studies and was repeatedly asked by his professors to serve as a teaching assistant because of his organizational and communication skills. He flourished in that capacity as well. He was on every law firm recruitment list, and he eventually chose White, Bear & Kirkpatrick as his new home. In less than ten years he was appointed judge of the Boston Superior Court. Four years later, he was on the Massachusetts Supreme Court.

The years had not changed his demeanor. He preferred settling back in his easy chair with many a transcript or document to review. Above all, he was approachable for friends and associates to discuss a variety of subjects, all the while being discreet. It was his small-town charm and upbringing that made him a classic. Few challenged him on the elements of the law. Yet he would listen.

His return to Harvard was prompted by his wanting to get back to teaching, so he opted to become the dean of the law school. Many of his professorial colleagues had called it a day, but he felt a resurgence, a need to get back to his roots and to share with others what he had learned.

As the dean, he also taught on a limited basis, and one of his students was a very bright and inquisitive Bailey Stewart.

Stewart Calls Brumfield

"Matt, Bailey Stewart," came the voice over the phone.

"Well, how is my favorite Supreme Court justice today?" came the jovial response from Brumfield. "What can I do for one of my favorites?"

"Matt, do you have time to come down to Fairfax and spend a day with Zach and me? I have something I need to share with you and it requires a face-to-face."

"Absolutely," was his quick reply. "What works for you?"

"This weekend okay?"

"Give me a time?"

"Make it anytime, and plan on spending the night if you have the time. Bring Barbara, too. Let me know when you will get to Washington and I'll have Yates pick you up."

"See you Saturday. Barbara is seeing her sister in Minnesota, so it'll be just little ol' me."

He remembered their meeting in her first year of law school. His memory of her rising up the legal ladder, eventually being nominated for the Supreme Court, gave him great satisfaction. He was there when she addressed the senate committee during her confirmation hearing.

What struck him was her collection of defining words from her philosophical views and determined speech when she argued cases in his law school.

When asked why she thought she was qualified for the highest court in the land by Senator Calvin McLish from Wyoming, she gave an eloquent response:

"Senator and members of this committee, I suspect we all have thought about ourselves as being at the center of our own universe, and I am no different. To paraphrase what I learned from my father, 'By listening, you can learn a lot; saying little doesn't mean you haven't said enough.' I do believe in those words, because as jurists we need to listen before we speak, hopefully using our skills to make qualified, fair, and reasonable decisions. I stand on my record as being honest, consistent, and fair. I understand that I would be holding the nation's trust in continuing to do that job to the very best of my abilities. I know the law and the Constitution."

There was silence in the room.

CHAPTER 7

Brumfield Remembers Stewart

Brumfield was as curious as one could be. Bailey was one of his best students, perhaps the brightest, and they had maintained a strong friendship through the years. When she needed a discerning ear or a friendly voice, she would call on the good professor. He had sensed her current concern, and the secrecy touched his sense of adventure.

Yates was there when Brumfield's plane landed at Reagan International Airport. The two had met before at Justice Stewart's confirmation hearings and twice again at social events in DC. They instantly liked each other and they had a common interest, that of Judge Stewart as well as Zach. The drive took less than thirty minutes on a Saturday morning, and the two struck up a conversation about Washington's NFL entry, treading water again halfway through the season. After the Washington Nationals had rolled over in the Major League Baseball playoffs in the first round, local talk soon targeted the Redskins.

Brumfield at Longfellow Estate

Bailey was there to greet her longtime mentor as the car circled the half-moon drive. After a big hug and polite kiss on the cheek, Zach was there with a firm handshake.

"Good to see you both," Matt said with a wide smile. "What's so damn important that I had to cancel my golf game with some pigeons from whom I planned to take some well-deserved friendly wagers?"

"We have something very interesting to share with you, Matt," offered Zach. "Let's go into the family room."

After some basic pleasantries and coffee, donuts, and rolls, Bailey began her story. It didn't take long for Brumfield to catch on to the potential minefield, what with the subject of government secrets on everyone's mind.

"As much as I would have thought there would be a simple solution to all of this, the more I became tangled up with what-ifs," she offered. "The first letter certainly got my attention, although I remained skeptical. After reading it four or five times, I became more intrigued. I couldn't wait for Zach to get home so I could have him read it."

"I had the same reaction," said Zach. "We both thought there has to be some corroboration to something as adventurous as this, but the where, why, and how were questions that had to be asked."

"I decided to at least establish a link, to see if this had any validity," Bailey said. "The second letter was like a bolt of lightning. We both read it a few times to grasp the depth of it all. I ask—we ask—that you read the letters and form your own conclusions. If we're missing something, or this is too far out there for anyone else to believe, then we need your scholarly opinion. We trust your judgment and value your friendship enough to include you."

Bailey handed Brumfield the first letter. He sifted through the six pages as an overview, as many jurists do initially. Then he carefully looked over the contents of the letter, pausing from time to time to raise an eyebrow or sip his coffee. His look of assurance after having finished the first full reading gave both Bailey and Zach a feeling of acceptance.

"Interesting in theory, but it's all about the facts now," said Brumfield, in a very Perry Mason type of way. He had the build of a Raymond Burr, but wasn't nearly as heavy. His demeanor, though, was very Mason-like.

He then picked up the second letter and seemed captivated by every word, as details rekindled the recollection of a blight on American history. The truth would come out one day, he always thought. Was this the Pandora's box that people had been searching for, and would anything else that was to be divulged bring on chaos? Brumfield took the time to reread the second letter, occasionally looking at the Longfellows as would a judge when facts came out in the courtroom.

"I am as curious as you are," he said. "I'm all in."

There was a smile on both of their faces. With the trusted Brumfield there to direct them, the possibility of getting to the truth seemed assured.

"Should we try on our own to verify, or is this something we need to get some expert legal advice on before we proceed? I could call the AG, Liz

Cookson, or Ken McDonald at DOJ," offered Brumfield. "But right now, the more we uncover, the more wheels will be spinning. Perhaps I can call Spencer Crockett—he served as a federal judge and became an excellent special prosecutor—to get his sniff of the wind. Spencer and I go way back. Let me arrange a private off-the-record meeting." Bailey and Zach looked at each other and nodded their approval.

"Let's set some parameters for communication since we all know what the NSA does on a regular basis," said Bailey. "And we don't want the FBI and any other agencies poking their collective noses in this investigation too soon."

"I have no problem taking the lead here, Bailey," offered Brumfield. "You might be in a precarious position for making subtle inquiries, and Zach, you wouldn't have the same connections that I might have, at least initially. I think we need to figure out who is on our 'team' and then plot our plan from there.

"For the time being, though, I think Spencer might give me some perspective. We have to go about our business as usual or someone might get suspicious when inquiries are made. The stuff about JFK is certain to raise more than a few eyebrows, so I think we should anticipate where we might get some initial pushback.

"How believable is this Ivanhoe as an informant?" continued Brumfield. "This person purports to have this information, which, on its face, sounds rather convincing. If what is purported can't be corroborated in some way, we might be opening up some doors that are better off left closed. And I think we need to know where it came from, in case there might be a freight train heading our way.

"Is there any way of getting a face-to-face with Ivanhoe? What we're talking about here isn't so much government secrets as it is not divulging all of the truth, so I wonder about the secrecy from their perspective."

"We both felt the same way, Matt," replied Bailey. "From the legal side we all are concerned about facts, the law, and what is considered admissible."

"From the medical side, I certainly could verify information in the JFK case, but I would have to have access, access denied for fifty years after the assassination," said Zach. "That time has come and gone and there still has been no release of any autopsy photos or reports or any related information. Get me that and I'll be able to decipher a lot of things on my own."

"This becomes more than a one-person operation, then," Brumfield said. "Let's draw up our own road map and see were the tangents will take us."

By this time, the sun was dipping into the western sky, but the unseasonably warm weather allowed the threesome to enjoy the back patio overlooking the terraced land behind the house, which included the lake-like pond. The pond water was fed by an offshoot of the Accontink Creek that ran in front of the house and was a part of the Potomac River maze.

"This is an amazing place. Every element—the water, the trees, and the land—is beautiful on its own, but together . . . just amazing," said Brumfield, sipping his lemonade from his vantage point on a large patio rocking chair.

"Serendipity," said Zach. "We needed a house in this area, and this had just been listed."

"The whole area is lovely. I've heard good things about George Mason University—isn't that nearby? I know it has a great reputation for its economics and law programs. The president of Harvard has to keep apprised of such things," Brumfield said with a smile. "George Mason, the man, was one of the greatest of the founding fathers of the United States. He drafted the Virginia Declaration of Rights, which became a model for the first ten amendments to the US Constitution."

"Yes, professor, we know," Bailey replied, with a smirk. "We love this area. Small-town atmosphere with just enough going on.

"Now, let's get one of our whiteboards and see if we can make any sense out of our new project."

While Bailey called for local restaurant delivery, Matt and Zach set up a couple of whiteboards in the family room.

With dinner enjoyed—the consensus had been Italian and there had been more than enough for the threesome—and some funny stories told, the three retired back to the spacious den for the subject at hand.

Brumfield started the conversation with an observation. "In that I probably have more latitude than you two, I suggest we set this up as a sort of moot court," he began. "Bailey, consider yourself as the judge; I will act as a quasi-prosecutor; and Zach, you become the jury. All of us will have questions, but if we frame this as a court case, if you will, it might help us focus on identifying our end game. Objections, thoughts, and questions can come at any time. I suggest we record this, as we won't have time to take valid notes if we are thinking about strategies.

"My thinking here is you and I, Bailey, have served in various legal capacities, but you may well have to be careful of your responsibilities if any of this gets to the court. And I don't think you can take much time away from the court to delve into the underpinnings of this information. I, on the other hand, can simply close my door and chat all day long. And I have the connections to get to whomever we need to get answers, certainly suggestions, even if off the record. Zach has the unique role of being in the medical profession, and with it, having access to pathology reports and other information that would require an expert's opinion."

"That is fine with me and I think we all can weigh in at any time," offered Bailey.

"Zach, you okay with being the jury?"

"Absolutely," he responded.

Brumfield, Stewart and Longfellow Discuss What Was Known

Brumfield stood in front of the whiteboard while Bailey and Zach sat on the couch.

"Some of our first decisions are to figure out whether any laws have been broken, if any power has been misused, or if suppressing the information is to be considered for the good of the country," said Brumfield. "After all, sometimes not telling all of the truth may have consequences, if all of that truth is needed to set the record straight. And we may well be dealing with hearsay unless we have corroborating evidence.

"Ivanhoe's letter details what are purported to be facts about the Kennedy assassination that generally are not known to the public. As a prosecutor, I would like witnesses, reports, studies, and pictures. Zach, the autopsy reports and pictures would be right down your alley. If you don't know all the facets of the pathology report, you could go to someone who could clarify.

"So, the fine line we face right here is whether there is classified information or just a number of reports that have been filed in a sealed area for so many years. The questions we are interested in are who knew before, during, and after, whether someone is to be held accountable, and if the public should be allowed to gain some closure with the whole truth and nothing but the truth.

"I, for one, believe in the Kennedy conspiracy. As a jurist, though, I would want substantive information to prove beyond reasonable doubt that Lee Oswald was a lone gunman."

"On face value, the public has a right to know if there was any conspiracy, that there may have been a government suppression of the facts, even a cover-up," stated Bailey. "I agree we need to determine what we are after here, and misuse of power is a good way to phrase it, Matt. I am concerned that there will be some high brick walls to overcome, even reverse inquiries that may lead to some very disgruntled folks. I can imagine that if names are divulged, there would be a strong will to block any further investigation, lest someone, perhaps already dead, be subject to further rewriting of history."

"This also has other consequences," Brumfield said. "Just how much information is good for the public to know? Is new information going to reinforce the public trust if the government had a hand in it, or will there be hell to pay? The Pearl Harbor attack sticks in my mind, and I would like to know what Ivanhoe has to say about that, too. Are government secrets really secrets or simply cover-ups to keep people from becoming unsettled?

"Perhaps we have to decide what would be admissible. If, as Ivanhoe purports, there was one person who had access to all documents on any one of a number of accusations or claims that Ivanhoe has made, can we subpoena that person's records?"

"That would be a sticky wicket," said Bailey. "There would have to be cause. We probably would have to connect the dots with other information before someone turns over Hoover's files.

"I might also object to Ivanhoe's assertions without proper foundation. It seems apparent Ivanhoe wants to and will remain in the shadows, like a 'Deep Throat' connection. Getting Ivanhoe as a witness seems like a zero. Perhaps asking for how this person came by this information might prove useful and take some of the suppositions out of the hearsay defense."

"Next, if I'm to meet with Spencer and give him a standard outline of what we are asking in order to get his legal perspective as a former AG," said Brumfield, "how much do we divulge? We could simply ask how opening the aspects of the Kennedy assassination would float in the justice maze. We could go further by including him our group, but would that compromise his access?

"All this time we have to be cognizant that the DOJ answers to the AG and the AG answers to the president. At some time, President McCade is going to hear something, and whether he has any knowledge or would let us loose to find supportive evidence is a good question."

"I have known JJ for a long time," Bailey replied, "and while he might be sympathetic to our efforts, he might be constrained by those who simply do not want all of the truth to come out—not just about the Kennedys, but all the other stuff."

"Leaks happen, and usually by someone with an agenda," said Brumfield. "Ivanhoe did say there were some fail-safe backup plans in the event something happened to them or to you, Bailey, for that matter."

"That reminds me of the movie *Three Days of the Condor*," said Zach. "In the end, the information that was considered sensitive was leaked to the *New York Times*. Daniel Ellsberg, and more recently Edward Snowden come to mind. If we don't pursue this with all of our connections, what's to say Ivanhoe doesn't drop the grenade somewhere? Ivanhoe has made a pitch to Bailey and I think we should get rolling. I'm also aware we may be walking through a mine field when a potential bad element gets wind of the information."

As each of them spoke, Brumfield made notations on the whiteboard. On the second board he wrote Crockett's name, hoping they all could agree on what needs to be asked of the former federal judge and special prosecutor.

His list included:

Overview
Ivanhoe
Kennedy
Crime
Cover-up
AG
DOJ

Additional mystery person who knows all

"From my standpoint, I think I would need a source of the material, at least how it came into the hands of Ivanhoe," said Bailey. "That at least would solve one of the hearsay questions that any prosecutor would want to substantiate. And I am genuinely curious as to what else might be in Ivanhoe's bag of tricks."

"I'm with you on this as well," said Brumfield. "Perhaps now is the time for you to drop another classified ad to Ivanhoe."

Two days later, an inconspicuous classified ad appeared in the *Post*: YOUR WITNESS, Foundation

Chapter 8

Ivanhoe Letter—3

Dear Justice Stewart:

Not being an attorney, I assume you are looking for some sort of proof that my information isn't contrived. While you have my word that it isn't, perhaps I can share with you the way I came by this, which was quite by accident. Rest assured, I looked at all of it, even the directions I was given, and I had my own set of questions. I, too, am a logical thinker, but I don't possess any legal background to ask specific questions.

Let me start with how I got this information. As I mentioned previously, I got an envelope and a note inside that merely said For Your Eyes Only. Seeing nothing else, I was somewhat confused and looked for some other notation on the envelope and letter. Nothing. So I tried a magnifying glass, a blacklight, lemon juice, just about anything I could think of. As I was sliding my hand across the top of the envelope and cancelled stamp, lo and behold, I felt a raised circle that was the eagle's eye on the stamp and discovered a microdot.

The microdot contained all of this information. How ingenious, I thought. An almost undetectable way to transfer material without drawing suspicion or snooping eyes. And this was for my eyes only.

I might add that I got a second letter from this anonymous source, explaining how the information got to them. In the event this seems pertinent to establishing validity, here is what that letter said:

Hopefully you have found the source of my message. To satisfy your curiosity about how this information came to me and in such detail and in digital form, think of moments in time when everything seems to focus on a point. Perhaps using the visual of the scene in Raiders of the Lost Ark *when Indiana Jones locked the Staff of Ra into a hole in the Map of Souls and the beam of light showed where the long-lost site of the lost Ark of the Covenant could be found. But I wasn't looking for anything; it just appeared, and I was alert enough to save it.*

Consider, if you will, no one person would ordinarily have access to all of this information—no president, no member of Congress, nobody from the likes of the CIA, FBI, NSA, or any of the other black-ops agencies, known or unknown, would have complete access.

I guess I was just lucky. I also felt afraid, knowing if I went public that I might be a goner. I had to pass this on, and I knew of you because of the lectures you have given in various circles. So, I picked you, hoping you would take up the challenge or at least pass it on to someone you knew would have great interest and at least make a go of it. I know I can't because I am a nobody.

The letter was unsigned and there was no indication I would ever hear from this person again.

It took me days to go through all of the material, and I was so captivated that I stopped from time to time to simply ponder what was and what wasn't possible. We are talking about rewriting parts of history, setting the record straight and perhaps giving closure to more than a few people.

My coming to you was a way to transition to the confirmation of the validity of the information, as I have no resources to contact the right people to get some answers to my own questions. I'm sure having seen what I have offered so far has led you to your own questions. So, it is my hope that you will carry this forward. I will give you what I have, but I choose to be in the shadows, so ask what you will and I will do my best to get whatever information I have to you as quickly as possible. I hope you will respect my position, not only for my own sense of anonymity, but perhaps for security as well. As I mentioned, if anything sinister befalls me or you, there will be other outlets.

I also sense that you are interested in the one-person reference. Think of FBI Director J. Edgar Hoover. He is the one person who knew of plots, questionable goings-on and cover-ups. His vast number of files on anyone and everyone who were suspects are mostly intact, and I have the proof that he indeed had all of that. He himself was threatened by many, and his trump cards were the files. He, too, was murdered, and some of his files disappeared, but what I have are all of his files that were transferred into digital form.

Are these files for the public buffet? I think not. But he had other information on suppressed documents, such as alternative energy sources, the Pearl Harbor fiasco, and medical technology advances. As you can imagine, information like this goes in every which direction and boggled my mind. Even today, when I read through all of what is here, I simply shake my head. But I wanted to know it all and I hope you do, too.

While I do not know what else I can add, except to offer up the information I have, I will do my best to get back to you with answers to your inquiries. Perhaps unfortunately, we have to stay with the cryptic form of questions.

Respectfully,

IVANHOE

CHAPTER 9

Stewart's Day

Mandy greeted her when the judge arrived home after seven, and was quick to tell her that another gray envelope had arrived. Bailey went straight to her office to read the latest, telling Mandy she would be down for dinner shortly.

The first read of the latest Ivanhoe letter left Bailey aghast, again. It outlined some very serious implications, ones that may well delve too far into government archives, albeit they were also close-to-deceitful if not downright unlawful shenanigans.

Dinner was waiting, and she and Mandy enjoyed lasagna, although the judge was not very conversant. Mandy offered most of the conversation, bringing the judge up to speed on some repair work to be done at the estate. She had her own plans for the weekend with her sister Kristen, a flight attendant for United Airlines, who was planning on being in the DC area for the next four days. Mandy could tell something was on the judge's mind, so she left her alone.

Mandy cleaned up the dishes and said her farewell as she got her things ready for the much-anticipated weekend. Bailey returned to the quietness of her office to reread Ivanhoe's recent letter. The bizarre had become more bizarre.

The court day had been a tiring one, but even the weary Bailey had time to reread the letter two more times. As Ivanhoe had stated, there were many more logs for the fire. She wrestled with the complexity of the "case" and wondered if laws were broken, even so many years ago, or if any of this would matter, except to provide closure. Was J. Edgar Hoover exempt in that he had the goods on so many? He died mysteriously in 1972 at age seventy-seven. To be sure, Hoover was as well known and scrutinized as any president or elected official in DC circles. Like him or not, he was in the know. Written pieces and the usual gossip were a part of his everyday life.

Hoover had a good public image, although there were some who didn't care for his alleged spying without cause on people from all walks of life, the rich and famous, the notorious, and the average. The fact the FBI had open files on well more than 400,000 Americans into the 1960s led some people to think there were some excessive things going on at the bureau, even if it was just the want and need of a dark side of Hoover as an individual.

Bailey had studied the former FBI director during her undergraduate years, yearning to find out how the investigative process of agencies such as the FBI, CIA, NSA and all the other known and unknown agencies interacted with the law, and in particular, what matters of theirs were discussed by the Supreme Court. Her senior thesis drew high acclaim not only from a pleased Brumfield, but from the entire faculty. At that time, Brumfield had an inkling Bailey Stewart might be one of the chosen few to serve on the high court. He had posed the question to her at one time, in a private conversation, and she had thanked him in a modest way, but indicated her wish to determine what phase of the law would command her attention—prosecution, defense, or becoming a judge.

The years would be good to her and the endgame was she was where she should be—an associate justice of the United States Supreme Court.

The latest Ivanhoe revelations left her more tangents to follow and the questions kept floating through her mind. Those involved in any aspect of the law knew that, with many a case, twists and turns were sure to come and there were many cliffs that posed disaster and required calculated responses.

CHAPTER 10

The World of Zach Longfellow

"Bails? Where are you?" Zach had had his own tiring day, replete with teaching medical students at Johns Hopkins Hospital about the intricacies of heart surgery. He valued his chance to share his skill sets with others, but it did require a lot of preparation. He was, in the eyes of many, one of the finest heart surgeons in the world, and his fifty-nine transplants were a testament to his attention to detail. He also had a great bedside manner and was constantly being asked to give guest lectures and attend medical symposiums.

He enjoyed the camaraderie with others in the medical professional field, but was also easily conversant with members of the media and those in political circles who were anxious to know the latest in medical science when it came to his area of expertise.

By all accounts, Zachary Longfellow, a descendant of the poet Henry Wadsworth Longfellow, was a pivotal player in the advanced research on heart disease and transplants. He, like his father and grandfather Henry, was an easterner who attended Harvard. Charles became a lawyer and statesman, serving in Congress before being appointed postmaster general and finally a federal district court judge.

In young Zach's formative years, he was accustomed to being around people of note and education. His varied interests could have led him in any one of a number of directions, but it was his interest in how the body worked that drew him into the medical field. A letterman in football, basketball, baseball, and track, he was drawn to challenges, whether on an individual or a team basis. No one else in his family had athletic interests, so he pursued his sports endeavors on his own, although his parents tried to make his games to watch and cheer.

His wanting to be a wide receiver in football, a playmaker in basketball, a long-distance runner in track, and a player of all positions in baseball except catcher seemed to characterize him as a runner, but perhaps a more apt description would be a racehorse with a wealth of energy.

Academically, he was challenged only by himself. Although readily accepted into social circles, he was quiet when it came to studies. He did what he had to do and excelled in almost everything, but he never made it a point to boast to others. He was an Eagle Scout at age thirteen, earning twenty-two merit badges. At fifteen, before the lure of the medical field actually took hold, he knew all the bones and muscles of the human body. He was an incessant reader and borrowed books from his father's medical friends. As a junior in high school he learned Latin, Spanish, and German and often tutored his friends when he had the time. As a senior he had aced his classes and was looking for more. While he missed scoring a perfect score on the SATs, he was satisfied that his one missed answer wasn't the end of civilization, at least as he knew it.

An inquisitive writer and pre-med student, he took his tireless curiosity about life to Harvard University. He raced through undergraduate study in three years, earned a graduate fellowship, and gained entrance into the Harvard Medical School at twenty. Although first drawn to obstetrics because of his fascination with the gift of life, he soon turned to the heart as his pathway to greater knowledge about the body. Again, his zest for knowing everything about the human body and the workings of all aspects of the heart spurred him on, to a point that even his professors were astonished that he seemingly knew more than they did.

One of his professors was so astounded that she gave Zach half credit for one of his answers in an essay-driven exam, even though, as the professor wrote in a note in the margin, the answer given was not correct. She further noted that though the essay did not comport with known medical science at the time, Zach's answer was so logical that she gave him half credit for its presentation. And, she added, not only had she scratched her head when offering comments, but she intended to do further research to see if anything like that would be possible.

All that brought a welcome smile to young Zach's face, and he subsequently related to the professor that he had been stumped by the question and had put on his thinking cap. It had earned him five points in a ten-point question, leaving him with ninety-five out of a possible one hundred points total.

Longfellow's quest to be the best in cardiology became his primary challenge. Surrounded by some of the world's finest doctors, he learned well. He also was going to join a select group of world-renowned specialists, some well entrenched in their area of expertise. He hoped others from his generation would take the baton and continue to race toward solving heart disease and better understand the miracles of the heart.

He became a resident at Johns Hopkins University, advancing to associate professor, professor, and finally head of cardiology. By this time, his credentials had advanced him into the international arena, where he was one of a handful of key experts in heart disease and heart transplants. He lectured all over the world, held seminars for his compatriots, and had a lust for teaching others what it meant to hold a heart, and someone's life, in their hands.

Bailey and Zach's First Meeting

Bailey and Zach literally bumped into each other in a tunnel while leaving the traditional Harvard vs. Yale football game, won by the Crimson 27–0, which left the *Hawwvad* folks mighty happy. The Crimson had just finished an unbeaten season, and putting a slap-down on the Yalies made it all the better.

The narrow tunnel meant people had to move slowly and avoid pushing, but as usual, some overexuberant Harvard fans who'd had more than one drink too many had other ideas. Zach was squeezed forward into Bailey and almost knocked her down.

"I'm sorry, I didn't mean to bang into you!" said Zach when he half-caught Bailey from falling face down and getting an unwanted concrete sandwich.

"Well, thank you for your chivalry," she said, composing herself while regaining her balance. "My name is Bailey Stewart, Mr. . . .?"

"Longfellow. Zach Longfellow. Pardon me for maybe being forward—or, I guess, more forward—but can I get you an ice cream cone or something?"

"Well, let's see. It's twenty-eight degrees outside, so maybe a coffee with some cream in it would be better."

"Your place or mine?" he inquired. "Err—do you have a place you haunt that would take in you and a stranger?"

"Quick recovery, Longfellow. How about Stickybeaks on Hobson Street? Meet you there in an hour?"

"Deal."

They looked at each other with a smile.

Now in the warm confines of Stickybeaks, where just about everyone knows your name, it was time for a friendship to blossom.

"So, Stewart," he began, "tell me something interesting about yourself."

"Well, I'm a transplant without a transplant, if you catch my drift, trying to make good on my quest to be a good legal mind. Born and raised in California, so the weather here sucks. But at the urging of one of my faculty advisors at Stanford, I took the leap to come east. Haven't regretted it, except the weather sucks. Did I already mention that?"

"Just what part of the law do you hope to challenge, seeing that you are up for a challenge?"

"I'm open. Wherever and whatever comes along, I will travel a path until a crossroads appears. Then I will make a decision and continue on my journey."

"What made you choose the law?"

"Not really sure. My sister and I were such competitors. She was going into finance and I just didn't like the black-and-white air about that profession. I've always liked interpreting things, offering opinions and, of course, listening. I think law has a lot to do with listening first and speaking next."

"Are you judgmental?" he inquired.

"Perhaps. But as I've studied more and more about the Constitution and the law, I've become more accepting of other opinions. Right and wrong need to be challenged by maybe."

The accepting smile on his face made her smile warmly back. There was mutual admiration in the less-than-fifteen minutes they had been together.

"So, Longfellow, what's your claim to fame? Where's your road going to take you? And, just curious, is Longfellow your real name or is there something you need to tell me?"

"Well, if you must know, Longfellow is my real name and my great-grandfather was, in fact, related to the poet Henry Wadsworth, so I am a shirttail relative. Henry wrote some notable pieces. Two of his brothers also had some fame of their own. One of my great uncles was an artist, but passed away well before I came along. My other great uncle was a member of Congress before becoming a postmaster general and then federal district court judge. My great-grandfather did writings of his own.

"As for me, I aspired to be in the medical field. The human body always has transfixed me and I have dreamt about being a part of science that discovers how to make things better, not only by saving lives, but determining what makes things fail. I initially thought of being an OB/GYN, but knowing I couldn't save all newborns bothered me, so I turned my attention to the heart."

"Did someone in your family inspire you to go into medicine?"

"My father had stories to tell about the family heritage, but he encouraged me to seek my own interests. He knew of my medical fascination and went out of his way to listen to me babble on about how the human body was so uniquely put together. Listening to his stories on how my grandfathers followed their calling was quite interesting, to say the least."

"So what was it like growing up knowing your great-grandfather was well known, not only when he was alive, but now, for his insights and words?"

"I got a chance to read all of his works, even the pieces not published. All was in his handwriting, so it was cool to see the actual script as well as seeing it in print."

"Anything jump out at you, since he was a poet and not necessarily a historian?" she asked, now mesmerized by Zach's every word.

"Well, the Midnight Ride of Paul Revere was a creative piece that snuck into American folklore and lives to this day. I read his original piece and felt like I was there riding with the folk hero.

Listen my children and you shall hear
Of the Midnight Ride of Paul Revere,
On the eighteenth of April, in Seventy-five;
Hardly a man is now alive . . .

"Inaccuracies be damned, the piece originally was titled 'Paul Revere's Ride' and later changed to 'The Landlord's Tale.' 'Paul Revere's Ride,' not 'The Midnight Ride of Paul Revere.' There is a lot more to the story and I was privileged to see a lot of the background information.

"Ernest Longfellow bequeathed some fifty-five paintings from his collection to the Museum of Fine Arts in Boston, including works by Jacopo Bassano, John Constable, Thomas Couture, Luca Giordano, and others. They remain on display there today. That's quite a heritage as well."

"So, what else do you have to say for yourself, Longfellow?"

"How about dinner?"

They clasped each other's hands and their smiles said it all. A Longfellow serenade of words followed.

Bailey and Zach at Longfellow Estate

His second "Bails?" call got a response from Bailey, who was in her office on the second floor, somewhat mesmerized by Ivanhoe 3.

"Up here," came her response. "Be right down." The two met in the foyer and Zach could tell that Bailey had something on her mind, something that seemingly lost in thought.

"Ivanhoe again?" was his first guess.

"This is the wildest E-ticket ride I've ever been on. I think we need a drink," she said.

Zach did a double take more than once as he read through Ivanhoe 3.

"It keeps getting more bizarre, doesn't it?" He gave Bailey a curious look as she was finishing off her glass of chardonnay. "I suspect Ivanhoe has a lot more information to share, and each time we get something back it will send our minds spinning with more questions."

"This information about Hoover is well beyond what I ever discovered in my original research, but my emphasis was on the development of the FBI and an investigative agency, not about Hoover as an individual," said Bailey. "This information goes to the man and may well prove to be a sort of 'smoking gun' as we try to figure what we can do to get access to documents to prove or disprove what Ivanhoe has presented. What concerns me is whether any laws were broken. Murder does not have a statute of limitations, and murder certainly was the focal point of the assassination.

"If there was a cover-up, on any level, then we'll be off in another direction. To investigate any of this, we'll need some supersleuths and access. Matt seems to have a handle on this, so we probably should get together now, while we have time, to see if he wants to go to Spencer Crockett now or continue to formulate our hypothesis as more information becomes available.

"This is not a simple black-and-white case. There are a number of questions that will need some expert attention. I realize we each have our own areas of expertise, but as others join the team, will we be able to control our investigations to keep everything from unraveling? I certainly don't want any of the others to become targets. There are those out there that would like nothing better than to disrupt, deny, and discredit someone who might get too close to something considered 'need to know' or 'none of someone else's business.' And physical violence certainly is not out of the question with the powerful, rich or not. That isn't relegated to just the Mafia or sinister types; it's been a part of the business and political arenas as well. Vicious, vile, and outright hateful rhetoric are a part of all of those worlds.

"Crimes against humanity are another consideration. Hitler, Stalin,

Hussein and Bin Laden remind us that evil lurks all around us. We need to identify it and neutralize it. But if you identify it, are you in harm's way? Will we be in harm's way? I'm struggling with that. I do believe the public has a right to know, but is there a fine line between telling all of the truth and leaving out some of the details?"

"Bails, you have said it over and over: if laws were broken, there is a demand to punish the perpetrators," offered Zach. "If we were to uncover and substantiate what happened in the assassination, for instance, would that bring closure for those who were old enough to be affected?"

"Think of the drill down, Zach. If some of those people responsible are still alive, shouldn't we feel obligated to punish them? If another country was involved, for instance, do we go after that country? Or a business concern or cause? Ivanhoe laid out the facts and it all seems to be convincing, so are we to assume that there are those out there who are hoping that there is a cover-up and they won't be threatened?

"I also think about all of the Nazis who fled to North and South America and elsewhere, that probably were given some sort of assurance that they never would be found—for a price. The Simon Wiesenthal organization and the Nokmim sought out thousands of those who were responsible for untold numbers of war crimes. The Nuremberg Trials only brought some of them to justice for crimes against humanity.

"We could be facing the same thing here, not just for the assassinations, but for other clandestine operations, even Pearl Harbor. I can hardly wait to see what Ivanhoe has on that 'Day of Infamy.' Crimes or cover-ups?"

"I'm in town for the next couple of weeks, so let me know what Matt thinks about getting together," said Zach.

"I'll call him tomorrow," responded Bailey.

CHAPTER 11

Order in the Court

For Supreme Court justices, law clerks, and even staff members, there is a certain glitz and glamor about being in and around the hallowed halls. During the court's term, schedules are hectic and include meetings, research, writing, a multitude of inquiries, and some long hours. All put a strain on the best of them. The justices are appointed for life and are used to the rigors. Law clerks, aspiring attorneys or judges, have a year, perhaps two, to fit in. Support staff have their limits as well.

As expected, the court's caseload has steadily increased over the years as more people seek justice under the law. Plenary review, with oral arguments by attorneys, is granted in approximately 100 cases per term. Formal written opinions are delivered in 80 to 90 cases. Approximately 50 to 60 additional cases will be disposed of without granting plenary review. What is striking is that the publication of a term's written opinions, including concurring and dissenting opinions as well as orders, approaches 5,000 pages. Some opinions might be revised a dozen or so times before they are announced.

The court hears three types of cases. Approximately two-thirds are appeals from lower federal courts, and one-third from state supreme courts. Rarely does the court hear the third type, a case that involves one state against another.

The normal court routine calls for oral arguments Mondays and Tuesdays, conferences on Wednesdays, and additional research and internal meetings Thursdays and Fridays. The meetings of the nine were held at least once a week to bring everyone up to date on the cases pending and submitted for review by the solicitor general. Determining final disposition led to long hours of debate about the merits of each case, choosing sides and deciding who was writing for the majority and who would write for the minority, if any. Those discussions were not for the faint of heart, as some of the cases seemed to hinge on a liberal or conservative view. But with this court, President McCade had inserted enough of what was considered a moderate view that the public felt there was not an ideology to be wary of as decisions were made.

It was the law clerks who spent a great deal of time researching precedents and court decisions. Justices spent their own time reading, a prerequisite to sitting in judgment, but any supplement that could help any and all arrive at a just decision was welcome. It was the duty of the clerks to dig deep and be at the ready when a justice needed support material. The justices had hand-picked their clerks, so the team relied on each other to make a case, either for or against. The trust value was inherent.

Brumfield, Stewart, and Longfellow Devise Strategy

In spite of all of the daily responsibilities Bailey tended to, she did find time to contact Brumfield and set up a time to meet that weekend.

Whiteboards and an assortment of fresh fruit, cheese, crackers and small sandwiches at the ready, the threesome was at it by 10 a.m. on what promised to be a beautiful Saturday.

"What we have seen from the Ivanhoe letters is startling, to say the least," said Brumfield. "Are we dealing with exculpatory or inculpatory evidence? Does it reveal a premeditated attempt to suppress and simply hide pertinent evidence?

"Bringing Hoover into the mix will cross several lines of investigation, so we need to be sure where we step. One of my first observations is that this information may well have come through the Hoover files. After all, he seemed to have had access where others did not. Even presidents, and government agencies, for that matter, couldn't come up with this stuff.

"But I also assume that Ivanhoe is sitting on other information and data that even Hoover didn't have knowledge of. The energy, medical technology, and space travel areas are ones that wouldn't have fit into his investigative framework. Stuff that involves elected officials certainly would have been within his scope of interest, as the FBI regularly vets politicos, including those running for office and those eventually appointed to high-profile positions. People have been denied nominations because of what the FBI has uncovered. Is there some political hanky-panky that goes on? Absolutely. It's all about power—and the abuse of same.

"Let's go back to our list of key words and determine if we are ready to get the wagons rolling."

Brumfield listed the words and asked, "What is valid and what needs to be added?"

Overview

- Ivanhoe
- Kennedy
- Crime
- Cover-up
- AG
- DOJ
- Mystery person

"I think the special prosecutor has a seat at the table here, but under whose direction—AG or DOJ? And perhaps we should say our SP will actually be a consultant, since his role would be a precursor to our or his contacting the AG or DOJ?"

"I concur," said Brumfield.

"As do I," added Zach.

"Do we have our facts straight and is it time to bring in Crockett?" asked Brumfield.

"Is this to mean that you meet with him, Matt, and give him the general overview without him seeing any of the Ivanhoe letters? Like an off-the-record sort of meeting?" asked Bailey.

"That would be my take," said Brumfield. "He would be able to determine if we had any legs to this and if so, determine if he was going to be a part of the team. I suspect he'll jump at this since he was a federal judge and an SP with authority. We might as well find out where we stand. I'll contact him and set something up."

CHAPTER 12

Spencer Crockett

Spencer Crockett was self-assured, inquisitive, and very perceptive. Raised in the comforts of Newport Beach in California, he professed that the law was his career of choice while at college, and after he graduated with honors from UCLA, he completed his schooling with a law degree from Harvard. He was among the top choices of recruits for the firm of White, Bear & Kirkpatrick, and it was there he met and became close friends with Matt Brumfield. The two shared some fun times at the firm, often sitting on the balcony after a law-filled day, sipping black sambuca. They were referred to as the Sambuca Brothers.

He, like Brumfield, became a superior court judge and was appointed to the state court of appeals before being recruited by the Department of Justice as deputy attorney general. A skilled analyst of the law and all its elements, he was appointed federal judge. After five years, he decided to accept an appointment as a special prosecutor. It was an area where he felt more comfortable, as it allowed him to investigate possible crimes and misdeeds as opposed to overseeing the variety of legal issues that seemed to plague every administration.

While his good friend Matt Brumfield gave one the impression of a Perry Mason, Crockett had the Gregory Peck look, along with his baritone voice. That actually worked in his favor, because he was the public-address voice of the Washington Redskins for six years. It was a recreational outlet for him and he was a fan as well. As his time became more consumed with SP casework, however, he had to give up his sports sideline.

He relished the investigative jobs, as the cases came to him. He also enjoyed conversing with old friends and colleagues. He didn't shy away from a friendly game of cards, and he and Brumfield were known to frequent social events—and they still were known as the Sambuca Brothers.

Brumfield and Crockett Meet at Old Ebbitt Grill

No sooner had Matt Brumfield and Spencer Crockett stepped into Old Ebbitt Grill, one of Washington's go-to places for lunch, then calls of "Hey!" "Over here!" "Old guys in the back!" "Matt!" "Spence!" and "Sambuca!" filled the air. In a place where notable politicians and people in the know met on a daily basis, Brumfield and Crockett were recognized by those who welcomed them at any time, at any place. The two shared friendly waves and smiles and shook hands as they wandered to their place in the back, sharing quick responses when they could.

Royalty, they weren't. Respected, they were.

Now in a somewhat secluded area reserved for private times when power brokers and politicians needed space, the two settled into the booth. The conversation started with an ongoing bet the two had with regard to the Red Sox and Nationals. Whatever team had the most wins at the end of the season, the loser had to buy lunch. Even though the Nationals had bowed out in the first round of the National League baseball playoffs, Boston fell well short of the post season. When Jake Dickson, the server for the most prestigious place in the Grill, asked what they preferred to drink and would they want any appetizers, Crockett had no problem going for a plateful of oysters on the half shell. Brumfield knew it was coming, so his expression was a mere shake of the head and smile.

Since 1856, this landmark bar and restaurant served DC's power class (including presidents Grant, Cleveland, Harding and Teddy Roosevelt). Rich with historic furnishings—even the head of a walrus allegedly shot by Roosevelt—the place never failed to satisfy. It was owned and operated by the well-respected Bonaventura family and run by the effervescent Angela. Known for its dependable American cuisine, the saloon featured a fantastic raw bar with seven types of oysters. Its popular lunch offerings included a terrific burger, a Reuben, chicken wings, and grilled filet mignon.

Crockett opted for the filet mignon while Brumfield stuck to his usual Reuben.

"Spence, I've got an unusual problem, a case if you will, and I would appreciate your take," Brumfield began. "I thought our initial meeting would be just to give you a lay of the land, and if this is something you want to get involved in, then we can meet and go over more intricate details."

"They didn't call you 'the Secret Man' for nothing, back in our day," said Spencer with a chuckle. "You were great at keeping people in just enough dark space that they didn't see what was coming. Very cunning and effective."

"As I recall, you were 'the Shadow,' with eyes and ears seemingly everywhere. How you came up with information stumped many. But we were a good team, weren't we?"

"The sambuca tag was classic," remembered Crockett, stroking his graying beard with a sense of great accomplishment for their travails. "Okay, I'm interested, since you are apparently all in, so give me the *Reader's Digest* version."

For the next ten minutes, Brumfield gave his version of the "case," interrupted only by the serving of their lunch. Crockett appeared to be transfixed as detail after detail was delivered. He didn't interrupt but gave nods to what was said, trying to analyze the whole content and how he might be a part of the equation.

Brumfield was truly all in, and Crockett had made up his mind early on that this was just preposterous enough to be totally true. How many times had he been involved in cases where elements were so wild that deciding what was true seemed like a crapshoot? And if it involved a jury, all bets would be off. Crockett knew his good friend all too well. He also knew Justice Stewart and Dr. Longfellow. To have all three of these people appear to be so passionate about such a case led him to believe that being another team member would be a dream come true.

Brumfield was enjoying the rest of his Rueben when Crockett simply said, "When do we start?"

The smile on Matt's face reminded Crockett of someone who had just won the lottery.

"What helped you decide, Spence?"

"Probably when I heard the word 'secrets,'" he answered. "As I listened to your words, I kept thinking about searching for the truth—isn't that what all of us in the legal field want to find? If this has legs, and I think it does, then I think we owe it to ourselves, and to everyone who has made the best of efforts to judge fact from fiction, to follow up.

"You realize that this is more than a can of worms, that once the hounds have been unleashed there is going to be some chasing going on."

"I do, Spence, which is why we have to get our ducks in a row, so we can counter attacks from different directions. We've seen this during our careers, from the bench as well as at the legal tables. Once I have shown you the documents it'll become even clearer that we are looking at lawbreaking, cover-ups on several levels, and what money can do. So, our challenge is to determine what form of wrongdoing has occurred and quite possibly is still going on.

"The public has a right to know, but to what extent, I do not know. The assassinations are one thing; the other stuff could cause some real problems. Truth be told, are we up to it and will anyone believe us? If we search for the facts and use our own sense of judgment, I think we can. Determining who else joins our team, as I have told Bailey and Zach, is just as important. We can't afford leaks, because as soon as someone knows we're making certain inquiries, well, once the lights go on, the rats will start running."

"What's to prevent possible witnesses from simply stonewalling us?" Crockett asked. "The assassination alone had so many firewalls that conspiracy theorists had a field day claiming cover-ups. Witnesses were coerced, paid off, even eliminated. I read a report on the JFK assassination that indicated that of 435 witnesses that were called before the Warren Commission, 379 died within ten years of the tragedy. And that figured out to be a one gazillion to one chance of happening, according to an actuary."

"What's to keep those firewalls from preventing us drilling further?", said Brumfield.

"Maybe nothing, but it depends on who's asking the questions," said Crockett. "Technology has changed the way the world does business. This Ivanhoe has dropped some very detailed information into our laps that may well help us break through those firewalls. When we ask witnesses to swear to tell the truth and nothing but the truth, we expect our own outcomes. If someone lies or we know they have, we can punish them with perjury, a jailable offense. Back when these cases were a part of government oversight commissions, hearings and investigations, there wasn't the technology to move quickly.

"I always felt Johnson was anxious to put the Kennedy assassination behind him because he wanted to lead. As long as there were some questions to be answered, he would be stuck in neutral. I personally felt the Warren Commission was a setup, and now Ivanhoe has brought all of this into the daylight, so to speak."

"We both were younger in that day and the uncertainty of the reports always has befuddled me. I guess the sealing of the documents sort of tells you there was something to cover up. Wouldn't you want to know all of the sordid details, however gruesome they might be? Why fifty years? Probably because those who were directly involved would have died or simply wouldn't remember pertinent details.

"Think of what goes on today. Social media and the ever-snooping print and electronic folks would be all over this. Which brings me back to Hoover. How much did he know and when did he know it? Did he break any laws and use his office to cover up, or was he saving his information for a rainy day?"

"All valid observations, ones that we are going to ferret out as we get more and more from Ivanhoe," agreed Brumfield "Any chance we can ever meet this Ivanhoe person?"

"Not from what I understand," said Brumfield. "If getting information in written form is our only option, then we will go with the team's perception."

"I'm all in, Matt," said Crockett with an assuring grin.

"Well, that settles it, then," said Brumfield. "If you want to join the three of us at the Longfellow estate, we can swing by your place and pick up some things."

"No need. I figured when the Mystery Man asked me to lunch, something was up. So, I am packed and ready to go," countered Crockett with a grin.

"What about Julie?" asked Brumfield. "She's welcome to join us. There's plenty of room."

"Once she heard me talking to the Secret Man, she knew something was up, so she decided to go visit her mother in Pittsburgh. Where's Barbara these days?"

"She's been going back and forth to Minneapolis to be with her sister who's been having some health problems.

"We can take the limo to Fairfax and I can share some documents with you along the way."

The din in the popular Grill seemed to be nonstop. As the two departed, there were those who had not seen Brumfield and Crockett arrive, which caused another stir among the patrons. More callouts, including that of FBI chief Randall Payne, resulted in more hand waving and smiles, and a reply or two. One person in the crowd whispered to his companion, "There go two of the most respected legal minds to ever hit this town." Her curious response was, "My, one looks like a thinner and younger Perry Mason and the other a younger Gregory Peck."

The two old war horses were riding again.

Brumfield, Crockett in Car Going to the Estate

The usual thirty-minute ride to Fairfax with no traffic took fifty minutes this Friday afternoon. The time was well spent, however, as Crockett read and reread the documents Brumfield had given him. Brumfield decided to not interrupt Crockett's reading or thinking time. He did notice a nod from time to time.

"Matt, how many people know about this?" Crockett finally said.

"You, me, Bailey and Zach, and of course, Ivanhoe."

"And you say we don't have any direct contact with Ivanhoe?"

"That's about it," Brumfield said. "The information Ivanhoe sends to Bailey leaves us forming our own questions, but wanting more. They have a system to alert each other and that has worked so far. I have a feeling that since everyone knows that government snooping is commonplace these days, the one fail-safe method of transferring information is by US mail. I guess a delivery service would work, but I think there is a way to back that up and see who sent what and when. I thought it was quite ingenious for the original informant to send the information to Ivanhoe by using a microdot."

"We'll have to be careful whose toes we step on, but we certainly can conduct our own investigation," said Crockett.

"How much do we have to divulge to the FBI or Justice?" said Brumfield. "I would expect we will hear 'we'll get back to you,' at some point."

"Having been on different sides of investigation and judgment, I would think the two of us would be able to weave our way in and out of any agency," Crockett replied. "I know those who I have worked with before wouldn't diss us, but answering our questions might require them to take the questions to the next level. I guess it depends on what those in the know don't really want to talk about and if they are concerned about suppressing documents considered sealed. In the case of the assassination, crimes were committed. A cover-up also is a crime. And if there are co-conspirators, they can't take the cover of statutes of limitations, as they don't apply to murder.

"How are Bailey and Zach on this? They might be vulnerable at some time, but we can launch our own investigations and keep them far from the public fight."

"Bailey took up the charge early, weighing the merits based solely on a want to know. She, too, has been a part of investigations and prosecutions and has sat in judgment, so she is eager to pursue this all-out. Zach wants to see the Kennedy x-rays and photos and match them to the pathology report, so he is just as anxious to see this through."

While Crockett had met and been around the Longfellows on a number of occasions, he never had been to the Fairfax estate. He was immediately impressed with the drawbridge. Bailey and Zach were waiting for them on the front porch. After the pleasantries and a first-time welcome to Crockett, the four found their way into the family room. Dinner would be ready in an hour, so they had plenty of time to plan the rest of their evening.

"I guess one of my questions for you, Bailey, would be whether you think there might be a conflict of interest as it applies to the court," Crockett said.

"I thought about that from the start," said Bailey. "If I believed there was a remote chance that anything I did or would do would draw unfriendly fire, I would step back, but I don't think so.

"The Constitution is based on three equal, but distinct branches of government. The Supreme Court was established to interpret the Constitution, not rewrite it. We don't try cases; we evaluate whether the law was properly applied. It's up to litigators to prove or disprove facts, criminal or civil. We don't adjudicate investigations, but the right to investigate might come before us if there is an infringement on someone's rights under the Constitution. Think of three words that drive the court—justice, freedom, and equality.

"I was drawn to the legal field because I wanted to know that the truth mattered. Having been a part of the Supreme Court, I still am frustrated that we can disagree on interpretation. So here we are, evaluating what we feel is fact and/or fiction and hopefully we all agree on the interpretation. We've read all that Ivanhoe has given us and I would assume we all are just as curious and perhaps startled as to what Ivanhoe presents.

"So, I say, state your case."

Brumfield rose to his feet and walked to the two whiteboards. "Now we need to start connecting our dots and determine how we will need to proceed. As I mentioned before, I think Spence and I have more cushion to work with and you, Bailey, can be the conduit with Ivanhoe. Zach, you will fill a valuable role of corroboration if and when we get access to the autopsy photos and pathology reports of the JFK assassination."

He rewrote the key words that they had discussed:

Overview
Ivanhoe
Kennedy
Crime
Cover-up
AG
DOJ
Hoover
Assignments for the Four

"Once again, Bailey, you've got Ivanhoe. Spence, you have the AG and DOJ. I'll take Kennedy, crime and cover-up. We'll let the Hoover connection simmer for a while. That okay with everyone?"

All nodded in agreement.

"Let's have some dinner and chat, then come back in here and figure where our tangents will take us," said Bailey.

Small talk and some funny stories dominated the hour-long dinner. They all were anxious to get back to the project and knew they only had a couple of hours before they would tire from the long days all had had.

"Let's approach this as an outline and use bullet points to drill down into the subject. Bailey, why don't you start it off and tell us what you know or suspect you know about Ivanhoe."

"Before we lose track of what we are doing, are we concentrating on the Kennedy assassination, or any one of a number of things Ivanhoe has divulged?" asked Bailey.

"Good question," said Brumfield. "We need to determine what our goal or goals are. Are we trying to prove or disprove something specific, reopen a cold case, or take a scatter-gun approach that will require more than the four of us to investigate? Is there one case that might be easy for us to gather sufficient information on, or should we take on only the JFK murder? The JFK murder still resonates in the public. There have been a number of shenanigans going on that have been passively forgotten or left alone. Even the cover-ups involving Ted Kennedy's career were open to suggestion.

"What Ivanhoe stated in the second letter in such detail makes me think we have a case that warrants our immediate attention. If we find credence in our investigations, then we will know the facts as presented by Ivanhoe are correct, or at least certainly believable beyond reasonable doubt."

Crockett concurred. "Rather than spread ourselves too thin, too fast, maybe focusing on the JFK assassination would give us some stability. I'm still okay with the assignments, but it would be helpful if we all offered our own bullet points to focus on what we need to do."

"Perhaps it would be best if we got back to it in the morning," suggested Bailey. "We have all day tomorrow, and sleeping on what we have to do might bear some fresh ideas."

Longfellow Estate

It was a clear and crisp Saturday morning when the four made their way to the family room after enjoying a breakfast of french toast, scrambled eggs, bagels, assorted fruits, coffee, tea, and what appeared to be a whipped-cream soufflé conjured up by chef Annette, who had stayed over by special request from Bailey to help her guests feel at home.

"You sure know how to set the table," said Crockett with a chuckle. "How can we concentrate on our serious debate when we have a food arrangement like that? And the view; goodness gracious, you two really have something here. Picture perfect."

"We've been fortunate to keep our home here, what with our jobs and other obligations," said Bailey. "I can't see ever leaving here, even when we retire."

"Shall we get to it?" asked Brumfield. "We've all had some time to think independently, so hopefully we can come up with a battle plan that will give us all a sense of purpose."

"Matt, I was thinking about our main purpose," said Bailey. "Are we here to solve a crime or give the public information they have a right to know? And how much is a right to know versus a moral obligation to let the public make an informed decision?"

"Very valid questions," said Brumfield. "Using the JFK assassination as our focal point, would our inquiries be to corroborate the facts as Ivanhoe has presented them or bring the perpetrators to justice? If we go on to other information listed by Ivanhoe—Pearl Harbor, energy, medical science—are we going to prove or disprove cover-ups as suggested?

"So, the question of the day is whether we are here to solve a crime or to decide what the public has a right to know," continued Brumfield, writing down notes on the whiteboard. "Spence, if you went to your sources in the DOJ, where would you start?"

Crockett Gives His Take

"Everything starts with the AG," Crockett began. "The FBI and any internal work by the Justice Department falls under that person's jurisdiction. But my read here is that I would call Randy Payne at the FBI and subtly walk him through what we are proposing. If that means getting his blessing to go to Liz Cookson at Justice, then I would know how difficult it might be for us. On the other hand, if he is unwilling to help or would refrain from giving Cookson a heads-up, then we might have to go through Congress.

"This takes us back to our purpose, though. Are we investigating a long-ago crime and trying to set the record straight and bring co-conspirators to justice, or might we perhaps go to the public and take our chances? Would

Congress have a horse in the race, so to speak, trying to show the public that it has the guts to investigate a crime from over fifty years ago, to bring some closure to people who lived through that horrific time?"

"Is this time to get additional information from Ivanhoe?" interjected Bailey. "Ivanhoe certainly outlined what I thought seemed credible in his letter. Is related info something Director Payne and any of his investigative folks would care to share, or is there a lid on this?

"The National Archives would have documents on the JFK assassination. Should we start there instead? Or should we make contact with Ivanhoe and ask for corroboration of the facts?"

"There must be millions of pages, including photographs, text, and even the Warren Commission findings in the Archives," said Crockett. "Ivanhoe seemed to have something that had been digitalized on all of this. How it all came together is anyone's guess. I guess when the stars align, they serve as a moment in time. And I agree with Ivanhoe's assessment that no one person would ordinarily have complete access at any one time—not the president or anyone else in government, even the most powerful.

"The public knows there are questions about the Kennedy assassination, but some of the other stuff like Pearl Harbor, medical breakthroughs, or alternative fuel sources could be overwhelming. And I'm not sure there isn't a mass of other information, things the general public never knew about, that would be mind-boggling.

"It would be nice to have a face-to-face discussion with Ivanhoe so we would know everything, but apparently that is not going to happen. So perhaps it makes sense to concentrate, for now, on the JFK assassination."

"Are we going to approach it as a right to know?" asked Brumfield. "We certainly can do our own investigations, but it would seem we need to get a lay of the land and see if we can trust Justice to help. Spence, Randy's response probably would give us a good measuring stick.

"Bailey, perhaps you could solicit another response from Ivanhoe; ask if corroborating evidence is available anywhere. Zach, want to contact the National Archives and see if you could get permission to look at any Kennedy documents and photos? I'm going to try my hand at any case law that delves into rights of privacy and see if the Kennedy family has sealed anything that would prevent us from digging deeper. I sense that if we don't do something quickly, and keep our lines of communication open with Ivanhoe, something might get leaked, and then there would be a horde of investigations going at one time."

The conversations had pushed them well into the afternoon and left them all with thoughts to ponder. Yates took Brumfield and Crockett back to DC while Bailey and Zach enjoyed seeing the setting sun drift behind the quasi-forest to the west of the estate.

"So where do we go from here, kiddo?" said Zach, draping his arm around Bailey's shoulder.

"I'll send something off to get Ivanhoe's attention. I agree it would be nice to be able to corroborate all of this. Having more information about the other subjects will add logs to the fire, but I think we need to get a sense of how deep Ivanhoe's information goes. A crime is one thing. Simply setting the record straight is another. And would we be doing more harm than good if all of the information became public?"

"Daniel Ellsberg and Edward Snowden didn't seem to care," said Zach. "They simply opted for the public's right to know. Did some people get hurt? Sure. Did it place a strong suspicion in the public eye that the government was up to no good? I would guess yes there, too. I'm interested in it all, but the cost has to be considered.

"Medical breakthroughs, like cures for cancer and other catastrophic illnesses, would be of interest to me. Trust in our government and of the rich and famous, the all-powerful; I think the general public has an appetite to know who has done what and for the good of whom. The public believes what it is told, through the spoken or written word, for the most part. Would rewriting history be accepted or cause more grief and turmoil?"

"How about a movie?" said Bailey, thinking a lighter activity would ease some of their built-up tension and swirling thoughts.

"Got anything in mind?" he asked.

"Well, let's just look it up," she offered, remembering what one of baseball's icons, Casey Stengel, used to say. That impressed Zach, as his baseball memory quickly clicked in.

The box of Pandora was about to be opened up.

CHAPTER 13

The Post in the *Post*

YOUR MOVE
Trust, but verify

A few days later, Ivanhoe 4 arrived at the unique white iron mailbox just outside the perimeter of the Longfellow estate. Mandy's continued curiosity had no bounds. She was in the dark on this and hoped at some time the judge would let her know what was going on. She would stay tuned.

The judge had had her fill of oral arguments during the court's day. Aside from forming her own opinions about the pending cases, she had more than a lot on her mind with what had been offered by Ivanhoe. Subsequent meetings with the Four, as she collectively referred to the group, added to the mix.

Mandy had dutifully stacked the day's mail in convenient piles for a quick run-through, but as she had done three previous times, the large gray flat envelope had been placed on top. That brought a smile to Bailey's face; she could only imagine that Mandy, the curious one, would have loved to be in on the caper, or whatever it was.

The rest of the mail mattered little, as Bailey quickly used her letter opener, leaned back in her easy chair, and began the latest installment from the mysterious yet informative Ivanhoe.

Ivanhoe Letter—4

Dear Justice Stewart:

While I sense you have some frustrations, believe me you will be satisfied with all of our efforts. As I mentioned, I have limitations, as do you, but I am counting on you to decide who might be able to help you connect whatever dots.

The National Archives has a lot of information on just about every subject, including people, places and things. What it does not have is a common thread to connect everything. That is why no one has been able to access qualifying information all at once—until now. The digitalized data simply came into view like an eclipse—momentarily, but not for keeps. My mysterious informant apparently was, as I've said, at the right place at the right time.

Your wish for verification probably can come through the National Archives because you would be looking for something specific. Since the Kennedy assassination is at the core of the original information, I suggest you search through what is available through public record and what remains sealed. Believe it or not, some records are said to be sealed for one hundred years, which means someone has something to hide. Obviously, no one who was around at the time of the assassination would still be alive.

That takes me to Mr. Lincoln. Not many people at the time knew Lincoln was going to Ford's Theater, at least not until the last moment. The security detail guarding Lincoln just happened to be gone at the time Booth snuck up behind the president and shot him. A horse just happened to be waiting for Booth to make his getaway. Just so happened that only one street was not sealed off when the search began for the assassin. Just happened when Booth was cornered in the Virginia barn that eventually was set on fire and he made an attempt to come out with hands up while dragging his injured leg, but it just so happened he was shot before he could be restrained for an interrogation.

Coincidence?

The one person who knew where Lincoln would be and had control of all of the other facets of the getaway and subsequent gunning down of Booth was Edwin Stanton—Secretary of War. Conspiracy? Stanton was the one who uttered, "Now he belongs to the ages," when Lincoln was pronounced dead the next day at a boarding house across the street from the theater.

This was a conspiracy for the ages. Eight people were convicted of being involved and were hanged. Four others received prison sentences.

As for Robert Kennedy and Martin Luther King, just think of the setup. Sirhan Sirhan was the one who got caught and he didn't even know how to shoot a gun (like the protagonist in The Manchurian Candidate*). He didn't remember doing what he did. As far as anyone knows, he doesn't remember anything today. What were all of extra bullet holes in the Ambassador Hotel kitchen doing there? The panels from the kitchen were taken by the police as evidence and subsequently destroyed. How convenient.*

James Earl Ray supposedly shot King and although he had used a gun before, he was not known as a sharpshooter. He, too, appeared dazed after the killing. He tried to retract his confession shortly after, but he eventually died of cancer in prison. Jack Ruby was a part of the JFK conspiracy, but he died just before he was about to spill his guts. Oswald and Ruby were interrogated and the notes, taped and written, disappeared. Coincidence?

So, I say look at the evidence that is in the Archives and see what is for public view and what remains sealed. That alone should raise some eyebrows. So would the analysis of forensic pathologists, both working the cases at the time and long afterward. Show me the autopsy photos and allow me to look at the reports and even I would raise some questions.

Why would anyone associated with the government want to hide the facts when we have an open and supposedly free society? And as I have said before, if you follow the money, you will come to some startling conclusions. Who stood to benefit from any one of the assassinations? Lincoln wanted to bring the country back together as if nothing ever was wrong. JFK was making overtures about the test-ban treaty, getting out of Vietnam, and legislating equality for the Black community. Bobby Kennedy was hoping to ride the Kennedy name into the White House and he would have been more inquisitive than Jack. And King was a true leader who was finding a peaceful way to move closer toward equality.

Some people simply did not want any of that. Is there any change in the way the world works today? People disappear, money changes hands, and it's still a power struggle.

Trust, but verify. Try the Archives.

Respectfully,

IVANHOE

No sooner had Bailey read and reread Ivanhoe 4 than she heard the door click and Zach was home from another trip. Although her days and her mind became more entangled with the court's process in early spring, she was mesmerized again by the Ivanhoe response and "factual" inferences.

As their eyes met, Zach could tell something was up and guessed it wasn't some court decision she was pondering.

"Ivanhoe?" he asked.

"Got it in one."

They went to the comfortable den and sat in their contoured chairs and readied themselves with a glass of wine. Bailey handed the latest from Ivanhoe to Zach. His nods seemed to indicate confidence in what was written.

"Ivanhoe is directing us to the Archives," he said. "I'm all for it, assuming we can get access to what we want and need. My only questions are whether someone would be monitoring inquiries and whether we are too high-profile to get into what could be a tangled web."

"I agree wholeheartedly," she said. "I am knee-deep in court decisions and written opinions and there is a lot left on my plate. I know you have your own responsibilities, but do you have any trips in the near future?"

"Not in the near future," he responded. "I have some tentative heart transplants on the docket, but all at Johns Hopkins, so I'll have some time to get through some of this. But should we perhaps have a trusted person or persons doing some of the initial legwork to see where this takes us? Isn't Matt's team on this?"

"I would say yes, I hope he's started, simply for time's sake," she said. "I don't think there is a deadline on this, but, like Ivanhoe inferred, if something happens to them, there might be some fallout if all of this information is dropped on the public's doorstep.

"I'm of a mind to call Spence and see if researching the Archives is something that goes through him, or if we need to do this on our own and then bring the rest of our team up to date. I think Crockett's team is planning on doing its own thing and getting back to us.

"I'll call Spence tomorrow when I get a chance. Since it'll be Friday, it means a justice conference to see who lines up with whom on the rest of the cases pending."

CHAPTER 14

J. Edgar Hoover Building

The office of the FBI director sits conveniently on the seventh floor of the Hoover Building, nestled in the corner overlooking Pennsylvania Avenue with the White House in full view. Although J. Edgar himself never had an office in that building, his was adorned with pictures of many well-known people, including political types of all leanings, foreign leaders, sports and entertainment personalities, even powerbrokers, scientists and a multitude of law-enforcement personnel.

Randall Payne didn't have the forty-three years of service to match that of Hoover, and wasn't known for his in-depth backgrounds on just about anyone. He had his own pictures, from the current administration to others he had met along the way as he rose up through the ranks to become the FBI chief seven years ago. He was known as a fair and honest chief, capable of talking to anyone at any time, rarely without an opinion, and steadfastly committed to getting the job done—no matter how long it might take.

Spencer Crockett had an accomplished career that interfaced with all the divisions of the Justice Department. He was one of the members of the select committee to vet the potential FBI chiefs, doing so as the deputy attorney general. Payne was his choice, and the committee deferred to Crockett's knowledge and comments when making its general recommendation to the US Senate for final confirmation. Payne had been President McCade's first choice and he relied on Crockett to see it through. And he did.

When the call came through to Payne's office that Spencer Crockett was on the line, the chief politely ended his phone conversation and took the call.

"Spence, so I see you at the Old Ebbitt Grill and now a phone call," began Payne. "What can I do for you?"

"Would like to set up a face-to-face, as what I have to chat about could be sensitive," said Crockett.

"Name the day and time and I will work my schedule."

"You tell me, anytime next week, just about any time."

"Tuesday at ten thirty work for you? Can you give me a heads-up on what to bring to the table?"

"We better save that until we meet."

"Then see you Tuesday."

Crockett Meets Payne

Spencer Crockett felt like he had been in every office of the expansive FBI building. And he was very familiar with the director's office, having been deputy AG and special prosecutor. But this time it felt different. His mind raced with how his conversation might be received. He felt like a stranger in a familiar place.

After the usual niceties, and holding a cup of coffee on what was another cold morning in DC, he settled in his chair and gave Payne his take of what was on his mind. The director was attentive, curious, and mindful that his friend and colleague wouldn't just come up with or be a part of some outlandish project or cause. All during Crockett's summation, Payne wondered how he, his department, or even anyone in the government might take any of this, let alone be called upon to take up the charge. Crockett's disclaimer that their conversation needed to stay between them—at least for now—stuck in his mind.

"Randy, I know this may seem preposterous, but from what I have been given in the way of facts and reasonable corroboration, I felt it warranted my look-see," said Crockett. "Verification is always at the heart and soul of all evidence. One man's fact could be another man's rebuttal. I have done my own investigations where supposedly-valid facts have been countered or strained, certainly enough to allow for reasonable doubt to creep in.

"But I believe in what I have seen, and Bailey, Zach, and Matt all feel the same. Obviously, there are sensitive areas here, including the position of Justice Stewart, and perhaps Matt and Zach, as all are in the public limelight to different degrees. I, too, have the weight of public scrutiny to deal with, as I have in the past while serving the president and the Congress. I came to you as they came to me.

"We have boiled down the JFK assassination down to whether we are trying to solve a crime or determine what the public has a right to know. As an investigative arm of our government, can the FBI help, or is there a chain of command that has to be recognized before we proceed? And if we do, is the cat then out of the bag?"

"As an interested observer, I am intrigued, but there probably is a fine line here," said Payne. "To open up an investigation, is it to dig deep into a crime or wrongdoing or to prove someone wrong? The Kennedy assassination has had all sorts of twists and turns, complete with a multitude of conspiracy theories, sealed documents, and a clash about what information would be suitable for the public.

"There were those who jumped all over the fact there was a foreign-government plot, but to my knowledge, nothing was proved beyond a reasonable doubt. And I can't even get into some of the documents that supposedly were FBI generated and held."

"Was this all Hoover?" asked Crockett.

"I would guess so, but so many of his files went missing that corroborating evidence has been hard to find," Payne responded.

"What if Ivanhoe has the goods?" countered Crockett. "Would the FBI open such a case?"

"Probably not without presidential or congressional approval. Of course, there would not be anything holding back an independent inquiry."

"Would doors be open or closed?" asked Crockett. "If someone doesn't want any information like this—or any one of the many scenarios—to be made public by Ivanhoe, would the government stand in the way? Obviously, if it could be proved beyond a shadow of a doubt who really killed Kennedy, would that shake the very foundation of the public trust? Would the government take a hit? Would anyone who had a hand in it would be subject to prosecution?

"As long as we can keep control of any investigation, I think we can get to this. My question to you is, can we count on you?"

"From a department standpoint, I would have to check above my paygrade. From a personal standpoint, I would be all in. I want to know about all of these things that you have alluded to as well. I would have to weigh any conflicts of interest from my side, perhaps as you would have to do, or what Justice Stewart, Zach, and Matt would have to evaluate, too."

"Can I have access to the unredacted FBI files?" asked Crockett.

"Let me think about how we could do that under the chain-of-custody provisions."

"I don't want to put you in a precarious position, Randy," Crockett stated. "I came to you, sharing a very sensitive subject that involves government documents, and I am only looking for a way to corroborate what Ivanhoe has stated as true. The Kennedy assassination represents one of a few of the facts purported to be true. All the other stuff will take just as careful an investigation. I know I am game, and I don't think this is a game to Ivanhoe.

"If we don't take the lead, this may well come out without any investigation, and, right or wrong, it will open up old wounds and put the public on notice that its government knew certain facts that the public should know. And if the energy and medical facts are proven to be totally true, someone is going to pay, and it will not be closure, but a potential war."

"You mentioned Ivanhoe as your source. Just how much do you know about this source?" asked Payne. "I would be curious to know how the source came by the information if it supposedly was firewalled to not just law enforcement, but politicals, powerful people, and more."

"We had the same concerns, as we discussed the project in its entirety," said Crockett. "The question we focused on was whether we were out to solve something or to allow the public to have knowledge. We won't really be able to make that decision until we're sure about the facts. If Ivanhoe's information is to be believed, we need to find verification somewhere."

"Why the Kennedy assassination?" asked Payne. "From what you said, there are plenty of other subjects to look into."

"That was Bailey's call, but I agree. I think the public remains fixated on JFK more than fifty years after his death. And we had hoped that documents ordered sealed for fifty years would now be readily available for inspection. So that brought us to you and the FBI since the agency was in charge of gathering and holding all of the evidence relating to the assassination.

"Was it a conspiracy, as some skeptics have thought all these years, or was the Warren Commission totally correct? The record says Oswald was the lone gunman. Ivanhoe says there is proof Oswald didn't shoot the rifle at all. Inquiring minds want to know, and if Ivanhoe has the road map to getting this mystery solved once and for all, will we be able to drill deep into valued records or will we hit a firewall?"

"I guess part of my curiosity has to with how this Ivanhoe got the information purportedly received from an anonymous source," said Payne.

"I realize the internet has changed the way people search and find things these days, but information of this type can't be found on any site. So how did this all come together for one person to find? And is this a part of a government leak and are we looking at an additional crime here? Is this a hacking issue?"

"You mean like Ellsberg and Snowden?"

"Those would be two of many who have either stolen or found encrypted government documents and laid them out for all to see. Are we looking at more embarrassing information to be divulged? I admit there are documents that are listed as top secret, for your eyes only, confidential, classified and the like. And, as you well know, a lot of stored documents have portions that are redacted."

"I wouldn't look at the Kennedy assassination documents as potentially embarrassing, but something that should fall under the Freedom of Information Act. Johnson had great misgivings signing the law because he knew where such access might lead in the future—maybe even to reports on the Kennedy murder."

"I will check on what files might be available, redacted or not," said Payne. "At some time I would like to see these Ivanhoe letters that you referred to. Is that possible?"

"Should be, but I think that would require you being a part of the discussion."

"Not sure that would be wise; I wouldn't want to be read into something where I couldn't deny inclusion. This would be a department read-in if I was in the loop."

"Can you assign any of your people to do a cursory check on any of this without directly including you?"

"Let me think through that. That might be a possibility, to conduct a surface investigation without having to go to Ken McDonald or Liz Cookson for approval. If there is something that warrants a deeper look, then we would have to include both."

"I could understand that. I don't think this calls for a special prosecutor, since we're not looking at investigating an ongoing case. I can remember many a case where the independent counsel was the right thing to do, but we aren't there with this—at least not yet."

"It may come to that, Spence, so we should at least put that sticky note on the board. And the identity of your group needs to be in the shadows. I have a couple of investigators that might be a good fit, but I'll get back to you on that."

"Any timetable for that? I wouldn't mind looking through the Archives."

"You're free to look through the Archives at any time, without anyone's consent. Whether you find everything you want or need would be your decision and analysis. What I'll be checking on is to see what documents are considered confidential or classified. I suspect there'll be some sealed documents that aren't covered under FOIA.

"I'll check with the AG and Ken at Justice to make sure we're complying with all statutes. Probably would be good to make sure the White House doesn't have a problem with it either. We certainly don't want to blindside the president."

"We have a meeting set with the chief of staff to go over what we know and want to know," Crockett said.

As Crockett finished his coffee he asked, "You ever have time a round of golf? You, Matt and I should get to it sometime soon."

"Nothing like springtime in DC in an election year. Give me some dates and times and I'll work on my handicap."

The productive meeting finished with a firm handshake.

CHAPTER 15

Brumfield and Crockett at Old Ebbitt Grill

The Secret Man and the Shadow were at it again, strolling into Old Ebbitt Grill to the looks and hails from many as they made their way to back of the famed establishment. While most people wanted to shake hands and say the usual hellos, the two were left alone when they reached their destination. The trusted Jake Dickson was again their server and knew when to make himself scarce.

"Met with Randy, and I think he's at least sympathetic to our inquiry," began Crockett. "He said he would check into what may be privileged, firewalled, or sealed. I also asked him if we could get some help from inside, on the basis that there might be some investigating that falls under the FBI jurisdiction. He said he would think through the process but cautioned that there may be a potential conflict that would necessitate bringing DAG McDonald and AG Cookson into the loop."

"All bets would be off then, I would think" said Brumfield. "Once the other people from Justice were apprised of what might be going on, that surely would get to the White House and certain members of Congress."

"We don't have any authority to launch an investigation, at least officially. But we do have the right to search the National Archives for whatever falls under FOIA."

"That is something I can probably do, but should we join forces here to minimize potential problems?" offered Brumfield. "The more people we read into this, the more we expose any investigation."

"That may well be something for Randy's inside help," said Crockett with a nod. "He mentioned he might know a couple of crack investigators that could take the lead here. My thinking is that we are high profile and people will notice when and where we go. Perhaps we need to be the silent leaders. After all, being the Mystery Man and the Shadow should count for something."

As outlined by Crockett when he met with Payne, the use of the US mail was seemingly the best way to communicate. The two knew well that surveillance techniques, publicly known or not, meant eavesdropping by the likes of the NSA or email account hacking by any one of a number of other sources, foreign or domestic, was commonplace. Yes, there were secure lines and methods of encryption, but the two did not have an established link, so the mail was the way to go.

Spence: Contact Curt Mitchell in our office. He heads our Special Investigations Unit as a senior FBI agent.

Stay tuned.

Randy

Mitchell and Crockett Meet at FBI Headquarters

Mitchell's office was half the size of Payne's and he, too, had an array of pictures displayed that chronicled his long law-enforcement career. At one time he was a cop, then an assistant district attorney, then an FBI agent. He rose through the ranks, stepping up the ladder where his interests took him. Now a twenty-five-year veteran with the FBI, he knew where everything was—or should be. He had assembled a crack investigative team that was handed the most sensitive cases. He was reserved, but not shy, listening to what others said or didn't say before drilling down for additional information.

His work as an ADA earned him high honors, even possible appointments to the bench, but Payne had seen the rising star and recruited him for Justice and his team before he ascended to the head of the FBI. Mitchell also knew key staff members at the White House, CIA, NSA and a number of other government agencies, was well versed in protocols, and knew when he could push.

Crockett and Mitchell had met on occasion in the past when Crockett was the deputy AG and special prosecutor. They were aware of the other's place. So, the call for an appointment and subsequent meeting went as if they had known and confided in each other for a long time.

"Director Payne read me into the project," Mitchell began. "If I understood his direction, he was looking for some investigation that would appear to be 'surface surfing,' as we call it, to see what we can come up with."

"That is what we talked about," said Crockett. "Since you have the overview, I guess the question comes down to do you have anyone who can handle this without sounding an alarm bell?"

"When the director told me about this venture, I knew exactly who I would tap—two of our top investigators who would jump all over this," said Mitchell with a smile. "Casey Kincaid and Jenny Warner would be excellent. I'll read them into this and we'll set up a meeting here to go over everything. Okay with you?"

"I'm familiar with both of them, so let me know the day and time and I'll be there," offered Crockett. "And thanks for getting to this, Curt."

CHAPTER 16

Casey Kincaid

Things came naturally for Casey Kincaid. From his earliest days when he would find things to do to occupy his time to the seamless transition into an alternate career that landed him in the Department of Justice, his instinctive thought processes were extraordinary.

Named Kevin Charles Kincaid, he was dubbed Casey by his father when he was four years old and he showed a knack for playing with trains. His father had given him his old Lionel train set with an assortment of engines, cars, tracks, houses and other supportive pieces. It didn't take long for the young engineer to develop a maze of tracks that traveled through towns and countryside. When he flipped the transformer for the first time, his "whoo whoo" could be heard throughout the house. He enjoyed his adolescent years when his father would take him to see the trains that came and went from their town. Young Casey knew a lot about big trains and what they meant to the infrastructure of American life. He was fascinated.

His zest for being busy all the time left his parents at ease. He made quick work of school assignments, played on almost every athletic field, and found time on weekends to get together with his friends to play football, basketball, and baseball. His love of baseball led him to collect trading cards, and he was captivated by statistics. He had what many felt was a photographic memory, and his recall of player numbers was astonishing to all who knew him.

A stellar high school career, mainly as a pitcher and first baseman as well as a good golfer, netted him a scholarship to Stanford University. He maintained his high level of academics and athletic prowess. A legal/communications dual major, he had every intention of becoming an attorney, but when the Philadelphia Phillies offered him a handsome professional package, he decided to take a chance on baseball to see where that led.

As is the case with many would-be major league prospects, competition and the chance to make "the Show" didn't appear to be on the near horizon for the still ambitious Kincaid, and he returned to Stanford three years later to pursue his law career. Surrounded by equally inquisitive minds, Kincaid swept through his studies and graduated with honors. Passing the bar on his first try brought a broad grin to his face and warmed his heart, but now he looked for new horizons.

Offers of employment were everywhere, but it was his Stanford Law School Dean Carlson Ward III that encouraged him to look closely at the Boston law firm of White, Bear & Kirkpatrick. So, he took his 151 IQ and spirit of adventure to the east coast, a place he never had been before. The relationship with the partners and legal clients was exceptional and he became a valuable and most-asked-for team player. His days at the firm were full and exciting, with many great results and much satisfaction. But a new adventure beckoned when Alexander Hailwood, another former Stanford professor, called him to try and recruit him for the Department of Justice.

If this were a match game, then game over. Kincaid had found a new window of opportunity, one that would combine his legal skills with his natural investigative abilities. He was one of those types of people who understood what had happened and wanted to know why. He dabbled in conspiracy theories—not just those that enveloped the mysteries behind the deaths of prominent figures, but also how companies, even foreign governments, manipulated what was known and left unknown.

Unknown it was.

Jenny Warner

Jenny Warner was self-styled. One of four children, she and her siblings were prompted to excel in academics, and they did. But the stir in her wasn't for academics; her love was for bicycles, from her first days with a tricycle to the more advanced cycles. Though she didn't consider herself an athlete, she stayed true to cycling and participated in a number of organized events. In her younger days, she was known to speed her bicycle through the streets of Redlands on her way to school. She became Jenny the Jet.

She maintained her hobby through her school days, but academics, as her parents insisted upon, were foremost. Her father was a judge, known in the community for having a great sense of fairness. Her mother was a music maestro who taught at the university and had several students go on to successful careers.

Jenny graduated from USC with a political science degree and furthered her education with a master's degree from Loyola Marymount. From there she entered politics, first with state representatives and then on to Washington, where she served as a legislative aide to three congressmembers and two senators before being recruited by the Department of Justice.

The first meeting between Kincaid and Warner did not go well. Both were in Southern California for an extended stay for research projects. They met on the driving range at the Riviera Country Club in Pacific Palisades in Southern California, where Kincaid took notice of the attractive Warner as she took her swings. He thought he was being a gentleman for offering his advice, but she wasn't too interested in his observations. She had picked up the game on her own, mostly to be a part of her own in-crowd. She never took lessons, but simply looked at the challenge and made it work, much like she had with the cycling outlet.

Kincaid took the initial hint, but he soon found out more about her by asking questions. Being a member of the Stanford golf team should count for something, he thought, so he made it a point to just be around when she was at the driving range. Persistence paid off. He got to know her, her golf game improved, and the two struck up a solid relationship. Both were fact driven and known in legislative and department circles for seeking the truth, whatever time it took.

The art of deduction came naturally to her, perhaps because of her strict upbringing. She was into the Nancy Drew mysteries in her younger days. The goal was always perfection, according to her parents, and she seldom got praise for anything less than an A grade. That bothered her in her formative years, but as she got older and more confident in her self-worth, she set her own goals and seemed pleased with her accomplishments. And so it was with cycling and golf, on her terms. She established her own goals and achievements as she raced and played against herself.

The Kincaid/Warner connection proved to be a valuable and proven asset to the DOJ.

Mitchell, Kincaid, Warner Meeting

When Mitchell asked Kincaid and Warner to meet with him, their intrigue piqued when he said he had a special case he wanted to discuss with them.

"So, when do we start?" asked Kincaid, replacing the usual "What's up?"

"What I am going to say here is privileged, so I need your assurance that you will follow the law but make every effort to follow any and all leads and understand what the end game is," began Mitchell. "We've worked well as a team, and rest assured, I am all in on this, as I hope both of you will be. If you have any reservations about the goal, now or in the future, you need to let me know. If either of you choose to withdraw from this investigation, now or at any time, I need your word as a member of the Bureau that you will not divulge any information about it until freed to do so.

"I will read you into this and then you can let me know how you feel about it. I have chosen you two because of the way you conduct yourselves individually and as a team. And I am very much a part of the team, too. You also will know who else is a part of the team, and that information is to remain confidential. Is that clear?"

For the next half an hour, Mitchell disclosed the information he had on the case. He indicated he did not have any physical evidence, such as the Ivanhoe letters. He did say he expected to see the letters in the near future, as soon as the director got back to him. The two special agents tried to comprehend what they were being told. They were not even born when JFK was slain, but they had read volumes about the case as part of the FBI historical training. Like all others, though, they did not have all the facts from all of the other agencies that contributed to the Warren Commission report. However, their natural suspicions about conspiracies heightened their interest to follow the trail.

"Are we constrained by firewalls?" asked Warner. "I would expect when people see or hear a couple of FBI agents are poking around, someone is going to ask questions. If we are asked what we are doing, what is our answer?"

"For now, simply say you have been asked to verify some facts and there is a preliminary investigation to get some answers to some questions."

"And if we are asked who told us to do so?" queried Warner.

"That would be me. Are we good?"

"Absolutely," they said in unison.

"For now," Mitchell continued, "I want daily or at least weekly reports, depending on how far you have progressed. This is not for further dissemination. It's just from the two of you to me—no cc's. I would suggest seeing what the internet offers and gathering as much information there as is available before tackling the National Archives. If you see a link to another agency, check with me first. I am guessing it will be okay, but we need to evaluate any inquiries because agency inquiries are timestamped. At some time other agencies will know someone is snooping and we will have to be ready for that. But that decision comes above our pay grade, and the rest of the team needs to know if anything has been compromised. Just remember, this is a preliminary investigation, and if anyone asks a suspicious question, then let me know as soon as possible.

"If you don't have any other investigations on the burner right now, get to this so we can see where this leads."

"If we run into some redacted information in our search, are we to assume that we will not be able to drill down further?" Warner asked.

"I suggest you stick with our Bureau matrix system and line up the facts with what Ivanhoe generally purports. That would include finding redacted information. Once you have your matrix filled in, it might be easier to see discrepancies."

"Are we to assume the FBI files and those in the Archives are correct, with or without redacted names, places, and suppositions?" countered Kincaid. "As history is written there is a tendency to believe what has been written or said, but Ivanhoe has offered revisionist history. Who is to be believed?"

"That, apparently, is what we need to determine," said Mitchell. "Conduct your investigation as a collection of facts and let your instincts drive you to get to the truth. If that's revisionist history, then it is up to us to prove it. There will be many more people who'll get involved in this, so beware of those who ask too many questions. As a rule of thumb, do not get chummy with people you do not know, even if they say they are seeking what we are.

"And for God's sake, use all of your skill sets—both of you—to avoid confrontation and be aware of danger signs."

CHAPTER 17

The Four at Longfellow Estate

The weekend meeting of the Four would be enlightening for all. Friday evening was more social, and the general conversation fixated on Bailey's upcoming Supreme Court decisions. While she did not disclose her for-and-against positions, she did have time to talk about cases that did not make the cut and were returned to the lower courts without review by the nine.

Saturday would be the key day, as everyone wanted to know what information had been gathered and what the next step was for them as individuals and as a group. Brumfield took the lead and stood with pen in hand next to the whiteboard.

"As we have discussed, the more we inquire, the more we're going to draw attention," offered Brumfield. "There will be some pushback, so we need to be ready with alternate routes when someone seems to be too inquisitive.

"Don't know about you, but I don't see leaks ahead of awards-show broadcasts, but somehow Washington and the political scene has more than an abundance."

"We have to be cognizant of the law, but I agree with Matt, we have to feel free to inquire and push for what we want, but know what our needs are," Bailey said. "Being stymied because of bureaucracy is one thing, but if we get tagged by Justice, we need to weigh our options. Heaven forbid that our efforts become totally public and the legal system takes over. We all know the law and have defended the Constitution, but there are challenges that are certain to come. And I pray that none of this elevates up to the court."

"I think it best that we bring in Casey and Jenny. They'll lead the investigative charge," offered Crockett. "Randy and Curt seemed okay with it since the FBI is the true investigative arm of the government."

"That goes back to how far they can go without raising a red flag with any one of a number of governmental agencies, let alone individuals that may have a horse in the race," replied Brumfield, now sensing that a broader outline of the entire project would be prudent.

"Imagine if dark forces got into a sensitive area where we have been and found documents, redacted or not, that led back to the FBI, perhaps another government agency or even the president? Or if some House or Senate member on a respective committee caught wind of an investigation and suddenly wanted to get more involved. I'm not sure this would be a partisan issue, but who knows with members of Congress? They insult and criticize each other in chamber sessions as well as committees during the day and then go to dinners or social events and act like they're cordial colleagues."

"And the legal system allows for every little thing to be litigated," Stewart said, leaning forward. "The court regularly declines to hear thousands of cases every year just because those petitions don't warrant additional analysis. What we have here is a montage of facts, proven or otherwise, that would interest the common person. The framers did not envision facts being suppressed, but did somehow structure the Constitution to allow for discourse by those who would follow."

"Which brings us back to the initial premise," said Brumfield. "Has the government willingly withheld facts, truths or not, from the public for its own good, or is this an issue of national security? Does the public have a right to know?

"I think we are in agreement that others should be brought on board. I think we all realize that the web will get broader, but we need to compartmentalize our efforts so we don't lose track of who is doing what.

"Spence, if you are okay with Randy and the FBI, then stay with that. That would include the work of Casey and Jenny. Bailey, I guess you need to be somewhat stealthy, but perhaps you can look at case files that might give us whys and why-nots of judicial restraints. I'm not sure how far you can delve into some legal areas since you have an ongoing schedule that will consume your time. But think about who you know who could do some sleuthing that wouldn't draw a horde of inquiries. I will do my own, but I think my follow-up with the Archives might prove interesting, at least to give Casey and Jenny some direction.

"Zach, as soon as you can get some clearance on the Kennedy files, I guess your efforts would be confined to forensics of cases in the government mystery box. Just what remains a medical mystery and how important any of it is now as we determine what is low-hanging fruit.

"Bailey, is there something we can get from our mystery guest Ivanhoe?"

"Was thinking of that," she said. "Perhaps I can go back to the classified section with a cryptic question."

CHAPTER 18

REDACTED appeared in the *Post* the next day.

Two days later, another Ivanhoe letter, the fifth of such, arrived at the Longfellow estate.

After another compelling day at the court and a satisfying dinner, Stewart had a chance to peruse her daily mail, locate the now-recognizable envelope on top that could only be from Ivanhoe, then settle into her easy chair, her chardonnay within hand's reach.

With a sly smile on her face, she looked forward to some moments of solitude with the words of someone she had come to admire for their insightfulness and candor.

Ivanhoe Letter—5

Dear Justice Stewart:

By redacted, I assume you are interested in information redacted by any government agency, not just by the FBI, CIA, NSA, White House or National Archives, for instance.

Governmental agencies, unlike private concerns, are required to document everything and are subject to the Freedom of Information Act, and that there is a provision in the Act that allows certain parts of any report or document to be redacted, for the good of the public, as they say. This goes to the very core of what I proposed to you at the outset. What does the government have a right to keep secret and what does the public have a right to know? Just who makes those decisions and is there anything behind the curtain?

I will tell you, as I have either alluded to before or would divulge when asked, I have documentation that is whole, without any redacted portions. Some of this information might prove strategic, and, I would offer, might not be suitable to be shared, but there are some things that simply should be evaluated. After all, are we talking strictly government cover-ups, lies, half-truths, or misinterpretations that shake out as sinister, or are we as citizens better off knowing?

Approximately one to three percent of all documents have a Top Secret tag, deemed not available to the public. Someone at some time created such documentation. I would venture to say that would include military information and national security issues. My coming to you involves information I feel should not be as sensitive, such as information on the Kennedy assassination, Pearl Harbor, medical breakthroughs, and energy sources. I do not profess to be head of the kingdom and decide on my own what would or should be told. That is my quest—to evaluate this information and make a decision.

As I mentioned, this information was given to me from an unknown source, delivered in an unusual way. I was told this was a perfect storm, where all of this information that has been collected and analyzed over many years came together in some electronic crossroads and this person, lucky or not, tapped into it. I hope you and whoever you choose to be a part of your team will make sense of it all.

I have made arrangements, as I have mentioned before, that if anything happens to me, this information will find its way into a much broader circle. This fail-safe provision comes from my own sense of responsibility to my fellow humans, certainly to the citizens of the United States. There would be no political gain on my part, although some of the stuff I have read and read again does point some long fingers at political types—and for good reason.

Like so much of the public, I always wondered about things like the Kennedy assassination, medical catastrophes, and all that, so this has been an enlightening experience. Since I have seen everything without redacted parts, I now feel more at ease rather than skeptical, untrusting of government, or relying on our system of checks and balances.

Your validation will come from your own sources. I will be happy to corroborate or verify. Like Deep Throat offered in the Watergate mess, there is a source to corroborate the truth. Some people may not believe the statements—or accusations, if you will—in my story. Others may simply deny, distract and distort. But this documentation is the real deal.

So as your word "redacted" floats out there, just know that I know the information that's been redacted and I can prove it. I trust whoever you care to have investigate the public interest subjects, as opposed to true government secrets that have to do with military and strategic assets, that they will drill deep into everything and know that a stop sign may well not be a brick wall, but a momentary slowdown on the way to the twilight zone.

Nothing sinister here. Just the truth.

Sincerely,

IVANHOE

There was a moment of feeling perplexed as more and more information came available. Bailey had come to understand more and more that Ivanhoe was searching for someone to confide in, rather than making a bold threat that if she couldn't help then all would be divulged to the public like the Pentagon Papers and the Edward Snowden revelations, even Wikileaks. This was different. Ellsberg and Snowden had crossed the line with military and strategic information, not with information about events, people, and history. She was a fan of Ivanhoe from the get-go but was even more enthusiastic about the idea that redacted documents would, in fact, provide a clear view when all was revealed. She, too, wanted to know about what really happened to Kennedy and how far medical and scientific research had actually progressed, along with the assortment of other topics Ivanhoe had referenced, and she knew the public would want the same.

She took no notice of her empty wine glass as she read and reread the latest from her mysterious correspondent. The Ivanhoe letters were a treasure all their own.

It had been surmised that only one to three percent of all records were deemed not available to the public and therefore beyond the reaches of FOIA. Stewart felt the Four had clear directives—Crockett would head to Justice, Brumfield to Archives, she would handle Ivanhoe, and Zach would look into the Kennedy assassination, perhaps with the help of world-renowned pathologist Dr. Cyril Wecht. She felt comfortable with that lineup and became even more anxious as she thought of subsequent meetings. They lived in a hurry-up society where stone carvings had given way to parchment scrolls, photography, microfilm, and finally the digital age.

Was this a search of a bottomless black hole, or would this provide enlightenment?

CHAPTER 19

The Brumfield Investigation

The ever-inquisitive Brumfield was off on his own adventure. One of his former students was Anita D. Wright, now the archivist of the United States, essentially the head of the National Archives. She had held the position for the past fifteen years and oversaw a senior staff of twenty-five. Brumfield had maintained contact with her over the years as she worked in and around the DC governmental circles.

His initial call to her was met was an enthusiastic hello from Wright, always anxious to chat with her former mentor. "Matt, what a pleasant surprise. What's going?"—one of her favorite expressions, one she learned from cowboy star Gene Autry, who used it all the time with friends.

"Annie, I need to meet with you sometime soon. I am working on a project that has some sensitivity to it and a face-to-face meeting would be best."

"What's good for you? I have my appointment book in front of me."

"Tuesday next week around ten?" responded Brumfield. "Your office?"

"Sure. Anything you can share with me, or is there something I need to bring?" she asked.

"Best that we talk behind closed doors."

"See you next week."

Brumfield Meets Wright at National Archives

Brumfield never lost his own sense of enthusiasm when he went to the Archives, whether with students or not, nor when talking about it with friends and colleagues that wanted to get a quick history of what to expect when they roamed the hallowed halls.

He was somewhat surprised and pleased that Wright, now the archivist, met him at the concierge desk when he entered the grand rotunda.

"Annie," he said with a smile as he moved toward her for a hug and a cheek-to-cheek kiss.

"Always a pleasure to see or hear from you Matt," she said. "I'm looking forward to our time. Your phone call sounded so mysterious."

"We have some interesting things to talk about, so thank you for taking the time," said Brumfield. The two rode the elevator to the fifth floor and entered what was a grand area with stately executive offices. Wright's office was to the left, a corner slot that had a panoramic view of the Washington landscape, including the White House and Capitol Building.

Wright motioned Brumfield to a more intimate table, used for small groups. The living room-style layout, with two couches and an ornate fireplace behind their table, provided an ambiance fit for favored guests.

The walls were adorned with a variety of pictures with political and donor notables as well as copies of documents that dotted American history. The oak décor provided a fine complement to the panoramic view. Annie offered her friend a cup of coffee and served herself as well.

"So, now that you have my attention, what's going on, Matt?" she said.

"What I say here is for your eyes and ears only, at least for now. If you feel that all is worthy of you and the Archives being involved, then we will proceed down perhaps an uncertain road. I am all in with this and so are the people who I will mention."

The quizzical look on her face turned to a half smile. "Lay it on me."

For the next twenty minutes or so, Brumfield gave Wright the *Reader's Digest* version of what the Four had surmised and planned to do.

"Is this verified information from this Ivanhoe?" she asked.

"We feel it is valid, based on what we have received from Ivanhoe. We all agree that there is an element of 'trust, but verify' here, and that is why we are looking at all aspects of what Ivanhoe has offered. Without showing you all of the Ivanhoe letters, I can tell you that the story is pretty compelling."

"What is the end game? Hasn't what you have said been investigated and proven one way or another?'

"I guess our initial questions came to that point. If we have a chance to reevaluate not only what happened, but why, can we dispel incorrect or outright false or misleading facts? As we have discussed, are we dealing with government-known facts, lies, and half-truths? And what does the public have a right to know? There are some subjects that have a cap on them, and we want to be sensitive to that. I think that is why Ivanhoe approached Judge Stewart in the first place. National security issues, for instance, are off the table."

"Where does that fit in with me and the Archives then?" she asked. "You mentioned some documents cannot be available for public scrutiny. And I am curious to know how this Ivanhoe came up with all of this information and, if true, how anyone would have such detail."

Brumfield gave her a quick synopsis of the background outlined in the Ivanhoe letters.

"Without making any commitment, where do you see me in all of this?" asked Wright.

"We have connections with the FBI, CIA, NSA, Congress, the Supreme Court and the White House. You are my connection with the Archives. If we face stop signs, we need to know if we can see what is behind the mystery door.

"For you, I would ask if we can see any one of a number of documents not on public display. And can we see redacted portions, for background? If our investigations lead to a suspicious road, can we see something that is not going to be copied, that wouldn't be betraying military or strategic government documents or legal issues?"

"I think you realize that investigations into Archives flagged as Top Secret would go before the Congressional Oversight Committees and surely would be on the White House radar," commented Wright.

"Interestingly, according to Ivanhoe, no one person in government circles would ordinarily have access to all the information, so this perfect storm simply happened, and the initial cache was passed on to Ivanhoe and then to us," he said. "A president, the FBI, the CIA, or whoever could not drill down to get this, based on certain safeguards—a safeguard to prevent leakage from a number of sources."

"I'm not sure how I can help, but I am willing to listen. The redacted information might be a reach and I believe a small percentage of our documents have blackened portions that are not for public consumption. I guess we'll have to see where your investigations take you and then deal with whatever whenever. Do you have anyone in mind to take up the challenge?"

"Casey Kincade and Jenny Warner from the FBI will be lead investigators," stated Brumfield.

"I'm not familiar with them, but I am not up on all those folks at the FBI. I know Randy, though. Is he okay with this?"

"Yes. Spencer Crockett talked with Randy and he brought in his top deputy, Curt Mitchell. He in turn recruited Casey and Jen. They are eager to get going and I suspect the Archives will be the first stop."

"They can get a lot of information online and I suspect they can connect some dots."

"The redacted portions might well be where they end, and knowing them, they will press further. I didn't want the investigation to get so far down the road that you would be put in a compromising position or be blindsided."

Now with a better understanding of her potential role, she said, "I appreciate the heads-up, Matt. Perhaps I should meet them so if they show up I can at least intercede and make evaluations without drawing unwanted attention?"

"I can arrange that. I could have Casey call you or, if you prefer, Randy or Curt at the Bureau could make the intro."

"Let's keep it at the Randy/Curt level, to cover ourselves, so to speak."

"I'll follow up with Randy and go by his recommendation. I appreciate your willingness to keep an eye on this, Annie. If you get any pushback, simply let me know and we will make course corrections. We are not in this to get anyone in hot water, but Ivanhoe has let us know that if anything happens to them some delicate information might get into the public sector—and quickly."

"We aren't talking about another Ellsberg or Snowden, are we?" she asked.

"Don't think so. The fact Ivanhoe went to a Supreme Court justice tells me they are wanting to share rather than indict.

"I realize you have many other things on your plate and this might well take up some time, so thank you from all of us. I only ask that we all share information internally and if there is a need for you to meet the Four, simply let me know and I will make that happen."

"I trust your judgment, Matt, so hopefully this will not be a nightmare that we can't awaken from. Based on what you have told me about who is involved, this is a serious undertaking, and I'd be happy to assist, even if in a small way.

"I'd like to include Elaine Meserve in this. She's our senior director at the Archives. She is extremely bright and knows where everything is in this place, both on-site and at other locations."

"Think I met her at a Washington gathering awhile back," remembered Brumfield. "Happy to have her on the team and would assume you can bring her up to date and then the three of us should get together sometime soon. That okay with you?"

After Ann's nod, he continued, "Every element of this is important and we all feel committed to seeing it through. We all have our own projects or responsibilities, so the fact that we have enlisted others who have their own areas of expertise should provide different perspectives."

"Sign me up," she said enthusiastically.

CHAPTER 20

Stewart Brings Justice Jim DeBarrow into the Discussion

Jim DeBarrow was the senior associate justice, having served thirty-two years on the high bench. Considered "the Wise Man" among his peers, he had been contemplating retiring before he reached his eightieth birthday, which would come in two years. He was detailed, asked questions in nearly all cases heard by the nine-judge panel, and wasn't afraid to offer comments when they met behind closed doors to deliberate. The bespectacled DeBarrow took a welcoming approach to everything, so he was easy to listen and talk to. He had written a book about his early days in the justice system, appropriately titled *One Man's Opinion*.

The Stewart and DeBarrow offices were side by side on the second story of the court building. Feeling the need to get another opinion, Stewart went next door and asked if Justice DeBarrow was busy.

"Let me check, Justice Stewart," responded executive legal assistant and scheduler Beverly Hempstead. A minute later, the two justices were sitting at a small conference table.

"You looking for an opinion?" was the familiar query from DeBarrow, made with a grin. The two had conversed on many a case, but he knew something else was on her mind now.

"Jim, I am involved in something that has stretched my imagination well beyond the bounds of simple justice," she began. "I'm not sure if there is a right or wrong, fair or unfair. So, I have come to you, Wise Man, for your counsel. There is a lot to this, but I ask that you hear me out and we can move on from there. I also recognize that this is not a court project, at least not now, so in sharing this with you I'm asking you to hold this in confidence."

"You can trust me, Bailey—always," he responded.

For the next thirty minutes, Stewart outlined as much as she could, from the Ivanhoe letters to the network derived from the inquiry to the Ivanhoe information to the outreach by Spencer Crockett, Matt Brumfield, and her own Zach, as well as herself. The attentive DeBarrow rarely interrupted or made comments. He made some notes but saved his observations for later.

DeBarrow had instructed Hempstead to not allow any interruptions unless urgent. The two justices felt their time alone without disruption would allow them to cut to the bone, rather than having to repeatedly start and stop, as was the case with so many goings-on with the court and its procedures. At eleven-thirty, DeBarrow asked Hempstead to order something from the court's executive dining room so the two judges could continue their discussion on what might be a clever way to proceed, given their status.

The two opted for Cobb salads, and DeBarrow pulled two bottles of iced tea from his mini refrigerator, which had appeared from behind a sliding wall after he had pushed a button underneath his desk. The justices all had their quirks, and all had hidden beverage areas behind sliding walls. Some such areas, as one could imagine, were more elaborate and better stocked than others. They all served the right purpose at any time of day.

Ever the thinker, DeBarrow oftentimes would put his feet up on his desk while looking out at the magnificent view of Washington. It was during those times he gained not only insight into his deeper thoughts, but a willingness to apply whatever legal interpretations he knew that would ensure a fair result, according to his view of the Constitution. Whatever he came up with—for or against—supported his own unwritten motto: Just the Facts.

It was under his tutelage that Stewart had found her way into a comfort zone on the court. She had her own set of standards, but it was her being watchful of others, while remembering the words of her father, that made her a quick study. She, too, professed to be ready for the words of her own motto: Prove Me Wrong.

DeBarrow Speaks His Mind

"It appears this Ivanhoe character holds all the cards," he began. "Is your whole theory based on what this person purports?"

"Ivanhoe has given us details and insights that apparently can be corroborated or dismissed with inquiries," she said. "To date I've received five letters, and while we can remember what we were told in school or perhaps along the way, there is that element of intrigue that captures the imagination. Like *what if* or *why* rather than the standard story as told by someone who may or may not have had an agenda.

"I don't know about you, but just hearing about facts perhaps not in evidence that point to any conspiracy, on any subject, certainly gets my attention."

"And that's part of the rub, isn't it?" he said. "If facts in evidence are dispelled or contradicted, then where does that lead? And, to your earlier point, what does the public have a right to know, and what is the right of the government to withhold information that might be harmful to the security of the nation?"

"That's about it. We are not looking to overturn purported facts unless they are proved to be incorrect. And that raises the question as to searching for the *why* something happened. We already know the *what* part of the equation."

"So, who interprets the value of the additional facts?" he asked. "If, like you say, there are redacted portions of an FBI or CIA file, does that agency claim privilege without access?"

"Perhaps that is where the road turns to us, Jim. I do not want to be in the middle, either as a recused jurist or as a conspiracy theorist. Ivanhoe sent this information to me on the premise that justices are appointed for life and are therefore above election cycles. I have no problem with inquiries, but investigations are a different sandwich.

"If what Ivanhoe has indicated actually has merit, could it not lead to advances in several areas that always have had their challenges, like cures for cancer and other medical maladies, energy options, or something as remote as space travel? I guess as a citizen I would like to know and utilize any and all for a better world, but if some of these unknowns are leaked to the public, would it disrupt any one of a number of areas—financial markets, research and development, food sources, all of that?"

"All solid points and worthy of discussion when you obtain additional facts to support or disprove some of Ivanhoe's theories. As you say, the more your network expands, the more you become exposed, so I would tread lightly if doors are slammed in your face."

"I think we all are aware of those who would try to quash any meddling, to protect whatever. Since the FBI is inquiring, I think we will get some answers easily, but as for redacted entries, that could be more than interesting."

"Who are you working with at the Bureau?" he inquired.

"Randy, Curt and his two top agents—Casey Kincaid and Jenny Warner."

"Know them all. Casey and Jen can hold their own against anyone."

Bailey sighed and smiled. "Thanks for the time and wisdom, Jim. It's easy to see why they call you the Wise Man.

"Not sure how wise I am, but I do like to listen."

Feeling comfortable with her discussion with DeBarrow, Stewart was on her way back to her office when she spotted Justice Yost reentering hers and asked for a minute.

"Sure, come on in," Yost replied.

Stephanie Yost

Stephanie Yost was the youngest of the Supreme Court justices, both in age and years on the high court. She was in her fifth year of service after having been nominated by President McCade during his first term. The Senate Judiciary Committee took its time in offering her nomination to the full body, as she espoused her disdain for political bias in making qualified decisions. She was, to all who knew her, a moderate. That set well with McCade, who was elected as a moderate and was happy to have a balanced court of three so-called liberals, three conservatives, and three moderates. If he had his way, he would have nine moderates. His mantra was "Leave your political rhetoric at the door and get on with the business at hand."

As a lawyer, Stevie, as her friends called her, rarely lost a case, and as a judge, she rarely was challenged with an appeal. Her rise to the highest court in the land wasn't planned, but she accepted the call each step of the way. When White House Chief of Staff Jim Fox phoned to ask if she was interested in being on a shortlist for the court's vacancy, she responded with, "How did my name get on a shortlist?"

Fox and Yost had grown to know each other years before, as she started climbing the judicial watchlist for possible federal positions. When he made this call, she was a judge on the Fourth District Court of Appeals. She tried to hide her enthusiasm, but Fox knew her all too well.

"With you it would be three," answered Fox.

"I'm flattered, but I wonder if I'm that qualified."

"If you weren't, the president wouldn't have added your name to that list and asked me to check with you as soon as possible. And that was about five minutes ago."

"Don't know what to say, Jim, other than thank you for even considering me."

"I'll take that as a yes, then?"

"That would be correct."

In that Stewart had taken Yost under her wing, they had developed an immediate camaraderie and easily spoke their minds.

"What's cookin'?" said the ever-alert Yost.

Knowing Yost was a quick learner and preferred a summarized version of legal matters, especially petitions before the court, Stewart gave her a quick synopsis of what she and DeBarrow had discussed. Without interruption, Yost listened. "I have to admit that there are conflicts," said Yost. "I guess that's why they were bundled. I agree this is a sticky one, and while we certainly will get varied opinions from the rest of our group, I can't say I know how we will be able to sort it out."

"I would imagine we will have some interesting discussions about these petitions. I just wanted to bring you up to date on what appear to be conflicts," offered Stewart. "As I mentioned, Ivanhoe is not saying anything about national security or even dumping on ideologies, just focusing on historical myths and outright falsehoods. I'm not sure I would call them lies, but misrepresentations of the facts."

CHAPTER 21

Longfellow Estate, Fairfax, Virginia

A rainy day and cooler temperatures made the entrance into the confines of the Fairfax estate a much-needed escape. The usual welcoming party of Mandy and Annette was greeted with a slight shiver as the warmth of the house gave Bailey quick relief. Zach was on his way home but probably would miss dinner. That happened more times than not, but fortunately he was good with warmed-over anything or even fixing a peanut butter sandwich.

The dinner with Mandy was filled with the usual updates about what mail was in the offing. When Mandy said there was another large envelope from "your friend," Bailey offered a surprised smile.

"Sounds like Ivanhoe has some more to say," the judge said, mostly to herself.

"Ah, Ivanhoe. What an unusual name," Mandy said. She was dying to ask about it but knew the judge must have her reasons for not explaining the intriguing envelopes.

Bailey recognized and appreciated Mandy's fortitude, and said with a smile, "I wish I could fill you in all of the details, but for now, that's not possible. Thanks for not asking."

Now with another chardonnay in hand and the comforts of her easy chair in the office, she began the latest chapter from Ivanhoe.

Ivanhoe Letter—6

> *Dear Justice Stewart:*
>
> *I didn't see any new reference in the* Post *but thought of other things to share.*

As I pondered seeking out someone like you to join me in my quest, I was reminded of all the things I learned in school or from other sources over the years that stuck with me, that made an impression. The subjects we have discussed through our channels have left me with unresolved answers. I am okay with the truth as I now know it, but if something that we were taught or believed was not necessarily true or was only half true, then I will seek closure.

I am not trying to be philosophical here, adding to conspiracy theories or simply refusing to accept the truth. I am excited about the information that has come my way. Yes, I was astounded by what I read. After all, if there is a cure for cancer, or an alternative fuel source that would revolutionize how we use energy, I'm all for it. But the consequences of utilizing those alternatives may bring on chaos. World markets would change, some for the better, some for the worse.

Consider for a moment the use of fossil fuels. We are using compressed resources from under the ground and basically putting them into the air. Good or bad? Is cancer, for instance, a disease that has been caused by such a transformation or has medical science simply become more exact as technology allows us to probe deeper and deeper into every life form?

I still think the most important invention of humanity is the wheel. The most important discovery, fire. The two things we cannot live without are air and water.

Undeniably, if we continue to pollute air and water, we are goners. What really killed the dinosaurs seventy-five million years ago? Lack of breathable air, no water, no food. What can we learn from history?

There are nearly one billion documents and artifacts held under the National Archives protection. Add to that some 140 million at the Smithsonian and untold millions at the Vatican, and research outlets such as the Mormon Church, and one gets the hint that there are places to look if the right doors are opened and eyes have access. While early records, documents, artifacts and the like weren't well kept, the Archives still has materials that date back 1,000 years. The Vatican, it is theorized, has items that predate the life of Jesus. The Nazis and their ilk confiscated treasures that are hidden even today. The disappearance of civilizations because of natural disasters, famine, and wars, means even more information has been buried or lost. There are discoveries waiting to be made. Even the existence of UFOs.

Interestingly, age groups really don't understand certain qualities of history. We understand biblical times because of the Bible, so there is some interest. But what really happened between biblical times and the Middle Ages? How is that we have what is believed to be a good accounting of those biblical times and much less of the Middle Ages? At least we have more documentation of our own Revolutionary War, Industrial Revolution and Civil War. The advent of technology and more accurate record keeping give us some sensne or nonsense of why we suffered through World War I, perhaps the Depression, then WWII. Baby boomers don't really understand either war and the millennials don't know who Elvis was.

The Archives has all of this in its records, for those who are excited to find not what happened, but why. Our search for truth as it applies to life's mysteries is our challenge. I hope you and your group can take such research to the next step.

Until next time,

IVANHOE

Zach/Bailey at Estate

Her neck stiffened and her hairs bristled, followed by an uneasy chill. The front door opened and the security beep signaled Zach had arrived. She jumped from her chair and went to greet him.

"Well, howdy, sweetheart," he offered.

She replied with a kiss, then said, "Got another letter from Ivanhoe, and this is getting deep."

"Care to share?"

"If you're hungry, I'll warm up the pot roast while you get a read on Ivanhoe number six."

They made their way to the breakfast nook where they often ate later dinners because of their differing schedules. Zach was well into Ivanhoe 6 when the aroma of warmed-up dinner tickled his nostrils and interrupted his thoughts. He loved meatloaf, so he couldn't wait for another plateful.

He quickly returned to his reading, and as he finished she could see the look on his face.

"Every letter seems to trump the previous one and I don't know about you, but this has all the elements of a great novel," he said. "Think it's time to get everyone together again? This seems to be moving at a quick pace. And I think there is a lot more to be learned if you keep getting letters. We probably should get our foursome back together and see what we've learned on our own."

"I agree. I'll give Matt and Spence a call. What are you working on?"

"I thought I would check in with Cyril Wecht and get his read on some of this."

"How is Cyril? Haven't seen him since the time the two of you were given the Lifetime Achievement Award."

"We run into each other at medical events from time to time. Thought I would give him a call and then get together for lunch or something."

"What's your sked for the next month, so I can try to coordinate our meeting?"

"I'll be in Philadelphia next weekend talking to the AMA. Otherwise, I should be good most weekends. Have the usual surgeries to deal with during the week, but don't recall any other conventions or something out of the area."

Bailey had the feeling Ivanhoe was getting anxious and rather than take a slow ride, there was need to ramp it up a tad. She also had every confidence in the two lead FBI investigators, who she knew were going to find something startling to stir up some letters in the alphabet soup. That would make it very interesting—and make some folks feel somewhat uncomfortable.

CHAPTER 22

Yates and Stewart Car Chase

Ever the observer, Yates constantly kept an eye on the highway in the rearview mirror while the judge sat comfortably in the lush back seat of the Lincoln MKT Town Car furnished by the Secret Service. It didn't have the same extra armament as those for the president and some others in the government, but it was still fortified with extras that were not available to the average person.

Of particular use was the rear-access camera, complete with a telescopic lens, developed by NASA for its docking procedures in the zero gravity of space. Yates had access to the technology on his dashboard, although he usually waited to check the tape until he wasn't driving.

He noticed a car that seemed to be following their course and became alarmed when the car seemed to speed up. Sensing possible danger and a need for a quick response, he pulled his SIG Sauer P229 from his shoulder holster and laid it in a customized holder on his right side and considered evasive maneuvers.

He had the presence of mind amidst the potential danger to give Stewart a quick alert.

"Hold on! Trouble here."

Although she routinely strapped in, her instincts and security training meshed as she braced for whatever might come.

It didn't take long for the Ford Expedition minivan to overtake the Lincoln and make a quick right turn in front of them, going seventy miles per hour. Having anticipated a sudden move, Yates had already put a foot to the brake as the Expedition swerved across three lanes, barely balancing on two wheels, then jumped the asphalt shoulder and landscaping, destroying roadside plants, launching three feet into the air before slamming down onto a descending off-ramp and disappearing into to the roadside below. Yates didn't stop to find out where the car went. Parts of the car and wheel casings had flown into the air.

A startled Stewart righted herself from her left side on the contoured back seat and asked what was going on. The whole encounter had taken merely seconds.

"Not sure what was going on, but my instincts tell me someone was trying to take us out. Whoever it was, they missed us by inches."

"What?" she exclaimed. "Are you sure?"

"No, but I'll be able to check the tape and get a license plate and other information."

"You have that capability?"

"I got it from the NASA folks. If they can pinpoint a rover on Mars, you can imagine how important this would be for law enforcement and government agencies if used properly. I'm going to run this through Secret Service, just to make sure."

The rest of the trip was uneventful. The two were shaken, the judge noticeably, Yates not so outwardly.

Yates left the judge at the front door, where Zach stood waiting after her call from the car to tell him what had happened. Yates couldn't wait to review the tape. He made quick work of parking, removing the tape deck from the car and heading for his cottage on the grounds, where he grabbed a beer before inserting the tape into his high-tech console that had everything any Secret Service agent had access to.

Thirty minutes later, after watching the chase a few times, he placed a call to Dennis Sullivan, head of the Service.

Inside of forty-five minutes, Yates got a response from his NSA contacts. Through satellite navigation, the network had spotted what appeared to be the burning remnants of a minivan off Haycock Road near Falls Church, where Yates had said the vehicle had careened violently off the road.

Yates also had followed Secret Service protocol and agents were at the ready to investigate the event. While the torched vehicle was a mere shell of itself, agents were able to pull a VIN and double-check additional identifying numbers.

While no human remains were to be found, it was determined that the vehicle had been stolen, but the quest to find out by whom and when remained elusive. He reassured Bailey about the investigation, but Yates was not one to potentially let the incident be written off by others. His well-honed instincts told him there was more to the story. He wanted to know what it was. And he would.

CHAPTER 23

Payne, Mitchell, Kincaid, and Warner at FBI Office

In the friendly confines of the director's office, Payne, Mitchell, Kincaid, and Warner met to plan a strategy the Bureau could follow.

"We've all been briefed and read in on this special project," Payne began. "If anyone asks, this is not an investigation, per se, but an inquiry based on facts now known to us. If you two are faced with an outsider seeming overly inquisitive, report back to Curt. I assume, Curt, you have a communication procedure set up to keep us all in the loop?"

"I do, Director, and both Casey and Jenny have codes when checking back, to alert us to whether they are alone or being detained or diverted," stated Mitchell.

"I would hope there wouldn't be any sinister roadblocks out there, but the two of you, Casey and Jen, understand that we are going into some uncharted waters here, and while this is not 'official' or part of our normal operation, we need to be wary of those who might not want us to poke around in some places," Payne said.

"We've got a preliminary plan to check internet sources to see what framework we have to work from, but I suspect that we'll have to tap into other sources, even our own files that may have redacted portions," said Kincaid. "Do we have access to our own files, redacted or not?"

"Curt will be the go-to person here, so when you come across redacted Bureau documents, make a note," said Payne. "Build your outline and see where the stop signs are, then report to Curt to see what course of action you can take next. The Bureau isn't infallible, so if someone with some clout starts asking questions, play the conservative card and make notes. As we well know, Washington is full of people wondering what someone else is doing. There are those who simply won't budge if we encroach into their territory. We will learn as we go along and stay within ourselves."

"Director, how credible is this Ivanhoe character?" asked Warner. "We've been briefed on the letters, but would it be a good idea to read all of them to see where this person is coming from? Is this a theory or totally factual?"

Payne replied, "All who have read the Ivanhoe letters are convinced this is the real deal and worthy of substantiation. Again, I do not believe the emphasis of this whole project is to necessarily disprove so-called facts, but simply to determine if the facts have been rightly displayed—the people have been given facts, just not all of them."

"So, we are not trying to argue the points, but simply to determine if what is known publicly is the whole truth?" she asked.

"In essence, yes. But bear in mind, there may be some evidence—redacted at this point—that may turn the qualities of those facts into a different reading. The Bureau is the scientific branch of the justice system. Investigations, or inquiries in this case, can turn up some interesting sidelights that need time to be evaluated or reevaluated. And we have other agencies that may have a vested interest, so we need to tread lightly as we gather our facts without dropping a grenade into someone else's yard."

"Not all agencies are that willing to share information, so as you encounter resistance, simply take notes and we will make course corrections to see where this leads us," said Mitchell. "I anticipate a stop sign when it comes to redacted information held by other agencies. Heaven forbid they all should be forthcoming and share what someone on the inside is trying to do. They will have their own set of contingencies and it may take having the director get involved. I know the two of you well enough that you won't be intimidated or denied, but for now, let's play it by the book and be somewhat conservative."

"Will do," said Casey, as Jenny nodded her agreement. "We've made a preliminary outline, and we'll get cracking on this right away."

The two agents excused themselves, leaving Payne and Mitchell leaning back in their chairs and sipping their coffee.

"Randy, those two are good. They're going to stir up the letters in the alphabet soup and someone is going to feel the heat and be very uncomfortable."

"I agree, Curt, and I, for one, am anxious to see if we have something here. Is this part of a government cover-up and what does the public have a right to know? Yes, Casey and Jen are well known outside this building. J. Edgar would have been proud."

CHAPTER 24

Zach Contacts Dr. Cyril Wecht

The two were acknowledged as world renowned in their chosen fields. Both were easily recognizable at a number of medical symposiums and conventions, oftentimes chosen as guest speakers. They also liked the sport of golf, which led them to many a friendly game or tournament. But perhaps most of all, they understood what they needed to do to add to the world's knowledge of their craft. It was no coincidence that the AMA had bestowed its Lifetime Achievement Award to them at the same time in the glorious setting of the Army Navy Country Club in Arlington, Virginia. The three-hunderd-fifty-seat room had been packed and the spotlight was well deserved.

Dr. Cyril Wecht had devoted his whole life to the science of pathology. He was beyond good. He was great. He had been called on for consultations in literally hundreds of cases, some widely known, such as the Kennedy assassinations. His marker was that he always sought the truth and did not care if there were political ramifications or someone's feathers didn't fit right. He spoke his mind and stayed true to his beliefs. His motto—Prove It.

Longfellow had star quality as a heart surgeon, but he and Wecht became instant friends because of the many times they had been together for whatever occasion. They had talked about the Kennedy killings more than once, so Zach thought this was the time to drill down into some of the details that might prove useful to the Four and their quasi investigation of what Ivanhoe had so carefully laid out.

The phone rang and interrupted his thoughts about a speech he was preparing for, but Cyril Wecht answered in his usual affirmative voice with "Hello."

"Cyril, Zach Longfellow," came the cheery introduction.

"Zach, you old dog. How the hell are you doing? Last time we chatted was at that Army–Navy course in Arlington for the World Heart Pathology symposium."

"Doing just fine, but my golf game needs some work. Hope I'm not interrupting anything. Got a couple of minutes?"

"For you, anytime. I'm just polishing off some remarks for a talk I'm giving in New York next week."

"We go way back and I felt I needed to turn to someone I could trust and who knows the landscape."

"This sound ominous."

"Well, it does have some intrigue, but we're not in any danger. I have something I want to discuss with you in private, if you have some time."

"Is this a phone conversation or should we meet somewhere?"

"Preferably meet so we can cut to the chase."

"My talk in New York is to the forensics convention on Monday. We can meet there or down your way if you're tied up."

"I'll be in Philadelphia next weekend talking to the AMA. Would that work?"

"I'll make it a point to be there as well."

"Thanks, Cyril. This is important and I need your counsel."

The two confirmed cell phone numbers and agreed to meet the following Saturday in Philly.

Zach Meets with Wecht

Dr. Cyril Wecht walked through the door of the Ristorante Pesto, one of the more popular restaurants in Philadelphia, and Zach Longfellow was there to greet him. Maître d' Giovanni Lucerno ushered them to the private room in the back. After taking their drink orders, Lucerno departed and the two notables began their conversation.

"I appreciate your meeting me. I'd like to tell you about an inquiry that may be of interest to you," Longfellow began. "A few months ago, Bailey got a letter from a person identifying themself as Ivanhoe. Without going into great detail, the whole scenario revolves around government secrets or perceived historical facts—what does the public have a right to know, given that some if not all secrets could or would be made public at some time? Think Ellsberg, Snowden and others.

"Where you come in is the reference to the JFK assassination. Ivanhoe purports to have intimate details of what, where, when, why, how. Bailey showed me the letters—there have now been six—and we have opted to bring in others who we trust to help us unravel whether this is true or a figment of someone's creative imagination.

"You and I have talked about the forensic information in the past, but I don't know all that you know in this area. I thought I would do my part and talk to you to see if you could add any clarification to what has been purported or what you found to be true or not true when you were a part of the Warren Commission investigation.

"Just so you know, Matt Brumfield and Spencer Crockett are on our team and Randy Payne from the FBI is also involved in what we describe as an 'inquiry.' I'm not sure we're in it to reveal all cover-ups or secrets for public consumption, or just to get to the truth about certain things that the general public would like to know or perhaps has a right to know.

"So, what do you think, Cyril? Can you help us sort this all out?"

Wecht had a half smile on his face.

"Wow. There's a lot to go on here, Zach. You piqued my interest with the phone call. When the government secrets card was played, I was all in. I know Matt and Spence, but I don't think I've met Payne at the FBI.

"I, too, have considered the Kennedy killings—and I use the plural here—to be huge cover-ups. I suspect your inquiries will meet with some dead zones and opposition, but there is too much information out there to maintain a cover-up for eternity. Assuming Ivanhoe has what has been surmised and is waiting for someone to prove any or all information wrong or off base, qualified analysis might be the best way to approach everything.

"As I told the Warren Commission and have written in books and articles, there is no way the pathology report could match up. Know that you have my complete support.

"Some of the conclusions from the Warren Report are simply preposterous. I told them then and I have pointed out those inaccuracies many times since. No one has proved me wrong or even called me out. The autopsy of the president was botched at the Bethesda Navy Hospital. I mean, how does it grab you as an American citizen to have two navy doctors, who had never performed a bullet-wound autopsy, examine the leader of the free world? And then there are the two forensics doctors working on the body of the president on the plane that brought him back to Washington from Dallas. No notes, but I daresay there were pictures that never have been available for public view, even under FOIA.

"It was an American conspiracy. It was a coup d'état."

Longfellow was mesmerized, as he was some years before when he was befriended by the learned Wecht.

"How accurate was the *JFK* movie by Oliver Stone?"

"Stone had the audacity to do the movie and Arlen Specter was a part of that, describing missteps by the commission and Chief Justice Earl Warren's push to get members to cut corners. One of the most damaging truths that came out was the outright failure to review certain autopsy photos and x-rays.

"Consider these salient points: One, Oswald was given a nitrate test on the night after the shooting. Results showed he had not fired a rifle recently; Two, Julia Ann Mercer, caught in traffic on Elm Street, saw a man get out of a truck and carry a rifle up the grassy knoll. She later identified the driver to the FBI as Jack Ruby; Three, more than five hundred photos were taken by seventy-five photographers in Dealey Plaza in the hour before, during and after the shooting. The Warren Commission examined twenty-six photos. The FBI examined fifty; Four, sixteen of the Dallas sheriff's deputies in Dealey Plaza believed shots came from the knoll and ran in that direction; Five, Connally's clothes were dry cleaned, destroying evidence; Six, Oswald's mother insisted he was an intelligence agent; Seven, there was more metal in Connally's body than was missing from the Commission's Exhibit 399, which is known as the 'magic bullet'; Eight, Connolly died in 1993; and Nine, Kennedy's brain is missing from the National Archives.

"Zach, I never intended to be the center of anyone's attention, but as a pathologist, conclusions have to be reached. I've served as a consultant on many other high-profile cases, perhaps because of the JFK involvement, and all I want is the real truth. FOIA is a part of our search for the truth, but are all of the facts available?"

"That's what we're hoping to find out," said Zach. "Aside from government, military and strategic redactions, this inquiry just may disprove a lot of historical myths, misconceptions, and perhaps lies that may hide under the government's carpet. And like you, I am not looking at being the focal point of any of this, either, any more than Bailey, Matt, or Spence want to be. But your help in substantiating certain facts will be invaluable."

"I look forward to our continued friendship and the symposiums we may be a part of."

Their firm handshake, warm smiles and a toast concluded another grand lunch.

CHAPTER 25

Stewart at Estate

The court's rulings stirred many a fuss, but the summer recess allowed time to catch one's breath. Briefs, documents and legal papers were beginning to stack up while the solicitor general waded through potential court business, but it wasn't yet ready for the justices' review. While there was time to take a step back, however, the justices were mindful that keeping a finger on the pulse was almost mandatory.

The August weather was at its usual hot and humid state and the days were long. Bailey was locked into some legislation that had found its way to the court in the past, but this time had been restructured to fight another battle. She loved the creative approach and braced for what might be another spirited discussion with her colleagues. One thing for sure, she did not back down, but she was willing to listen.

Satisfied with her normal day at the court, she had a peaceful ride back to the estate, as she called it. She wished for a quiet evening with some light reading and maybe some TV. She also looked forward to seeing Zach, who had returned from yet another world symposium in Zurich.

Zach was planning on a barbecue, complete with chicken, roasted potatoes, and zucchini. He was enjoying a glass of chardonnay when she got home and was quick to offer her a glass of merlot when she found him ready to "Q" on the extended back patio. The spa would come later.

Mandy had sorted her mail and left her notes on the inquiries of the day. The pile was on the table next to the Brown Jordan lounge chairs. The glass-topped table seated six comfortably and Zach and Bailey often would use the area to simply relax during the warmer months. The enclosed lap pool, spa, and sauna were nearby.

As Zach was nursing the gas-flamed barbecue and sipping his wine, Bailey reached for her daily updates and was surprised to see a large flat envelope that could mean only one thing. She had come to wish for and look forward to such deliveries, as they were insightful as well as entertaining. She felt more learned after working her way through the multitudes of facts and presumptions.

"Oh, what do we have here?" she said as she sliced through the envelope.

CHAPTER 26

Ivanhoe Letter—7

Dear Justice Stewart:

I suspect by this time you have come up with many more questions and have made efforts to search for additional clues to solve this maze. And I suspect you have called on people you trust to help you in your quest.

Let me reassure you, your efforts will not go unnoticed or unappreciated. While the main topic of discussion probably was your chosen subject—the JFK assassination, medical research, energy, extraterrestrials, religious documents, the environment and all that certainly would gain attention if someone started poking around.

It no doubt would be interesting to send you everything I have, but I don't think that is wise at this time. Rest assured, though, if something happens to me or you, the information and all of its treasures will be opened for all to see. I suspect some would doubt that such information really exists, but I believe what I was given to be the whole truth and nothing but the truth. Doubters will be believers. Stonewallers will face the wrath of more than many, and history truly will be rewritten. Then again, for all those who believe one way, there will be others that look at everything in a different light.

Politics comes to mind.

So, in keeping with bringing certain facts to the table, I offer up some tidbits that may help in your collective investigations. I also realize that you may not be able to communicate with a one- or two-word line in the Post, *but I will continue to look for an inconspicuous or cryptic reference. It is paramount that we not meet, for fear of jeopardizing your position or perhaps mine.*

Irrespective of my own personal thoughts, philosophies, and observations of the materials that have been given to me, I ask that you consider the following:

Medical Research

As cultures comingled through wars, conquests, and trade, certain diseases were sure to devastate civilizations. The conquest of the Americas that all but wiped out Native American populations was at least in part the result of native communities not having immunity to European pathogens.

But what has happened in more modern times? Do you actually think that AIDS, Ebola, or Zika just started up somewhere? These diseases were planted to help eradicate overpopulation. Medical science comes up with antidotes for just about everything. When something gets controlled, something else comes along. The research into this clandestine procedure is well documented in the information I have been privileged to see.

On the really good side, medical research has developed many cures such as heart bypass, artificial hearts and limbs, and more. We are on the cusp of using advanced technology to reconnect and restore damaged nerve endings, enabling people to walk and use limbs that have been debilitated through heart attacks, strokes, and accidents. Laser optics, fiber optics, artificial connectors will pave the way for people to become more functional.

As for actual cures, the files I have in my possession show we do know how to eradicate cancer, at least as we know it today. But divulging that information now, for public consumption, probably would destroy continuing research that may prove valuable for other to-be-seen diseases. For those whose lives have been impacted by something as stark as cancer, a cure would be a welcome relief. But if I told you we knew about this twenty to thirty years ago, would the public be outraged? I think so.

And that becomes the core principle we continue to think about—what should the public know? The earth already is overpopulated in terms of life-sustaining nutrients. There will not be enough food and water to handle the increasing population, so does wiping out scores of people fit the puzzle on how to survive?

Energy

For years we have relied on oil and its refinement to propel us through all manner of travel. As I mentioned in one of my previous letters, take away the use of oil, at least in its general sense today, and what fossil fuels we take from the earth would become by-products that circle the earth—carbon dioxide.

The fact we have known about alternative fuel sources, namely nuclear, electromagnetic, solar, wind, even silicon, prompts one to ask what should we be expecting in the future? Technology will determine that.

World order would be the answer.

Consider what it would do to the world order if oil consumption was substantially cut back. Cultures would be vastly disrupted, money flow would be drastically altered. Energy is the one resource that allows us to expand our horizons. Water and air are the resources that are absolutely mandatory.

For those who are stuck on global warming, tell them to look up history and delve into the ice ages and warming trends of the past. If we were more sensitive to the use of clean water or the immediate need for desalination, the weather trends would reverse much quicker than they would if we eliminated fossil fuel emissions. But if we did couple that with the decreased use of oil from underground and spewed into the air, you would see a completely different atmosphere.

In fact, if one were to raise the question why civilizations have disappeared over time, the simple answer is water, or the lack thereof.

Some civilizations were overrun with rising seas or oceans. This was not the result of global warming, as has been presented today. It was caused by natural changes in the earth's atmosphere—like the ice ages. Volcanic eruptions, earthquakes, and plate tectonics also played a role.

For those civilizations that disappeared in the mountains of Peru or the relative flatlands of Mexico and South America, all simply vanished because water sources made it impossible to grow food and have water to tend to normal needs. As I said before, the two things we cannot do without are air and water. They both lead to food, and without those, we perish. The mysterious disappearance of the Incas and Mayans is rooted in the loss of water. Those civilizations went somewhere just to survive. Treasures were moved to a safe haven and now are ready to be found. Some of my information might just lead someone to find long-lost treasures. They are closer than you might think.

Extraterrestrials

I can't speak for other individuals, but I find it interesting that there are pyramids on every continent in the world. There are structures that were built millennia ago with stone slabs that seemingly fit together with a precision that our present-day builders find extraordinary, given that there was no known machinery at that time to produce such perfection.

The data I have been given explores all possible theories, and the common denominator is that these megaliths were produced by extraterrestrials with advanced knowledge of building with the materials they had at the time. The fact that pyramids had similar shapes without the people of various lands connecting with each other in some way is astonishing.

Consider that civilization may well have started in the Southern Hemisphere and migrated north. Lost civilizations are more prevalent in that part of the world as archeologists are finding many centuries-hidden settlements and cultures that have been overgrown by vegetation. There are some tribes and peoples that never have seen the outside world. And there is a strong consideration that the pyramids of the southern regions of the

American continents predated those of Egypt and elsewhere in the world.. The coastal deserts of Peru and the Andean climates of some ten thousand years ago were lush and green before El Niños buried their existence. The same could be said of the deserts of northern Africa. The Incas and Mayans came later to South America.

The cave drawings and other artifacts that have been recovered also give some credence to air and space travel, complete with rocket-like propulsions. And our visitors had knowledge of space flight given their unknown forms of propulsion were not made of what we know as common materials. They had mastered nuclear fission, fusion, and magnetic warp to go with what we think is the limit of travel—that of light speed. Gene Roddenberry had the connection and Star Trek *became a phenomenon. Coincidence?*

The advent of incandescent light, sound reproduction, flying, even computers goes back well before any modern-day inventor tackled the prospects of reinvention. Were Archimedes, Cai Lun, Isaac Newton, Leonardo daVinci, Albert Einstein, Jules Verne and others of their time just 'make-it-up' kind of guys? Perhaps, but there had to be some basis from which their ideas grew.

Some theorists even think earth was populated by beings from another world and we have evolved into what we see today. There are a multitude of documents outlining all such possibilities, given that research has been going on for a long time. Mind you, some of these reports are postulates and thus open to interpretation, but the evidence suggests with all likelihood that we have been visited and helped on our way.

As for actual physical evidence, the government does, in fact, have objects that are from elsewhere, including what we call spaceships and robot-like beings. Would any of this evidence be of interest to the public? I would say yes. Would it startle people to find out we are not alone and there are others who have reached us? I would say yes. The public, for the most part, lives in a vacuum and is okay with conflicting information, even threats to existence. But I venture to say, the great majority of people do not believe in the end of civilization.

Alien beings, for instance, have been robot-like. The depictions of and the actual remains show a synthetic-type skin with a Kevlar or Speedo look. Notice that these beings do not have actual mouths or what we know as genitals. The skin is extremely flexible and we have no clue what makes up its composition, since there are no cells to analyze.

The crafts have brought us materials we do not recognize, although scientists for years have been trying to duplicate any and all. The stealth aircraft, even our space shuttles, have some elements of this technology, but apparently we do not have the resources to duplicate exactly. Yes, Area 51 is involved. There is more than stolen technology from our earthbound friends there. Even inventions devised hundreds of years ago have found their way into our developed society. Just how did those folks way back then come up with this advanced technology? Coincidence?

That brings me to the religious element.

Religion

Consider why we have different God-like images, cave drawings and other artifacts showing descriptions of something out of our perceived universe. There are heads and masks of all sorts on every continent. Does that mean one being or a collection of them visited so long ago that those who depicted them thought of them as gods or simply something from the stars? From what I have seen in the decrypted notes of this material I now have, these different cultures could not have evolved without some sort of connection.

That brings me to the Vatican. There is a bevy of information within the walls of the Vatican, corroborating and/or disproving some of the things linked to religion over the years. This information, to a great extent, is listed in the documents. The Vatican's secret archive holds many important and historically significant documents—some believe it is hiding *important pieces of history, too.*

We do know what some of the contents are: Galileo's trial transcript, and letters from Abraham Lincoln and King Henry VIII.

These archives were created by Pope Paul V in 1612, and four hundred years later, some of those documents are finally on display. However, there still are questions as to whether or not the Church is hiding documents that put it in an unfavorable light, like anti-Semitic sentiments and other backward ideas.

You can't just waltz into the archives that are available for viewing; you have to be a scholar and pass Swiss guards. Credentials for access expire after sixth months and tourists, journalists, students, and armchair historians are never granted entrance. There is more than entombed popes buried in the bowels of the Vatican.

There are at least seven different safe houses and warehouses around the world that hold millions of artifacts, documents, and support materials, including what is thought to be lost treasures of the Library of Alexandria, Phoenician and Babylonian collections, and more. The list of all such materials is a part of this cache of information.

At least the internet has given wide entrance to subjects of all kinds. But there is some material in here that would simply rewrite history as we know it, the history we were taught in school, or that we learned through something printed or said. This information is the holy grail of the world.

Perhaps that is what we are sitting on here—the holy grail of humanity.

I hope this has given you some background on what I have delved into. From what I have read, there is logic in the presentation, leading me to believe what I am reading. I hope you share my enthusiasm and quest. And I apologize for being a bit more philosophical than normal, but I think we all need to make our own interpretations as more of this information comes forth. I also hope that those who you have shared this information with will see it through, complete with overcoming obstacles.

IVANHOE

CHAPTER 27

Bailey and Zach at the Estate

She sipped her wine and read the letter with astonishment. An occasional utterance, such as "Oh my god," "Really," and "You have got to be kidding," came through loud and clear. Zach kept turning the chicken, potatoes, and zucchini, grinning slightly when she offered up her words. He knew she was enjoying every minute of the latest of the Ivanhoe letters.

Having read through the first volley of the four-page letter, she went for the reread. Now done, she looked at Zach and said the letter needed another pair of eyes.

"It can wait. Dinner is served." Knowing full well Bailey was trapped with the contents of the latest letter, he surmised that she was excited to tell him all, so he countered with, "Why don't you give me the thumbnail version, and I'll take a hack at it when we're done with dinner?"

While she tried to eat her dinner, she spent most of the time distilling the elements of the letter and trying to give Zach his own time to evaluate. Zach sat patiently, listening to all before adding, "Is this fact or is this Ivanhoe becoming philosophical?"

"From a logical standpoint, it makes one wonder how this could be contrived. After all, we have interest in all that Ivanhoe says, be it health care, medical research, energy, even extraterrestrials. If someone wrote a book with all of this, wouldn't it be a best seller based on the fact people are transfixed by mystery? I've always had interest in facts, preferred nonfiction to fiction. To say history wasn't reported exactly or correctly, based on new and inviting discoveries, means I would be all ears."

"But if some of those new discoveries undermine what we perceive to be our basis for structure and trust, should such information be out there for all to see?"

"Look at what we already have and have had for almost two hundred fifty years of this nation. We have government meetings, be it on a congressional level or within the executive or judicial branches, that warrant some form of secrecy. I see that every day with the court. This goes back to our original question: What does the public have a right to know?

"Read the latest letter and tell me if this is going deeper than even we thought."

Settling into his lounge chair, Zach read with great intensity, occasionally giving an approving nod. He went through a second read and put the letter on the adjoining side table.

"Want another glass of wine?" he said.

"I thought you would never ask," she responded.

CHAPTER 28

FBI Building

The bottom reaches of the FBI building were cavernous, with no buildouts for offices or other amenities for the goings-on of the Bureau. With over two hundred thousand square feet of space, there was enough room for the stacks of documents and artifacts that were a part of an unknown number of FBI investigations. As was the case for the National Archives, the FBI secure area was considered a double-lockdown facility, complete with a multitude of security checks that not only included a human presence, but cameras, sensors, and laser capabilities. If someone were to breach one door, a second one had an even more secure command.

"The Pit," as it was affectionately referred to, was temperature-controlled and lead-lined. The well-organized special viewing areas where documents and artifacts could be analyzed were nearly soundproof and had chairs, couches, and tables, some of which could accommodate up to twelve people.

While the National Archives had documents that were sent from various agencies, the FBI vault had unredacted documents that pertained strictly to the Bureau and its investigations. Access to the depths required a special clearance and an agent presence. No photographs or document transfers were allowed without a sign off by the director.

The Hoover files, what there was of them, were housed in a corner area further secured by a gated entrance, accessible only by a separate code, retinal scanner, and laser system. The eponymous director had set up the area as his own secret lair, complete with a washroom, couches, and a more-than-adequate seating space. His files contained dossiers on individuals, associations, businesses, and societies, the likes of which no one had ever dreamed about.

He was meticulous about filing even scraps of paper. The information in some of the dossiers certainly was not meant to see the light of day, so some of the documents had been reclassified after his death as top secret, classified, executive clearance, and for your eyes only, referring to the director himself.

It was the missing files that caused a constant stir among Bureau operatives, who knew that some 25 percent of his known files disappeared after his death.

The well-catalogued documents were cross referenced. Other agencies such as the NSA and CIA had similar fail-safe security operations. When sharing information with another, unredacted data was not transferred. Every governmental agency that dealt with sensitive information had its own agents keystroke and encrypt its own documentation.

With the advancement of the internet and its almost-full disclosure of information, it was paramount that certain documents that dealt with military and state strategic procedures be kept secure.

While there was respect and professional courtesy among interagency personnel, there was also competition. All thought of themselves as the number one in anything, so to cooperate meant to edit out a bit of info here and there. Even state and local law-enforcement agencies felt burned by the fed operatives. Just how much information was shared seemed to be determined by agency individuals rather than the agencies themselves. In some circles, grandstanding was the rule rather than the exception.

How deep Ivanhoe's information dug into any and all agency data remained to be seen, but the fact that so much was referred to in the letters left a now-very-intrigued Bailey Stewart ready to find out. The possibility of breaches in what was known as classified or top-secret information, and that the information somehow had been downloaded from a single source, had more than raised her eyebrows. She was all in to learn more.

CHAPTER 29

Longfellow Estate

It was time for the group to meet again. Stewart's recent Ivanhoe letters had stirred a constant pot for her, and while she was committed to the exercises of the court, she was determined to see this puzzle completed. She had developed many theories about the outcome and was willing to add more logs to the fire while her other compatriots were doing so as well.

Brumfield and Crockett had confirmed their time for the weekend, but Zach was off to Buenos Aires for an emergency symposium on the growing concerns of advanced bacterial content of the water supplies. The country was experiencing a rise of heart conditions and the death rate was causing alarm.

Saturday morning, the three were seated at the solid oak dining room table with their own laptops and sets of files. Yates had set up the whiteboard in the dining room and erected a screen for viewing downloaded information from the internet and the personal laptops.

"Zach had wanted to join us today, but with the growing concerns about bacteria and viruses that are sounding sirens in not only in Buenos Aires but most of South America, he agreed to stay a few extra days to add whatever expertise he could to the cause," Bailey began. "He did at least do a brief summary of what he has been up to, so I decided to print out what he gave me. In short, he met with Dr. Cyril Wecht, who was a key component of the Warren Commission from the pathological side, and I think that report alone gives credence to what Ivanhoe has told us.

"I realize we all have other things that are going on. But I thought we needed to at least summarize what we've found out since meeting two months ago, so we have a focus on what we need to do next and call for additional help if need be."

Brumfield and Crockett both nodded in unison and Bailey asked Brumfield to share what he had learned.

"I met with Annie at the Archives and she said she would do whatever she could within the confines of regulations to get us to whatever questions we had," he said. "She did not seem reluctant to step in herself if we met a stop sign, since Archives is a public house.

"She did note that Archives has redacted information, that information sent there already had been sanitized. I asked whether we could have access to documents on whatever subject and see if any redacted documents would be useful. She said yes, unless there is a special read-in only. I would think we could formulate an outline from there."

"What are your upsides and downsides at this time, Matt?" Bailey asked.

"I suspect we will gain enough access initially, since a great percentage of Archives data is available online, but for the more sensitive stuff, we might have to tread lightly. I guess my overall assessment is that we'll get more access to the Archives than we will at the Bureau."

"Spence, what's your take?"

"I have the same charge," offered Crockett. "I've talked with Randy Payne and his top guy Curt Mitchell and they have assigned Casey Kincaid and Jennifer Warner to work with me for FBI information. I've worked with them before when I was an SP and found them to be diligent and trustworthy.

"Both Randy and Curt have promised full support as long as our inquiries are just that, not termed an investigation. I told them I would keep them apprised of what comes up as we look for corroborating evidence or information. I also assured them that if we came up against a security issue—such as national defense, or anything that may compromise the works of the NSA or CIA or others—that we would make note and keep them in the loop.

"At the same time, I told them that if they heard of anything that might trigger a protocol or sanctions on any of our efforts, that they needed to let us know immediately. The last thing we need is for someone to get hurt or be put in harm's way—and that those goes for all of us as well."

"Totally agree, Spence," replied Bailey. "I think we all face a possibility of someone tapping us on the shoulder, so to speak, and I want to know that all of us, including our own teams, are not in this to cause any flare-ups in any federal agency. As long as we have the support from our sources, I see no reason why we can't ask questions and expect reasonable feedback."

For the balance of the day, the three shared documents and other inquiry information they had learned. There was a common sense of relief when they all felt they were up to speed and they were doing the right thing to follow the Ivanhoe leads. Bailey shared the latest letters from Ivanhoe, and Brumfield and Crockett had the same aghast reaction. The latest letter, outlining the areas of medicine, religion, extraterrestrials, and weather patterns left them wondering how Ivanhoe actually came into all of this information—if, in fact, it was to be believed as totally factual.

"I think we feel the same way about Ivanhoe's representations," offered Bailey. "Every time I think Ivanhoe has said enough to whet anyone's appetite, another letter arrives with more and more information that sends me into another world of thought. It certainly has made a great read. And if this is, in fact, all true, then some historical 'facts' need to be changed. Those changes are going to bother some people, even at the Vatican."

As the day was wilting into the afternoon sundown, Yates was ready to take Brumfield and Crockett back to Washington.

Dusk brought on a moment for solitude for Bailey, and she cupped her chardonnay and got lost in thought as the sun drifted beyond the silhouetted trees outlining the pond. A time for the sauna would come later.

The early-morning phone call from Zach the next day rousted Bailey from a comfortable sleep, unusual for her given that the court was about to render its decisions on several pending cases.

"Good morning, sweetheart," was Zach's greeting.

"What rooster woke you up this early?" countered Bailey.

"Just wanted you to know I will be coming back a day early, so should be at the compound by late afternoon. Anything new from your meeting with the guys?"

"It was a good session and we all felt reassured we were up to date. You read the recent Ivanhoe letter, and both Matt and Spence seemed even more concerned that while we had our own areas to drill into, this constant stream of new information was starting to become overwhelming. I hope we don't lose our focus."

"Sounds like a pool discussion to me."

CHAPTER 30

Brumfield Adds Dean Polkinghorne to His Team

The past few months as a member of the Four had more than whetted Brumfield's appetite for knowledge. His legal mind swirled with anticipation of finding clues that led to a true answer. While his administrative duties had consumed his daily calendar, he still found time to wade through options and possibilities. His team's search of the Archives would necessitate expanding his team. As he rose through the ranks to become the dean of Harvard Law School and onward to become president of the university, he had hired and been associated with some talented people whom he knew he could trust.

His reputation as a fair-minded and articulate legal expert had followed him throughout his career. Once he was named president, he had tapped Megan Polkinghorne as his replacement for law-school dean. She, too, had learned the old-school ways and was quick to incorporate the uptick of changes in the legal profession. She was the third woman to hold the prestigious post at the school.

Brumfield now met with Polkinghorne and, after revealing the identities of the members of the Four, gave her a broad outline of what he was interested in doing. She was asked to recruit deans and professors whom she could trust, allowing them the minimum of information under the guise that this was a project. Her challenge was to organize a small group to do research at the National Archives. Some of that research, he surmised, might be available online, but the bulk of their work would be done at the Archives.

"I'm good to go on this, Matt, but is there some goal here?" she asked.

"Suffice to say that what you're doing will go a long way toward proving or disproving theories. I expect there will be a lot of frustration because I anticipate a lot of redacted material, but have your team plot its travels so we can determine where we need to jump a barrier. Perhaps down the road I can read you into more of the backdrop, but it's better that I don't tell you too much now."

"Seems like a fascinating reach and I'll get right on it," said an enthused Polkinghorne. "Want me to correspond with you or just talk with you?"

"No emails for now. Let's do this by meeting here from time to time. No one will think of our meeting every once in a while. And your team members should do the same with you. Data can be copied and saved in a Word file and disseminated later."

"Sounds so mysterious, so inviting. Can't wait to get started and see what we come up with."

"Let's plan on meeting at least twice a month. I am inundated with administrative protocol, so I won't be able to have my hands on this all the time, which is why I turned to you for your input and expertise. You, too, have a lot of administrative duties, so pick your best to follow this through."

"Well, you taught me everything I know, Matt. I appreciate your confidence. I've got some people in mind that I think can help move this project along. I'll get back to you in a couple of weeks."

Polkinghorne left Brumfield's office with a smile on her face. He sported a matching grin, satisfied that he had a staunch supporter, one he felt might even be a strong candidate for his current job when he decided to call it a day as the school's top administrator.

CHAPTER 31

Crockett Meets with Kincaid and Warner

Spencer Crockett decided it was time to meet with his crack team to get an update on its findings, joining Kincaid and Warner for lunch at the Army Navy Golf Course in Arlington.

"Spence, we've been outlining our plans to review documents at the Bureau," began Kincaid. "We're sure we'll meet some initial roadblocks, so should we go directly to Curt Mitchell or check back with you first? Obviously, we don't want to jeopardize our project, let alone put our jobs on the line."

"Curt Mitchell as well as Director Payne will be your contacts to curtail initial stop signs," stated Crockett. "Remember, everything you do is a part of an inquiry and all you are doing is reviewing, not launching an investigation. We're all aware that the FBI files are unredacted, and if there's something that's really sensitive, then we might get tagged. Simply make note of where you're stopped by top secret or classified designations and we'll see what Curt and Randy might be able to do. Above all, we do not want to start an inquiry about our inquiry."

"We're ready to delve into it, so should we meet at any time or place when we have something or simply set up regular meeting times?" asked Kincaid.

"Let's meet monthly unless something jumps out at you," suggested Crockett. "Your analysis is the center point of what we need, so whatever you feel is important, note in a journal entry."

"Spence, we can't take photographs of the FBI files without prior written consent from the director, so how do we substantiate our findings?" asked Warner.

"Your notes will suffice for now. Also, I expect you will be working separately at times, so it might be best to compare your notes when you're away from the Bureau."

"We're ready to rock, so see you in a month?" Warner asked.

"I'll call you with a time and place."

CHAPTER 32

Judge Gordon O'Driscoll at Ruth's Chris Steak House

Gordon O'Driscoll, now into his seventeenth year as an associate justice of the United States Supreme Court, liked dining out with his wife Caryl on weekends, whether the court was in session or not. His favorite haunt was Ruth's Chris Steak House, where all the waiters couldn't wait to serve the two. Laughter was always part of the evening.

As was the case with all court justices, there was a driver/bodyguard, and Laurel Barksdale was up to the task. The former marine had numerous decorations for bravery while in the service and her uniform showed a variety of colors of badges and ribbons. She became a special agent of the Secret Service after twenty-some years in the corps and was recommended by Dennis Sullivan, now head of the Secret Service. The two had grown up together in Republic, Michigan, a small town in the upper peninsula. They had stayed locked as friends after high school. While Sullivan had opted for naval intelligence as a career, Barksdale had taken up the fight.

When the O'Driscolls went anywhere, she was with them, even when shopping. The usual protocol for dinner would be for her to drive up to the curb, escort them into the restaurant, and sit in the car and keep tabs with her earpiece. She would therefore know instantly if they needed assistance, as well as when they were ready to leave.

The justice was well known in many circles, and as a moderate on the court, he was looked on as a mediator when the liberal- or conservative-leaning justices simply chose not to agree. The court's currently balanced makeup was something the public had taken a liking to.

All was well with the O'Driscolls this night, with the justice ordering his favorite filet mignon and Caryl her shrimp scampi. They shared a bottle of their favorite merlot and topped off the evening's meal with a crème brûlée. Soon after finishing his last bite of the dessert, however, the justice started having convulsions and felt nauseated. His quick summons of Barksdale brought the agent into the restaurant in less than thirty seconds. Thinking that the justice was having a heart attack, the agent felt his pulse and looked at his eyes. Seeing standard signs of a possible heart attack, Barksdale called her own 911 contact, and the emergency crew was there inside of three minutes.

The justice was having problems breathing and was therefore intubated by the EMT crew and whisked off to Arlington Memorial Hospital in a flash.

Dr. Alan Smithson, the attending emergency room physician, came out quickly and conversed with Caryl and Laurel.

"What did Judge O'Driscoll have for dinner?"

Caryl offered up the menu and the timeline.

"It appears Judge O'Driscoll was poisoned, something slow acting but deadly, had you not been alert and got him here when you did."

"Poisoned?!" Barksdale asked sharply.

"How?" was the response from Caryl. "We each ate a standard dinner, so why didn't I get sick?"

"Apparently there was nothing unusual about the food you two ate, so we'll need to get samples of everything else," Dr. Smithson replied.

"I already locked down the place and told all waiters and management to bag any food or drink that may have been a part of their dinner. Standard procedure," said Barksdale, with a befuddled look. "Not sure we will get the meat portion back, but if there was something in the wine or dessert, we should be able to run enough tests."

"This wouldn't have been deadly unless ingested over a period of time; this was no food poisoning incident," said Dr. Smithson. "Get us the food and drink samples and we'll run the tests here, though, to be certain."

"Should we check with the Service or the FBI?" Barksdale asked.

"We can save some samples for them," said Dr. Smithson, "but our labs here are quite thorough."

As is the case when any member of the court falls ill or is involved in an accident or something else more sinister, everyone, from the members to the staff, are alerted, as are the Service and the FBI. When word reached Bailey Stewart, she immediately contacted Zach, who was in Minneapolis at the Mayo

Clinic for a two-day set of meetings with the rest of the world-renown heart specialists. Her angst came across loud and clear. Her churning mind led her to imagine a conspiracy theory against members of the court. She did not know why, but this was the fourth incident, each of which involved a different member, and she was becoming alarmed.

O'Driscoll was cleared to go home after a battery of tests showed he was stable, and it being a Friday, he preferred to be at home in their Arlington estate. The 0.65-acre, 6,800 square foot home was valued at $3.5 million and drew a lot of attention because of the up-lighting and grand look from the street with windows galore. The O'Driscolls had been there for all of the judge's years on the Supreme Court.

The chase is on....

CHAPTER 33

Stewart Meets with Towner and Hailwood

In that information was readily forthcoming from the sources of the Four, Stewart felt there was a threshold staring them all in the face. As an officer of the court, she had an obligation to determine when the flags of right, wrong, fair, foul and perhaps illegal were flown.

Rather than wait for the next meeting of the Four, which came in the form of monthly sessions in Fairfax, Stewart decided she would read-in her chief of staff Candice Towner and her experienced senior legal counsel and confidant Alexander Hailwood. Both had been with the justice well before her appointment to the court and had provided valued input on just about every subject imaginable. Even personal matters were discussed from time to time, and the three were at ease with sharing.

Now alone in the justice's office, she laid out her involvement in the search for corroborating documentation. She didn't pull any punches, either. She wanted their take on what Ivanhoe had divulged and where the Four had each planned to take a segment and see it through. The elements of legality had to be discussed as well as the integrity of the justice's position as a member of the highest court in the land, one that quite possibly could be called upon to render a decision about the very information they were investigating.

"I think you can sense my interest and intrigue here, but I also want to protect the sanctity of the court and, of course, all of us," said Stewart. "This isn't a 'no-fly zone,' but if this falls under the Freedom of Information Act, then I think it is in our best interest to find out just how far we—meaning the three of us—and how far anyone else—including all those I have mentioned—can go.

"My thinking now is to have a chat with Jim Fox, the president's chief of staff, and at least give him a heads-up. I don't want the president to be blindsided by some snoopy member of the media that is looking for a Pulitzer Prize. We've had enough of that. Starting a range war over something as sensitive as this would be very counterproductive. I want to know the details, as a citizen, just as much as anyone else. But our job is to protect rights and prove wrongs.

"Alex, your take?"

"My first reaction is this sounds like FOIA, since Archives has documents for the eyes of all. But if redacted information gets out, through the FBI or another source, then I think there might be a congressional hearing and looming court battles," responded Hailwood. "I guess it would come down to whether someone felt the information was classified or privileged or would in some way cause some embarrassment for a powerful person or entity. It's the redacted information that could prove to be a high bar."

"Candy, your thoughts?" asked Stewart.

"I definitely would read Jim Fox in on this, not in great detail, but to let him know there have been some inquiries, under the guise of FOIA," she said. "I don't think the president would have any personal problems with any of this, but there might be some powerful people in the wings that could throw a grenade his way if they might be compromised in any way. And I agree with Alex on the redacted information aspect."

"I guess we have to formulate some sort of a talking-points session, off the record of course, with Fox," said Stewart, holding her reading glasses. "Can you both get together and draw up a non-fileable white paper? We can get together the first of the week for about an hour and plan a meeting with Jim."

With the usual "yes" from both Alex and Candy, the meeting was over.

Jim Fox

Jim Fox was an accomplished neurosurgeon, but he gave up the practice when he became close friends with John Jefferson McCade, JJ to those who knew him well. They had met playing golf as amateurs in the famed Pebble Beach Tournament on California's Monterey Peninsula. The two hit it off immediately, so well that they had side bets on just about every shot and hole for the four-day tournament.

McCade was in line to run for governor of California and somehow talked Fox into joining the fun and games of political life. Fox had already anticipated hanging up his noted career sometime soon, as the usual steady hands were not as strong as they used to be. So, he took a leave from his practice and signed on as a confidant to then-candidate McCade.

Within a year, Fox was hooked and retired from his days as a neurosurgeon. The McCade bandwagon rolled through two successful elections. The run for the presidency was next on the rocket ride to the top. McCade won his first term with a comfortable electoral college margin, and he made it look easy with a landslide victory after the first four years. Fox, now sixty-six, was what some people referred to as the ultimate shotgun rider on a popular stagecoach.

Fox was known for his wisdom and knowledge of the facts as stated. He always professed he would be honest, consistent, and fair, so for the people who knew him, there was no need to beat around the bush. If he caught the gist of a discussion, he would ask pertinent questions.

He would also study the person's presentation and mannerisms. As McCade had relied on his judgment to keep everything orderly, he was quick to make assessments as to whether the conversation, with all of its implications, would be considered high priority, give-it-some-thought or "we'll get back to you."

The phone call announcing Candy Towner was on the line stopped Fox from what he was doing. The two had been longtime friends, even before Fox came to Washington five years ago.

"How's my favorite Candy?" said an enthusiastic Fox when he greeted Towner on the phone.

"Well, just fine, my friend," said Towner with equal enthusiasm.

"To what do I owe the pleasure?"

"I'd like to set up a meeting—your place or mine—about something that needs about 30 minutes."

"Can you brief me on the meeting?

"Would rather not on the phone, as this remains off the record, at least for now. Nothing sinister, just potentially sensitive, so I thought a brief meeting would bring you up to speed.

"Can do. Give me a minute to check my schedule and we'll get it done."

CHAPTER 34

The Drive Back to Fairfax

Justice Stewart was grateful that Yates knew when she needed some solitude. Instead of making small talk, he merely did the driving as she pondered whatever the day had left for her. This had been a contentious day, filled with opinions and controlled arguments, as issues before I court often turned out to be. While there were many 9–0 counts, there were others that split into 5–4 battles with compelling arguments on both sides.

But Stewart was away in her thoughts. Not about cases, but about the letters and Ivanhoe, who had made a compelling case to push forward with what appeared to be factual accounts. As a citizen, an officer of the court, and now a part of an engaged group, she was all in. Was it Ivanhoe she sought, or was she going to have to rely on the rest of her team to help unravel whatever was presented? The maze was there. Was her interest there as well?

Ivanhoe Letter—8

> *Dear Justice Stewart:*
>
> *I thought I would give you some additional information to ponder. Whereas we have learned from those who have supposedly written down facts that actually are true, I daresay that words can be deceiving. What I divulged to you before were the facts as they really are. History books and now the internet are filled with facts and purported facts. I did not approach you to rewrite history, merely to*

clarify it. Yes, there are those who would seek to discredit what someone else says—look at politics through the years—but my information, as stated before, is real, not imaginary.

The facts I have were cleverly deciphered into digital form, thus eliminating many of the mazes those of the past wanted to cover up. This real information just happened to be available at one moment in time and just happened to be saved and recorded. To my knowledge, the person who gave me this information is the only one who had it, and that person gave it to me for safe keeping and to protect it against being destroyed. I know that person is alive and safe.

While I didn't mean to digress, I felt it was necessary to reassert the authenticity of what I have divulged. I, too, wish to be safe and away from the public eye and what would be public chaos, should all of this information be divulged. I also want you to know I do not want you or anyone you might be working with to be in harm's way. As I read and watch what happens here, I will make sure any people that intend to do anyone harm will find it a difficult road to travel. This goes well beyond what J. Edgar Hoover had on literally millions of world citizens. This is beyond huge and it will have a profound effect on what we have known and what we have not been privy to.

I totally understand your use of "befuddled," but I ask that you stay the course, however slow and tedious it may be. I also understand people on your team are doing this without funding, so this becomes a labor of love, as well as being for the good of this country and the world.

As I read through the first portions of this vast information, I was struck with the way it made so many things become more logical. The fact aliens have visited the earth explains such things as the building of structures that were well beyond the capabilities of earthlings at the time, the existence of a supreme being for so many varied cultures, the inventions of the Greeks, the development of the internet, the lost treasures of whatever . . .

Again, the question is not so much what, but why? Why not be factual about the real reason pyramids were built on several different continents? That fascinated me from the get-go. I haven't given you the specifics, but check into the existence of the Topaz Crystal with one of your archeological friends and see what reaction you get.

The main thrust of my first intrigue was the Hoover files, as they dug deep. That seemed to open a Pandora's box, and I was sold. I say stay with it because that information alone will lead to the rest of the tentacles that have diverted our attention and led to unreliable accounts of more recent historical happenings, such as the JFK assassination.

I think going forward that it might be best to offer specific caches of information that may well give your team a strong basis to explore. If you are all ears, I am all in.

Stay tuned.

IVANHOE

CHAPTER 35

Ivanhoe Letter—9

Dear Justice Stewart:

I find myself wanting to share all of what I know, albeit I do not know the scope of what I have to share. Make sense? The information I have shared with you so far is, as they say, the tip of the iceberg. In that some of this collection of information grows exponentially with every day and has a profound historical significance, there is some information that simply is meant to be shared with the world.

While I do not profess to know what all of the government cover-ups mean or have been stayed to protect our way of life, I am curious enough to want to know more. To wit, I would like to know about The Aegeus Phenomenon, The Whippoorwill Project, The Ponce Directive and the Topaz Crystal.

Consider, if you will, 70 percent of the world's population lives within fifty miles of an ocean, there is no more fresh water on the planet today than there was two thousand years ago and the population two thousand years ago represents three percent of today's population. In space the pressure is to keep air from escaping (out), under water the pressure is to keep the air from crushing (in).

The deep sea is where we should be headed. The unexplored oceans hold mysteries more compelling, environments more challenging, and life forms more bizarre than anything the vacuum of space has to offer. Plus, it's cheaper to go down than up. In the Old West days there was a fight over water rights and people moved west. Imagine what will happen when underdeveloped countries run out of water. That spells chaos. Imagine what it will be like when water and food become so scarce that the have-nots will swarm to the haves.

You can conserve all you want, but it comes down to the world's burgeoning population. If not desalination, then what? The world is going through a climate change, irrespective of a ramped-up industrial revolution in areas like China and India. The displacement of refugees because of civil unrest is only a small part of it. What if the earth's rotation is changing ever so slightly? There are those who think that is happening now, as they investigate theories of reverse polarization.

Isn't it interesting that the northern hemisphere is more developed than the southern? There are places in Africa, South America and even Australia that seem like they are light years away from what we think of as the modern world. Consider the forests yet unexplored. And we have explored space with great enthusiasm to seek other life forms, yet two-thirds of our planet is covered with water and we have only scratched the surface of knowing what's down there. If we could only drain the oceans to see what's really there. How do we know that certain life forms in the sea aren't really from some unknown planet or galaxy?

Just sayin'.

IVANHOE

CHAPTER 36

National Archives Gets a Visit

While the main storage centers for the National Archives are in and around Washington DC, there are other outlets around the country. With the advent of new technology, nearly all documents can be digitally shared from any place on the planet. Actual artifacts are maintained in a secure location in seven such storage facilities in the DC area.

Archives, as the DC location often is referred to, maintains its own set of security measures, but it allows for public disclosure of unclassified documents, allowing archivists to do their research. Documents listed as unclassified are on the first subfloor, with sensitive, restricted, classified and top-secret listings below. Members of the nation's security platforms—such as the FBI, NSA and CIA—have special privileges to filter through most of the holdings, but the door to classified and top-secret information requires clearance from the heads of the pertinent agencies.

The reviewing rooms are clean and well lighted, with areas to spread out what is being analyzed. But no photographs or reproductions can be made without express written consent of the heads of Archives or whatever agency's information is being reviewed. When someone from the FBI is making an inquiry, however, more than one person notices.

Members of the respective branches of government, be it the executive, judicial or legislative, have only limited access to classified documents, as a safeguard against any one person having access to compromising information that could be politicized.

In that Casey and Jenny were senior FBI agents, their pass through the secret doors of security was easily handled, but even they had to get clearance when it came to classified and top-secret documents. That meant Curt Mitchell and ultimately Randy Paine had to be aware and sign-off.

Once the two agents had drawn up their strategic plan, they were anxious to see it through. The first two weeks of inquiry meant analyzing where documents were and how any links could be formed. To say it was a maze would be a mild understatement. Fifteen-hour days were the norm, and both were exhausted when they left the building every day. Initial questions brought more inquiries and off they both went, often in different directions, to find the missing pieces of the puzzle they were trying to recreate.

Once they completed their first round of research, they were set to turn over their findings to Matt Brumfield's team to drill further. Casey and Jenny were moving on to concentrate on the FBI files.

The Wright and Meserve Tag Team

If one looked up the term *tag team*, the names and pictures of Anita Wright and Elaine Meserve might appear. Wright, a former student of Matt Brumfield at Harvard, had studied the law and became an expert in forensics. Her career took off when she decided forensic investigation grabbed her interest. Her skills allowed her to apply scientific methods and techniques to the investigation of crime quickly and efficiently.

The FBI didn't hesitate in hiring her as its go-to person in many issues considered high stakes. She constantly was asked to be an expert witness, was called upon to give graduation speeches and other keynote talks to a variety of organizations and managed to write three books, all novels, in her spare time.

As the senior archivist, she was allowed to pick her own "wing person," as she referred to Elaine Meserve. One would have thought they had grown up together, because they were great at anticipating each other's next moves.

Elaine Meserve was tapped for Archives by President Bush, with whom she had become friends when he was governor of Texas. At the time, she was custodian of the state's treasures in Austin.

A quick study of literature in her youth, she was dedicated to all the humanities, and her master's thesis on arts, sports, and entertainment had earned her high marks and admiration when she graduated from the University of California at Irvine. Her ongoing interest in sports and entertainment came from her days as a national champion tennis player and as a movie buff, the latter one that led her to be a trusted movie critic.

She authored a book for children that provided a sneak peek into what the Great Books of the Western World were all about. Her hope was that she would reach at least a few students who would want a career in preserving literature.

Initially hired as a director at the Archives, she eventually added the title of deputy archivist alongside Wright, who was appointed by President Bush. The two formed a valued team, and those who knew them were comfortable with their collective knowledge of what was in the Archives—all nine stories and satellite locations.

Brumfield Team Explores Archives

Paul Hooper was also a Matt Brumfield protégé, a student of the law so well versed that Brumfield would consult with him when someone brought a ticklish question to him. Hooper scared Brumfield, not in a literal sense, but in a way that the stately president at Harvard felt like he was looking at a younger version of himself. He treated him like a son, as the studious and alert younger Hooper was fixated on learning more.

Even though Brumfield was a part of the Four, his duties as president of the university often had to take priority. He therefore needed a confidant and savvy person to run his inquiry team. When Brumfield discussed this with Polkinghorne, she recommended Hooper and he was all too willing. It was up to Hooper to field his supportive team to drill deep into the National Archives.

Hooper, the deputy dean of the Harvard Law School under Polkinghorne, tapped five top-of-the-list TA's, who were excited when he said he had a project. Welcome Alaine Huffman, Gary McClain, Ben Traylor, Wes Burr and Tom Garrett. All were graduate students working on PhDs, and they were ready for the task at hand.

After Brumfield met with Anita Wright and Elaine Meserve at Archives, he felt he needed to take the Hooper team there to meet with the two top archivists. Brumfield felt he was with one of his classes, composed of extremely gifted students that earned their A's, and all were either in quality jobs or were bound for stardom. The smile on his face when they all gathered around Wright's conference table was that of a grandfather who was proud of his family.

"Well," offered Wright after the usual pleasantries of introduction, coffee and tea, "Matt says you are the A team, and it didn't take me long to want to meet you all. And from what I've heard about you, Mr. Hooper, I would not be surprised to see how quickly you climb the tallest ladder." Hooper was somewhat embarrassed, but proud to be commended in front of others.

"Matt, I guess we should have another catch-me-up version of what you want to do."

"Sure, Anita," Brumfield said. "As you and I discussed some time ago, inquiries into various government documents under the Freedom of Information Act have begun. That Act, initiated in 1966, was to allow public access to government documents that were not held back as a threat to national security or had anything to do with the military or strategic plans. I have briefed Paul and his crack team as to what we are up against, given that time may well be a factor.

"As the team knows, we had two top-notch FBI investigators in Casey Kincaid and Jenny Warner do an initial check here before moving on to the Bureau. They completed their initial analysis and have dug deep into the Bureau files. Paul's team here has been put together to see where we can go and what we can see, without touching what is deemed so top secret that it would get into national security on any level.

"What you and I discussed before, Anita, is that we need to know what our parameters will be. Each member of this team has been sworn to secrecy and everything we find will be summarized by Paul, shown to me, and then to the two of you. We understand the intent of FOIA and will be mindful of what can be divulged to Justice Stewart and Spencer Crockett. We intend to be truthful at all times."

Casually looking at the members of the team as Brumfield spoke, Wright then explained that there were approximately "a gazillion files held in trust by the Archives. Maybe I should give all of you a brief description of what we have here.

"As of today, the main Archives building and the Archives II facility in College Park, Maryland, alone preserve, protect and provide reference on six billion pieces of paper and over eleven million still pictures; 112,469 reels of motion pictures and 236,557 sound and video recordings; 2,760,890 maps and charts; 3,639,571 architectural and engineering plans; and 20,687,173 aerial photographs. Those numbers, of course, increase periodically.

"Only one to three percent are so important for legal or historical reasons that they are legally transferred to the National Archives and Records Administration and kept by us forever. While the majority of our holdings are declassified and open to the public, an estimated five percent are closed to research due to classified national security concerns or other statutory restrictions.

"For the record, I was a student of Matt's some time ago, and when he approached me with this project a while back, I was somewhat skeptical, but true to his ways, he convinced me we could be of help. Elaine knows every nook and cranny at the Archives and she will be your main contact.

"I think it wise to bring in Ralph Buck, who has worked for the NARA since 1991. Prior to his current assignment, Ralph was the supervisory archivist in charge of textual processing, textual reference, and tapes review for the Bush Presidential Materials Staff. He currently is the chief of the special access and FOIA staff. His office is responsible for tracking all FOIA requests for archival materials in the Office of Records Services, Washington, DC, and for processing FOIA requests for closed records.

"His office also is the custodial unit for the JFK assassination records collection, records of independent and special counsels, and other collections with special access restrictions. His duties include being our liaison for any one of a number of governmental agencies. That being said, when documents or records are set to expire their security under the cloak of classified or top-secret designation, Ralph is the coordinator. He is a master at what he does, so contact with him will be essential if you are to wade through the masses of documents and records."

"If we need to ask for specific records and/or documents, should we contact Ms. Meserve or Mr. Buck?" Hooper asked, ready to start his team's job at the word "go."

"I would start with Elaine. I will be available most of the time as well," responded Wright. "I assume you, Matt, will be the coordinator for Team Hooper, so we don't get too many inquiries going in too many directions?"

"Yes. Paul will keep me in the loop and provide whatever summaries," replied Brumfield. "I will take a look at all, get in touch with you and then we will proceed up the ladder."

"Okay then, we have a presumptive plan of attack," said Wright with a nod. "Matt, I'll assume you will let me know when the team wants to start drilling or when they might want to continue their dig some more. Elaine, Ralph, and I are here to assist, at least within the law, and will wait for the starter's gun."

"We'll have a team meeting and outline our sequence of inquiries and then I will personally call and let you know our plans," said Brumfield.

The looks around the room made Matt Brumfield and Anita Wright feel like they were a part of a new history, one that would be telling, resourceful and enlightening. The meeting ended with everyone nodding in agreement.

CHAPTER 37

Kincaid, Warner Drill Down in FBI Files

Meanwhile, a mere two-minute drive time away, Casey Kincaid and Jenny Warner were continuing their investigation. Not only were the two of them instinctive, they were quick, yet they worked at a measured pace and rarely were thrown off course. To those who knew them in the Bureau as well as the DOJ, they were relentless and the best of the best.

Having met with their immediate boss Curt Mitchell, Kincaid and Warner had to lay out a plan to move forward.

"So, what's you take on where we should go first?" Warner asked.

"My play would be to review the files we have here and see where that takes us," responded Kincaid. "Curt sort of left it to us to explore, but I sense once we start deep diving into some files, especially the Hoover files, as soon as we come across anything redacted, a red flag will be raised. Randy and Curt said they would have our backs, but who has theirs? Let's start the process, make notes, and get it all cleared by higher-ups and then give the Archives a visit."

"Wasn't Matt Brumfield going to lay the groundwork for us there?' Warner replied. "We've been led to believe that each one of the Four laid whatever groundwork and we should have general access without going through more red tape."

"That was my understanding, but I sense that when we get into someone's 'closet,' there will be an attempt to block or divert," said Kincaid. "That happens in politics every day and that is why the powers that be are going to try to protect their territory."

"It's not like we are inquiring into legislation or appointments or, for Heaven's sake, a vote on the budget or immigration."

"DC is a special place, full of know-it-alls and power-hungry people that would do anything to keep what they have and make sure their adversaries don't have access to anything they consider private or confidential."

"But we're talking about historical facts versus half-truths or misleading information. Don't people want the record to be corrected if not totally true?"

"You would be surprised at how the political world works here. The two political parties could stand before each other and have a completely different version of the same story. It's all about who do you believe."

"This Ivanhoe person seems to have the goods, so if we uncover something in our own way, wouldn't that be good enough to correct wrongs and set the record straight?"

"It's all about power and maintaining it. When we met with Randy and Kirk, they said we would have some stumbling blocks because someone will raise the flag and say 'why.' And it's our job to say, 'why not.'"

Encrypted FBI files, including all of Hoover's documents, were digitalized for posterity, but all original documents and collateral were saved in a separate vault. Whoever did the digitalizing would be an interesting person to talk to, assuming everything worked on had not been sanitized first. But what happened to the some 25 percent that seemed to have gone missing? Those files were taken and stored elsewhere. Who else but Hoover knew of their existence except someone who had time to digitalize same?

Kincaid and Warner would find references to encrypted files and other support material. Not knowing what was behind the encrypted wall would hinder their investigation but not dilute their perseverance. There were plenty of files to delve into, and the missing pieces would be found.

Ivanhoe would see to that.

Kincaid and Warner had decided to tackle the Hoover files together, hoping to get a general overview of what was there and what perhaps wasn't. The two started their day around seven in the morning, reading the list of files that had been catalogued with a numbering system that included cross-referencing.

Wading through some seven thousand entries on the first day told them this was going to take a while. Names, investigations, and dossiers included people they had heard about and a great many they had not.

Aside from an occasional break for food and for exercise to limber up the body, the two had relied on coffee and water. In all, the list of Hoover files comprised slightly more than 450,000 entries, so the task would be daunting. The two spoke from time to time when finding a recognizable name or situation, but for the most part it was like two people sitting in a library, deep in thought.

As the clock reached nine p.m., Kincaid decided he had seen enough for the day. "Don't know about you, but this could drive me to drink, so why don't we call it a day?"

"I'm with you, partner. I think we need to figure out how much of this we can do on back-to-back days or in a week."

"I was intrigued from the beginning, and having sifted through just these entries today certainly has piqued my interest. Figuring out how some of these files interact with other investigations or background information, though, will be a tall task for whoever does it."

"I'm still in."

"Let's grab some rest and evaluate our initial findings tomorrow."

In the Line of Fire

As partners, Kincaid and Warner spent a lot of time together. From time to time they also shared a dinner, or a night out for a movie or the theater, and they shared their personal triumphs and tragedies. For the most part, however, they had separate lives outside of work. But at any given moment, they knew they had one another's back, no matter what the circumstances, day or night.

Kincaid made his home in Arlington, while Warner lived in a modest brownstone in Georgetown. Her neighborhood was semi-quiet, well-kept and safe. After an exhausting day in the depths of the Hoover FBI headquarters, she was ready for a quick shower and a chance to kick back and read a book not related to her investigation.

Close to dreamland, she was startled by a strange series of sounds—a clang, a bump and then a click. She grabbed her weapon out of the bedside drawer and sprang to her feet, at the ready.

She looked for any light sources from the hallway. Seeing the red laser that signaled someone was in fact inside what she thought was an alarm-secured townhome, she stayed low and tried to flank the laser point. Now behind the light, she shouted, "Freeze! Drop your weapon!" The intruder started to lower the weapon to the floor when a bullet whizzed by Warner's right shoulder.

Having been in harm's way many times in her years with the Bureau, she knew shooting, agony, and sometimes death were a part of several scenarios. Though this was on her home turf, leaving her confused as to how this could happen, she quickly calculated her defense, given that she was alone. She dropped to the floor and fired four quick rounds in a line at the light source. A grunt and shrill cry of agony told her she had hit her mark.

But now she wondered where the second shooter was. A spray of bullets in her direction told her she was at a distinct disadvantage; she could be seen, but she couldn't see her target. She crawled along the floor away from the kitchen area, assuming the second shooter would tend to their comrade. She heard chatter with the continuing cries of agony. Now down her hallway that led to the back of the townhouse, she opened the window, then retreated back down the long hallway and pushed a button disguised as a decorative portion of the wainscoting. That led her to a secure room. The door closed quickly.

She pushed her safe-room monitor to view all rooms in the townhome and saw the one perpetrator trying to help the other. She reached for her cell phone and called her partner.

With light traffic at now three a.m., he was there in twenty-five minutes. No sooner had he arrived on the scene, now buoyed with members of the FBI emergency alert team and local law enforcement, than two shots creased the top of his car. Duck and cover was the order of the day. What was going on here?

Kincaid called Warner just after his arrival and sniper shots. He and his SWAT cohorts entered the townhome and let her know all was clear inside. The other members of the support team scoured the area for the whereabouts of the sniper.

Kincaid was shaken by the near miss, but was more worried about where Warner was. The two veterans were tight, and what happened to one was taken to heart by the other. Both had been wounded in battle and had the scars to prove it.

His call to her cell phone was answered with a sharp, "Casey, where are you?

"I'm in a rather messed up kitchen," he stated. "I thought you were more tidy. I've searched the place and can't find you. Are you alright?"

"I'm in my safe room, in the middle of the long hallway."

"What safe room? You never told me about any safe room."

"Oh, sorry. It's one of the reasons I purchased this place ten years ago."

As the safe-room door slid open, he was impressed by the secrecy.

Although slightly rattled by a home invasion and another look at death, she just smiled. For the next thirty minutes, they tried to make sense of what had happened and who the assailants were.

The coincidences in outright attempts on the lives of people who were a part of the investigation now were sinister. But in what direction would anyone turn to find any answers?

CHAPTER 38

Stewart Rereads Ivanhoe Letters

Having reread what now was tagged as Ivanhoe 7, Stewart was just as consumed with the latest letters, Ivanhoe 8 and 9. She had read the latest when she returned from the last of the week's court days and rustled through the mail Mandy had sorted. While the court goings-on consumed her daytime, she was fit to tackle other things when she had time to relax. That meant sipping a chardonnay and sitting in her easy chair in her home office or, as she did this evening, outside on the veranda when the summer months allowed her to sit outside without being overwhelmed by the heat and humidity of Fairfax.

The summer breeze felt good and she embraced the setting sun in the western sky. She decided to reread all the Ivanhoe letters, to further give her the scope of what this mysterious writer was offering. The letters totaled more than twenty-five pages of information, all bent on allowing her to imagine the what-ifs and why-nots.

Had someone been monitoring her as she read, they would have noticed a variety of facial expressions. This wasn't some court case that needed a "simple" evaluation; it was a revelation. She had read each letter as they had been sent to her, but in rereading them all at once, she began to connect more dots.

For Supreme Court justices, if not all judges, lawyers, physicians, and other professionals, a handheld recorder—which sometimes meant a smart phone—was the preferred way to make notes, as talking was much easier than writing. She had done this every time an Ivanhoe letter had been received. That made for a quick synopsis to share with the Four.

The phone vibration broke her out of her concentration. It was Zach, calling from Bern. Given that it was one o'clock in the morning there, Bailey hoped it was nothing serious.

"Well hello, Prince Charming, and just what is going on in your part of the world at one in the morning?" she inquired.

"Just about to get out of here on the Ready Jet," he responded. "Should be back there around twoish your time."

"What's Ready Jet? I thought Learjet was the way to go."

"The association made the plans. Readyjet is a direct competitor, so it was whoever gave the association the best deal, and with five of us coming from the United States, I guess that worked best."

The International Association of Cardiologists, which is located in New York, usually made plans for the symposium that collected the world's most renowned cardiologists to talk about new advancements in the treatment of the heart.

Longfellow was a favorite guest speaker, given his sense of humor and quick wit, so they worked the entire event around his schedule. The sites of the symposiums moved around, and this year Bern, Switzerland, was the place of choice. He was good to go anywhere, so getting a free ride to Switzerland for seven days didn't bother him at all. He was frequently asked to chair or be an integral part of many other such events throughout the year and he complied when it didn't conflict with his surgeries or consulting practice.

"So how did it go?" Bailey asked.

"There are some new technology advancements that are going to make not only heart surgeries more successful, but others as well. I've always been fascinated by new innovations and prospects for bettering life, so some of the things we are privy to before that technology actually is in place are inspiring. Patience for patients.

"Gotta go. See you in a few hours."

Bailey was back to reading. She had more questions than ever, and as the light of the day started to fade, she thought a return to her Bailey Cave might be best, as her easy chair would be great about this time.

In what seemed like a short time, she noticed it was nine o'clock. She had been mesmerized again, as more and more pieces of the puzzle were being put into place. There was much more to learn, for sure, but she was starting to see the bigger picture. And her voice-recorded notes would prove invaluable. As was her custom with court cases, subsequent notes of recorded dialogue gave her instant recollection as to her thoughts were at a given time.

Ivanhoe was a mysterious conduit, but certainly well learned and informed. As if reading a book, her piqued interest begged for more. More than a page turner, it was "show me a road not yet traveled."

Longfellow Estate

Among the many renovations Bailey and Zach had made to the estate was the addition of a family entertainment center just off the more formal living room. This allowed them to enjoy television on a big screen, with surround sound and seating that gave them comforts of being in a small theater.

Zach had returned from Bern, and Bailey was enjoying some rare downtime from the court, so they had time to simply relax at home for a change. It was just the two of them, as Yates was in his own place and Mandy was with friends for the weekend. Annette, the cook, had most weekends off.

"So, you said you heard from this Ivanhoe character again," said Zach, enjoying a black sambuca as they listened to some soft and soothing music.

"I reread all the letters and seem to be getting a grasp of what is being purported, but I find myself wanting to meet Ivanhoe, to have a one-on-one conversation—to know more, maybe all, of what this story has to offer," she said.

"Maybe Ivanhoe wishes to stay mysterious and out of the way, maybe staying in the shadows out of fear or something."

"Perhaps, but I say the depth of the information I've received goes well beyond someone guessing or making something up. Some things are shockingly believable, though they go against what we were taught in school or picked up along the way. Ivanhoe is well learned and wants to let someone else in on their knowledge. I find myself captivated and wanting to know more. I am a skeptic, but I am intrigued.

"I wonder, though, why he chose me and not some news outlet or someone looking to make a name for themselves?"

"Didn't one of the first letters say you were picked because of who you were and that you would search for the corroboration to any and all if that was divulged?"

"Yes, and I wondered then why me, and now I have an even stronger feeling that I was picked."

"I wouldn't focus on why here but on what we have to do to carry this forward. You have the four of us and now who knows how many others working the case."

She laughed. "Working the case. Takes me back to my prosecutorial days and reminds me of the responsibilities of being a judge, an arbitrator."

"Then trust what you are given," he said. "Ivanhoe is obviously going to keep feeding you information that will leave all of us wondering just how such information is to be divulged and how that might change our view of history as we know it. There's a reason Ivanhoe has gone this far and I venture to say that we'll see a lot more such letters. Matt and Spence are with us all the way."

"I guess my concern is who would make the final decision as to what can be divulged and what simply is best left covered up or redacted," she said.

"Now that I'm back, is it time for the four of us to assess where we are?"

"I think yes," she said."But maybe not right away, since we have our vacation hideaway waiting."

"That be true," he said with a wide smile.

The Poet's Lake House

Even with their professional obligations and the many social events Bailey and Zach attended each year to support charities and local groups, they did find time to get away. The two had been invited to spend some time with friends at Smith Mountain Lake several years ago and just fell in love with the place as a home away from home.

Located in the middle of Virginia, Smith Mountain Lake was thirty-two square miles with five hundred miles of shoreline, and was the largest artificial lake in the state. The area had twenty-two thousand inhabitants and offered a small-town atmosphere that allowed frequent guests to feel relaxed.

Zach had suggested buying a place and renting it out during their busy work months, opting to take a two-week sojourn every August when the area was ripe with activity. Historical sites, fine dining, unique shopping and marvelous sunsets were part of the everyday fare.

The lakefront property, affectionately named by the Longfellows as the Poet's Lake House, was nearly two thousand square feet, with three master suites with adjoining baths, a hot tub, a sauna, a pool table, an entertainment center, and a large deck and fire pit, as well as a sizable dock for excursions on the lake. It had a separate boat house. The back of the house had large windows for a beautiful view of the sunsets fading against the western sky.

A mere four-hour drive from their Fairfax estate and halfway between Roanoke and Raleigh, North Carolina, the August trip had become standard from their very first stay as owners of Poet's.

It was a night out for Bailey and Zach, and they were headed to Waller's for one of the house specialties—crab legs. Yates normally went with the two of them everywhere, but Bailey and Zach suggested tht Yates and his fiancée should enjoy the comforts of Poet's and watch the sun fade into the distance.

Having enjoyed their wine and seafood entrée, Zach was ready to order the double fudge brownie with its generous scoop of ice cream when Bailey looked across the lake and saw a fire. Startled, she grabbed Zach's arm and exclaimed that there was a fire and it looked eerily close to their place. Zach's head jerked around and he snatched Bailey's hand before they bolted for the door.

"I'll be back to settle up," he said to the hostess. "Here's my card. Give it to James."

No sooner were they in their Lexus RX than they got a cell call from Suzie Blanton, Yates's fiancée.

"Zach, come quick, the boat house is on fire and I can't find Yates."

"What happened and where was he?" Zach asked, his alarm rising.

"We were sitting on the deck watching the sunset and Yates went to the wine cellar next to the boat house for another bottle of wine. The next thing I knew, there was a loud boom and the roof blew off of the boat house!"

"Suzie, get as close to the fire as possible and see if you can find him. I've called 911 and the nearby neighbors. Keep this line open and tell us whatever you see."

Suzie scrambled around the side of the house that wasn't endangered by the flames and saw Yates lying prone on the grass. She rushed to him and was relieved to hear his groans.

"What the hell just happened?" he said with a grimace, clearly in pain. "That felt like an explosion, and either someone doesn't like me or the wine isn't any good."

Helping him up and away from the carnage, she was able to walk him back to the house as the fire department tended to the flames. They were done in short order.

Zach and Bailey arrived shortly after the fire department and found Yates and Suzie in the main room of the house. Yates was blackened and holding his left arm, but he appeared to be in satisfactory condition.

"Yates, Suzie filled us in on the explosion and was horrified that she couldn't find you. At least it looks as if the boat house was the target, but was there anything you noticed before or after?"

"Nothing struck me as odd, but the second I closed the wine cellar door, I heard a click, moved quickly to the door and all of a sudden was catapulted about twenty feet toward the house. I've been shot, kicked, tortured, knifed, but never blown up. I'll just add that to the resume."

Zach turned to Bailey and said it was time to call in some sleuthing help. "The home invasion, car chase, odd accidents and now this aren't coincidences anymore. "I'm calling in someone who has helped us in the past, Preston Doran. He'll know what to do."

"Is Preston even in the States?" she asked.

"He will be after I call him."

Doran would be at Smith Mountain Lake the next day.

CHAPTER 39

Ivanhoe Letter—10

It was late and Stewart knew the morning would come soon enough, but she felt the urge to reach out to Ivanhoe again. She felt the Hoover files may well prove to be the key element to their research and discovery. If there ever was a keyword in legal matters, "discovery" was probably at the top of the list. She was ramping up for the opening of the new court year, but this case, the one Ivanhoe had presented and seemed to be pressing, had her spare-time attention.

Her cryptic ad in the *Washington Post* was simple. The header: J. EDGAR. The next line: How So?

Ivanhoe's response was a tad slower than in the past, but the words sparked more intrigue.

> *Dear Justice Stewart:*
>
> *By now you probably have put a lot of pieces together for this complex puzzle. I presume from your post that your legal mind is asking how J. Edgar Hoover is so important in a lot of this. While Mr. Hoover's information relates more to people and places of the present and immediate past, his files contain a lot of facts that simply get overlooked. To use an analogy, the sands of time have covered over many a city, including monuments, artifacts, and more.*
>
> *Hoover's files are intact, although some seem to have disappeared moments after he was murdered. Yes, he was murdered. To say a lot of unsolved murders don't have links is a mild understatement,*

especially when it comes to politics and power. His files prove a great deal of the cover-ups, some of which you will have to decide needs to be clarified for the public view. My caution to you originally had to do with making judgments on what the public had a right to know and what simply could not be divulged. Most of the double-secret entries have to do with national security, but even some of those do not bear out the evil that lurks in the shadows of civilization, looking for a way to endanger our way of life and undercut our government and its agencies.

As I have professed before, there is a lot of material to be analyzed, not just from J. Edgar, but other sources. Some of this is available in the National Archives, but just so you know, Mr. Hoover had copies of a lot of that information, unbeknownst to anyone else. He was a secretive man, to be sure, and his quest to know as much as he could about anyone and everything kept him in control of his own destiny. The fact he was taken out did not wipe out that information. It is at the crux of information I have received and share with you.

Hoover's files, the ones he held under close security at the FBI building that now bears his name, contain unredacted documents, whereas the ones at the Archives have redacted portions. The painstaking research has to do with reading every file, and I suspect that since there are more than a million, it will take time. To the curious and trained observer, the information is there and provides a valuable compass through a strange maze of quality information.

We have discussed normal public curiosities, like the JFK assassination, extraterrestrials, medical research, the power grab bag and all, but there is a lot more to be had, since the information that was given to me included checks and crosschecks of every bit of information that has been collected, evaluated, and affirmed over time. As I said, this was like the perfect storm, because at one moment, all of this came to one focal point, and when it was copied for posterity, it became the find of all time. Praise to the technology age, as the internet has proved. We can find almost anything on the internet. This information, with the Hoover files being a sort of roadmap, is like looking into the heart and soul of the American part of human history, if not the history of all of humanity.

So, this comes back to Mr. Hoover. I believe what has been deciphered and collected, even the summations and crib notes he kept on anything that caught his eye. Remember, he was the opposite of what we think of as a black hole in space. He became a collector of information that transcended political, cultural, and geopolitical lines. That included good and evil as well as good vs. evil. I have read all of this collected information and still am overwhelmed as to what it implies, contradicts, or confirms about what we have been led to believe in the annals of history books.

We do not know who confiscated the 25 percent of his files when he died and maybe that is immaterial now since the collection is intact through electronic means.

In that I know your time is valuable and that you no doubt have others working with you on uncovering information that will corroborate or dispel facts we have been led to believe over time, I am hopeful that divulging these small pieces a few at a time will allow you to analyze and choose to follow.

If the FBI, CIA, NSA or any other world intelligence organization throws up a stop sign, I will release information for or against. This, again, is not to punish the intelligence community or the government, but to decide what is fair for the public to know—national security excepted.

In addressing the fact I have all of the Hoover files secured in memory form, I feel safe in knowing that no one can subvert what the director had compiled. I look forward to your requests for direction.

Good hunting.

IVANHOE

Bailey Stewart

One thing Stewart was known for among her colleagues on the court was that she was very detail-oriented. It had been her nature throughout her life. Although initially cautious so as to assess every situation or problem, her inquisitive mind longed for more. Her quest for the truth, or at least all of the facts, gave her a brave disposition. Now that she had intertwined the intrigue of the letter with her always-important duties as a Supreme Court justice, the word "driven" was front and center.

The Ivanhoe letters, with their plethora of information, including documented facts and believable keys to help unlock some of history's mysteries, had added more to her everyday thoughts. There were times when she questioned whether she could see this all through, given the constraints of time in a day. But her father had taught her when she was an early age, *Do not doubt your ability to seek and find, no matter how much time it takes.* That, along with Vince Lombardi's quote, "*Perfection is not attainable. But if we chase perfection, we can catch excellence,*" drove her on whatever wild course she chose to accept. And she hoped to gain wisdom along the way.

CHAPTER 40

The Search for Ivanhoe

The Four had decided to make every effort to meet once a month, hopefully on a weekend when busy business schedules allowed, carving out at least a day at the Longfellow estate to get caught up on the happenings.

After another delicious breakfast, they retired to the family room where the usual whiteboards and the professional Christie projector and screen were in place.

Now settled into their well-cushioned chairs, Bailey spoke first. "Before we get into our usual recaps, I would like to know how everyone feels about the information we have received from Ivanhoe." She handed them the most recent letter, number 10 for those who were counting, and then continued.

"As for me, I find myself wanting to know more and then more again. We all do our own inquiries, but I feel it is the information we get from this Ivanhoe that keeps us on the prowl for something new, most of which I find somewhat startling. As a citizen, I do want to know more. I feel like I am reading a book and continue to visualize what Ivanhoe has shared.

"That being said, I wonder if we shouldn't reach out and have a face-to-face with Ivanhoe, to see all the cards in the deck? Would that be chasing an invisible person that doesn't want to be found? The facts that have been presented leave me intrigued at what might be in the offing. Wouldn't it be better to cut to the chase?"

Brumfield chimed in, offering that if Ivanhoe really wanted to be seen, that they would have made an appearance a long time ago. "Seems to me Ivanhoe wants to stay on the sidelines for a critical reason, and if the only form of communication is by these letters, then that's what we have to deal with.

Though of course I would like to meet up with this person and learn more, then more after that."

Crockett concurred. "In my research and work from the prosecutorial side, informants are best left in the shadows, so they don't get compromised, or worse, taken out. From what I can gather from the letters and my end of the research battle, the information has been a roadmap as to where to look and how to corroborate information.

"Ivanhoe has professed to have much more information than even the cleverest investigation might turn up. I, too, am intrigued. I do wonder, however, who Ivanhoe is, and whether we'll ever get a chance to meet."

The laid-back Zach said, "Ivanhoe obviously has a grand story to tell and has the means to get information to us without being exposed. I think I am okay with that, but I would like to know who this is and how they came by this information through whatever means, and that all is true and stored securely.

"I seem to recall one of the letters indicated that the information was available to the one person through a digital source, sort of like a perfect storm—right place, right time. The fact such information was carefully collected and stored is overwhelming in the first place. To think this historical accounting has been uniquely deciphered blows my mind."

"Do we reach out to Ivanhoe and ask to meet, or do we leave well enough alone at this time and hope that our trails lead to consummate understanding?" Bailey asked. They all were in agreement. Ivanhoe would remain in the shadows.

Stewart Questions Conspiracy Theories

As much as conspiracy theorists loved to counter claims of historical fact, the rest of the public rarely followed the same trail for the whole truth and nothing but the truth. History books were supposedly based on facts as known at the time, and who was to say those facts were misleading or false? In more recent history the JFK assassination, Pearl Harbor, perhaps medical research, alternative fuel sources and alien visits warranted much of the public's attention. There were those though that had other balloons to float and publishers and talk show hosts were all eager to cop for ratings.

The Ivanhoe letters had captivated Stewart's mind, perhaps due to the more recent subjects. The Kennedy murder had stained the American history landscape, but the Pearl Harbor attack was one she never could let go of. It was part of her history upbringing, being that her father Verlin was there and survived. His devastating account of the ninety-minute attack had captivated her early teen years so much so that she, too, had done some research.

She believed the government had knowledge of the impending attack, given that President Roosevelt and Director Hoover had to know something, which led her to believe there was a cover-up. When Stewart saw a secondary name in the Ivanhoe text—Dusan Popov, a known Serbian spy—she was transfixed. She had not seen that name before. Now she was going back on the trail. It was time for a reach out to Ivanhoe.

Stewart's drive for the facts and would-be information kept her interest ramped up. Ivanhoe had done it again. The assassination of Kennedy certainly was a main interest, but there were so many other subjects that deserved to be investigated.

The one-word cryptic line in the *Post* simply stated "Popov."

CHAPTER 41

The Pearl Harbor Conspiracy

Ivanhoe Letter—11

The expected letter arrived only three days later, giving Stewart the sense that Ivanhoe was close by.

Dear Justice Stewart:

Yes, Hitler had a hand in this.

Perhaps unbeknownst to Hoover, Roosevelt caught wind of the impending attack at Pearl through intelligence sources and had been in contact with Winston Churchill. It was Churchill's long-held belief that if the Americans got into the World War II fray, victory would all be but assured. Roosevelt, at first happy with the US involvement only as a provider of munitions and goods, standing as an isolationist, was eager to know everything about a war on a different continent. He was sympathetic to and empathetic about the plight of friends in Britain, but wasn't convinced the American people would buy in to total involvement.

When more and more details came forth about the Japanese plans, Roosevelt knew he was playing a dangerous hand and accepted the fact that America eventually would be dragged into the war. An attack so dastardly certainly would incite and inflame public opinion, so much so that the cause for war would be accepted and met with every piece of strength the US could employ. Roosevelt knew he had to take the gamble, hoping that minimal casualties would ramp up public opinion. His "Day of Infamy" became the single worst happening in American history.

Now it was time for Churchill to have empathy and sympathy. The loss of life on any front was devastating, as both leaders detested aggression and conflict. On that day of the Pearl Harbor attack, Hoover got the news and cried. He had not read the president in on the Popov revelation because Hoover and Roosevelt did not trust each other or share delicate information. Hoover would write his own thoughts and dedicated facts into his secret files. When a portion of his files were stolen upon his death, the Pearl Harbor file was among them.

Good hunting,

IVANHOE

CHAPTER 42

Bailey and Zach at Estate Discussing Ivanhoe Letter

Summertime was anything but the blues. While the July and August weather presented a hot, humid daytime, the evenings usually were pleasant, especially at the Longfellow estate, with the pond that had a golden glow about it as the sun fell behind the tall pines westward. Bailey and Zach were enjoying the tranquil evening, the court and Zach's continuing work and travel set aside for the moment.

Bailey sipped her chardonnay in between snacking on some dry-roasted peanuts, and slumped back in her easy chair, catching the last remnants of the sun in the western sky.

"Did you get a chance to read the latest Ivanhoe letter?" she asked.

"I did, and I find it amazing that Ivanhoe has so much intricate information, as if we were reading some history book for the first time. Did you tell me that all of the information from the previous letters has been corroborated by our crack teams?"

"That's what I have been told through emails and chats with Matt, Spence and the rest of the team. I don't know about you, but we have to give careful consideration to what we should divulge without bringing more of the players together."

"You mean like the president, members of Congress, maybe media?"

"I would say the administration and selected members of Congress, maybe the oversight committees, but not the media. Not yet. There are some media outlets that can't be trusted to report fairly, and the bias sends people into a tizzy when wild accusations and false statements are made before all the facts are known."

"I guess you've seen enough from the court side and all the grandstanding that goes on."

"Trust me, Zach, a lot of what eventually is released by some media outlets is so twisted that even the originators don't always recognize what was said or done in the first place. It's not as bad at court. Attorneys come before the court and make very plausible arguments, but someone winds up taking a step back and accepting a decision that is not to their liking. Same goes for what is offered for public opinion."

"Does this go to the public's trust in government, the media, even history as we know it?"

"I think I get the concept, but some of these people in the media are so far left or right that it raises the question, Do they really listen to an opposing viewpoint or are they only interested in grandstanding?

"That brings me back to our dilemma here. If all of what Ivanhoe purports is true, will the public be able to handle it, given that there will be opposing points of view? Being on the court, my job is to determine if the facts are correct and that judgments in lower courts have been fair in interpreting the law as written. Our job isn't to make the laws, only interpret them. To that extent, if we determine this information is for the good of the people of this country, will there be some who oppose such a stance, given that it may disrupt our sense of history, right or wrong?"

"Aren't you convinced that Ivanhoe has the goods and wants this to come out, so the public can make up its own mind?"

"I think I am okay with that, but as an officer of the court, I think I need to be aware of what is good and not good, although I don't think there is a law that states what is good. I think we both are looking at this as citizens and probably have enough curiosity to want to know what history has said about people, places, and events. What concerns me is how any of this might change someone's mind about people, places and events—for the good or not so good?

"As time marches on, is there enough interest in knowing about past events, given that people who lived through the events are older and may not care much anymore? I also think that a lot of history as presented was meant to be misleading because knowing the true facts may well have startled people into doing some wild things. The Kennedy assassination cover-up—and I truly believe what Ivanhoe has divulged—might have toppled an institution, such as our inner government agencies, even the structure itself, back in the '60s and '70s. How many people would have been pissed about our involvement in World War II back when it was happening?

"The average person believes what they see or hear. It's the folks who understand the inner workings of governments, big business and controlling organizations, that have a vested interest, as public opinion can be a powerful locomotive hard to stop."

"So, what's next? Do we keep the team digging and explain all at some time?"

"That would be my take. Rather than divulge a few historical anecdotes, I think we need to see this through."

"And you think Ivanhoe has all of the goods and that all will be there for everyone to see?"

"I think Ivanhoe is well-meaning and has said he/she want me to see it through. So yes, I'm in it for the duration."

"Well, then, my dear, I'm with you."

"Care for a swim?

"Thought that might be in the offing."

They shed their clothes and jumped in feet first.

All of this would be known to the Four as the investigations continued. The Ivanhoe letters continued to shed new light on old darkness and they all knew that history was about to have some rewritten pages.

Zach on His Way to Medical Symposium

The quiet and restful weekend gave way to another trip, this one to Toronto, where Zach was to be a part of a medical symposium on "The Art of the Heart." as one of the world's foremost cardiologists with an emphasis on transplants, Zach relished being a part of the ever-advancing technology. Among his panelists was to be his friend Cyril Wecht and they hadn't spoken since they met about Ivanhoe.

Zach's thoughts, as he sat comfortably in his Readyjet seat, were about Bailey's interest in finding out where the Ivanhoe trail led. Knowing how relentless she was when she wrestled with cases before the court, he wanted to make sure he was there for her when the quest for the truth stirred the mind into a feverish pace. He, too, was anxious to see this through, even when more and more supposed relaxation time was consumed with the advent of a new Ivanhoe revelation.

The letters gave a new sense of adventure to the two and, he suspected, to Matt and Spencer and the rest of the team as well. He was all in for sure, but wanted to make sure Bailey didn't pull back, considering her position as a jurist, when facts or partial truths led to varied interpretations.

He didn't presume to know the law as she did, but perhaps by osmosis, her career as well as his allowed each to become a fairly knowledgeable person. They both enjoyed it, even if some of the intricacies of their respective professions were too detailed at times.

Zach often wondered if she had time to pause for daydreaming about her cases as he did with his. The continued search for the truth was first and foremost on her agenda. He was the ever-learner, constantly thinking of what he had done to promote heart care while teaching others the craft with advancing technology.

Of the thousands of heart transplants that had been performed since Dr. Christiaan Barnard successfully did the first one in 1967, Longfellow may have had a hand in nearly nine hundred during his career. He followed Dr. Denton Cooley and Dr. Robert Jarvik in the advancement of the artificial heart, and that number had increased significantly when heart donors were not readily available. And two of the early pioneers in the heart transplant research, Dr. Michael DeBakey and Dr. Keith Reemtsma, had become inspiring mentors to the aspiring Longfellow as well.

Although he was looking forward to the symposium, Zach was anxious to get back to the continuing quest for the Four to find its own grail.

CHAPTER 43

Chief of Staff Jim Fox Briefs the President

The general public's perception of any government, or big company, for that matter, was that the top-tier executives simply oversaw any one of a number of departments and senior officials, who give them pertinent information. For those who filled those roles through time, it all came down to how much information one individual could infuse into their mind and to being a quick study as to what to do and how to do it.

So, delegation was important, and trust was a key element in making valued decisions based on the best knowledge available to whomever for whatever, for whenever. The trickle down from department heads to middle management and lower tiers can be critical to any success.

The president of the United States often is considered the most powerful person in the world, based mainly on the strength and resources of the country. The United States could, for instance, be an isolationist country—because of all of its natural resources—and survive. But it is indeed the United States that has looked after the world, and people have depended on the Americans to be in the middle of everything. Even when other ideologies have differed from what the US has planted on the world's doorstep, there has been an understanding, even if not said, that the Americans were not going to back down.

In politics, the US displayed a different mindset as administrations came and went. All had their agendas and secrets, as most countries had their agendas and secrets. But for sorting those out, the US intelligence community has been considered second to none. Its vast historical data banks have held collected information that predated any modern society. With the plethora of knowledge from the FBI files, there seemingly had been nothing the Americans didn't know about whomever, whatever and whenever.

President McCade was considered one of the most affable leaders in modern times, always shaking hands and extending a warm welcome in the form of "How are you doing?" to everyone, whether he knew them or not. His good-natured, good-humored, courteous and professional attitude lent itself to getting along with members of both parties, even those who held a conflicting ideology. Those who stood on the opposite side of the aisle were willing to listen, and that was all he asked for. From that came respect. For those who did not offer such a balanced rapport, he simply moved on.

He trusted his advisors, especially those closest to him. He also felt a trust with the leaders of Congress as well as those of the rest of the world. Yes, there were adversaries, but he simply spoke his piece, gave anyone a chance to offer opinions, and then moved on. He was a student of the inner workings of government, shook off the critics in the media, and took time to listen to the voters when the polls showed trends.

His Hotline for America allowed people to call, write, or send email to a specific location, and if time allowed, he followed up with a response through his intermediaries. The people felt a buy-in, and some 150,000 inquiries poured in each day. All of that kept staff members busy, and the data showed promise.

As was the case for most electeds, there was time to go to meetings, make special appearances, even be a member of an audience to see a play, attend a sporting event, or enjoy entertainment. The White House also had its own theater, among many other amenities, and McCade, as others before him, liked seeing recent movies and documentaries in his spare time. White House dinners and dignitaries from other countries also filled valuable time.

The carefully choreographed scheduling of any president's day or evening was a monumental job and it took a lot of coordination between the scheduler and the president. The gregarious McCade seemed to manage it all in stride.

During his daily briefings with his inner circle he was all ears and relied on information from those trusted confidants to keep everyone up to date, hopefully without fear of leaks like those that had hampered previous administrations. With McCade's way of doing business, there were no unwanted leaks, only planned leaks to launch a trial balloon to see which way the wind was blowing on a particular subject.

Time was precious each morning, so any briefings were kept to a certain time allotment. After that, Fox and McCade would retire to the study just off the dining room for their own private conversation. The two longtime friends talked to each other as if they were kicking back, although mindful that their conversation was steeped in confidential exchanges.

This time, it was Jim talking to John, without the formality of titles. In the public domain, Fox always referred to John J. McCade as Mr. President.

"What else is on your mind, Jim?' the president said. "You indicated you had something to talk about between the two of us, so of course you have my attention. It sounded serious."

"I'm not sure how to explain this fully; it's not a disaster waiting to happen, but it is complex," said Fox. For the next twenty-five minutes or so, he gave the president his read of what he had come to know.

The narrowing of McCade's eyes left no doubt that he was intrigued, yet somewhat dumfounded.

"Let me get this straight. Someone—this Ivanhoe person—came across some historical facts and has asked Justice Bailey Stewart to see it through? It always has been my understanding that no one person could have all access to all historical records, for security as well as politicalreasons. There have been attempts by presidents and their well-wishers to gain access to all of this for political reasons, but the safeguards—the fail-safeguards, if you will—were put in place to make sure that never happened.

"I was okay with that, but who, for instance, wouldn't like to know about the Kennedy assassination, or Pearl Harbor, or space travel for that matter. History books and conspiracy theorists are filled with what-ifs, what's and whys, but now someone has collected all of this together and wants to know what is right and not so right about the public knowing?"

"That's about it. I've talked to the Four, as they are known in their circle, and I want to see Randy at the FBI, Liz at Justice and even folks like Mike Manchester at CIA and Dan Sweeney at NSA. I would ask generic questions and not divulge what I really wanted. They would ask questions, of course, but I want to know if they had been contacted by anyone about classified information that is housed in the Archives."

"And you don't think that might raise a red flag and start an internal inquiry in their areas?" asked the president.

"It might, but at least we will know who is in whatever loop and if this Ivanhoe is playing us," said Fox, his hands palm up.

"From what you've told me, Ivanhoe's information has been corroborated. And is most of this coming from the Hoover files?"

"As I understand it, the Hoover files corroborated the facts. Whoever this person is, they came across the computer documentation of all of this—I mean everything—by chance, along with a detailed analysis of what was true and not true. Circumstances just happened to converge; it was a perfect storm."

"Perfect storm?" asked the president.

"The internet and digitalization has introduced us to a whole new world. It's up to us to learn from all of this."

"So, where does that leave us?"

"Well, we have to determine what information, be it actual facts or distortions or outright lies, has led our historical accounting to be corrupted. And in turn, we need to determine what of that information should be released."

"Would that be good for all, or just some?"

"Depends on who you ask. Conspiracy theorists will be around forever, and some are committed to setting the record straight. They have an agenda, and to me, that could pose a problem—spreading to the entire populace their distrust for our system. In short, has our government been lying to us and can anyone be trusted? Like I said, I'd like to know all of the true facts of the Kennedy assassination, or Pearl Harbor, extraterrestrials. Could I handle the truth? Could I accept the revised account of history and be okay with that? I don't know. Do *you* think our people would be accepting of revised history, or would that cause an uproar?"

The president leaned back in his chair and continued. "That I don't know. The more people who find out that someone is delving into what has been stated as facts that may not be necessarily true—especially historical facts—the more questions will be asked, ones that we may have to answer without much to go on. It's not like elements within the government did anything to keep information from the public, but think of the people who darkened our history by lying or withholding pertinent information from everyone, including the sitting president.

"Think about the possibility of people wanting to retaliate against the Russians for having a hand in the Kennedy assassination, or perhaps wonder why Roosevelt and Hoover knew about Pearl Harbor and didn't tell us, or that the proof of extraterrestrials exists and is simply being withheld.

"Jim, this could be a disaster if everything was left for the public to analyze. Should we meet with the Four and determine what course would be in the best interest of the nation and all of its citizens?"

"That might be wise, but we have to be careful about any conflicts of interest. I think Justice Stewart may well have to recuse herself if this became a legal battle, and she has made reference to that."

"But Ivanhoe picked her."

"Yes, for the basic reason that she was independent of politics, that she was a woman of distinction, character and common sense, and perhaps most important, that she couldn't be expelled from office."

"I get that reasoning, and Bailey is at the top of the charts on all those counts. I know Zach, Matt and Spence very well, too. They're straight shooters."

"One of the things we're faced with here is whether any investigations can delve deep into the Archives or the FBI files without congressional or executive orders. We need to check with our in-house counsel before we involve ourselves with the FBI, Justice or any other agency. All of those entities may well be implicated, and we don't want this to be a house of cards. I would guess as well that there will be some power brokers in this city that would not want to get their hands soiled by any implications of past wrongdoings, albeit under the veil of it being 'for the good of the country.'

"The fact the CIA apparently found out about how the Mafia intended to hit Kennedy through our covert operatives Gary and Nancy Graylon in Budapest three months before the act, would lead one to believe enough people could have said something to prevent the assassination. From what the Hoover files divulged, J. Edgar knew and actually let the FBI look the other way. Then came the bogus Warren Commission saying that Oswald was the lone gunman. To say horse is only half a word is a mild understatement."

"What about the Hoover files? Where are they and can they be tapped?"

"They are under lock and key at the FBI, but access can be had. The fact some of the files disappeared when Hoover died—mysteriously, I might add—adds to the story."

"How did this Ivanhoe get all of this information if some of the files disappeared?"

"Apparently, Hoover had all of his files put on microfilm some time ago and then transferred to a secure location and eventually digitized. And that is what Ivanhoe or someone who gave them to Ivanhoe found."

"So, the truth is out there with Ivanhoe?" the president asked.

"That's why this whole thing came down as a perfect storm. Ivanhoe has said that if anything happens to anyone seeking the truth through their communication—including whoever they are— it would result in all of the information being disseminated to the public for all to see. If that happens, all bets are off."

"Jim, we need to get to our next meeting with the Joint Chiefs, but I think we need to think this through. Look over your schedule and mine and let's get back at it as soon as we can, keeping a smile on our faces while we do it."

"John, I'm glad you're the president. Can't think of anyone who would be able to handle this without letting it get way too political."

"We've been through a lot, Jim, and I can't think of anyone who I'd rather be joined at the hip with."

No sooner had McCade said his last words when a ping hit his phone to remind him of the upcoming meeting with the chiefs. The day was just beginning and yet the two of them felt they had talked for a week.

Fox and McCade Part Deux

Four days had passed, including a busy weekend with nine personal appearances, and the president couldn't shake enough hands. His curiosity about what he and Jim Fox had discussed the previous Thursday, though, had kept his mind racing. Although deeply interested in his Monday-morning briefing, he was anxious for the hour or so he had between that first meeting and the next—a collection of congressional leaders who were hot on the trail for finalizing a budget. That meeting figured to be intense as usual, but McCade was determined to get some solid time with Fox on the side.

His first briefing concluded, McCade asked Fox to stay and thanked everyone for their updates and assessments. The door to the Oval Office closed and McCade couldn't wait to ask Fox what he had learned.

"I talked to all four and they are agreeable to meet, but they do not want to be in any spotlight or have to answer questions—at least at this time," said Fox.

"How about having them up to Camp David?" the president said. "The snoops may well see who is coming and going, but there is no way they could know what we would be talking about. After all, we're old friends, and for all they know we're playing cards or shuffleboard."

"That might work. Is there anyone else you want to include at this time?"

"Think we need to get a feel for what the Four have going and then we can filter. I certainly do not want to break their code of external silence, but if we need to help them move the needle, then I need to know what our options are."

"Should we invite spouses or leave it to the Four?" asked Fox.

"Adding spouses might confuse the snoops that are hanging around. At least we can jam any outside listening devices, and there are plenty of social things we can offer that will distract those looking from the sky. Get Triden on this."

The president looked out the window and wondered if any of this would put any of the Four in harm's way or cause them to be criticized in any one of a number of forums. DC naysayers were always looking for something to cause turmoil and chaos. It was a game both sides played, keeping those in power from achieving a climb up the mountaintop without sliding back occasionally.

"Ever wonder, Jim, if proof of the likes that this Ivanhoe has submitted could topple our way of life? Would blame come down on us, even though withholding a lot of this information was approved a long time ago?"

"We would be the ones who would have to have the answers—whatever they might be," Fox said. "Ivanhoe has the goods, I am sure of it. We either need to find out who that is or be ready for an onslaught of questions without reasonable answers.

"This Ivanhoe has said that if anyone tries to find out who Ivanhoe is there would be dire consequences, and when I talked to the Four, each one made it plain that they needed to stay clear of doing the searching themselves. The information Ivanhoe released to them has been handed over to one person—Bailey Stewart—and she has enlisted the help of Zach, Matt and Spencer. That's a strong foursome and I trust them to lead the way. I'm guessing they will find Ivanhoe or Ivanhoe will literally find them. I'm intrigued."

"Aliens, cures for cancer, energy sources?" the president said. "Just think of the exhilaration for people from every culture to find out this information is true and available, that we have a redefined sense of exploration, that stricken people would have access to life-saving services, and that transportation as we know it will look like a horse and buggy compared to what it actually could be. Has Ivanhoe explained about aliens or delved into specifics about medical science and substantiated the alternative fuel opportunities?"

"I haven't read the Ivanhoe letters—apparently there are twelve of them—but would like to," said Fox. "When I talked with Bailey she said she would bring copies for us to peruse when and if we meet. She has concerns about her role as an officer of the court and a potential conflict, but she also wonders if Ivanhoe would clam up if she did recuse herself.

"Ivanhoe could have released all of this stuff at once but chose to drop it piece by piece, probably to see how Bailey would react. I get the feeling

Ivanhoe knows her, or least knows enough about her to sense that she is beyond reproach and can handle herself on any ground. She's honest, consistent, and fair, and she knows the law. That alone is why I have confidence this is being handled in the best way possible."

"Let's set up a meeting at Camp David and see if we can pull this off. I don't want any leaks, so this stays between you and me."

"On it," Fox said, with a grand smile on his face.

"Aliens, a cure for cancer, a fuel source that would eliminate a lot of the greenhouse gases we seem to talk about all the time . . . I'm pumped," McCade said, returning his smile.

The hour had passed quickly and the congressional leaders probably were waiting. The Fitbits used by both the president and his chief of staff buzzed on their wrists and they closed their secret folders and left them on the table so no one could steal a glance. They had all of the information they needed in their heads, and it was like Christmas morning to them both. There was a bounce in their step and smiles on their faces as they moved on to the rest of their day.

The cavernous city block that housed the Archives had rooms with hermetically sealed drawers and display cases that could be accessed only be a select few, including Head Archivist Anita Wright and Deputy Archivist Elaine Meserve. The whole complex had the most sophisticated surveillance and security systems in the world, like what was in place at the FBI, CIA, NSA and other high-security governmental agencies. In the digitalized world, nothing went unnoticed.

Either Wright or Meserve had to sign off on any entry to secure areas, and with their history they knew where everything was or should be. Thieves had tried to have their way, but any attempts they made were counteracted with a quick response. The system was fail-safe.

Jim Triden

Jim Triden was one of those people who had a sixth sense, which in part led to his nickname as "the Magician." As head of the White House Secret Service detail, he seemingly was ahead of almost everyone he came into contact with, a much-valued trait in the position he served with three administrations. The one-time FBI counterintelligence agent was recruited by the department's Mike Norris after working on some deep state assignments where he showed his exemplary skills.

To some he was like a long-distance runner who simply never stopped running, and chasing down the undesirables was his end game. With the development of the Department of Homeland Security and the Treasury Department, the connection was a natural. The presidents he served trusted his instincts and often asked questions of him before going to public appearances outside the confines of the White House.

He had taken his lumps along the way, having been shot twice, hit by a car, and thrown off a three-story building, surviving each to live another day. His response to what happened: "You should see the other guy." He demanded discipline, teamwork and self-control of himself and his team. He also maintained a great sense of humor and knew what line not to cross. And his ability to show up at the right place and time—or perhaps ahead of it— was simply uncanny.

CHAPTER 44

Payne, Mitchell, Cookson, Brumfield, Crockett at FBI Headquarters

The room was filled with experience, well over three hundred years if someone totaled up all the time of FBI Director Randy Payne, Deputy Director Special Investigations Unit Curt Mitchell, Attorney General Liz Cookson, Matt Brumfield and Spencer Crockett had on their collective resumes. All had distinguished careers with few downturns. They had risen through the ranks with the respect of their peers and when any of them had knocked on a door or made an inquiry, people were quick to respond.

Payne had called the meeting, having talked with each of the other four individually as well as with other now-interested parties, including Jim Fox at the White House. The spacious glass-walled FBI executive conference room just off the director's office was the perfect setting. The midmorning meeting was expected to last for the better part of two hours and Payne had his staff prepare a brief on what they had to discuss. After the usual pleasantries and a chance to settle in with a cup of coffee or tea, Payne dug right in.

"Thank you all for being here," he began with his usual smile. "I thought it might be wise to come together for a brief overview of what I feel might become a more intense inquiry, if you will. You all know of the subject matter, but in that DC has a way with snooping, leaks, innuendoes, and misinterpretations, I think we all need to determine how we react when a negative force throws a grenade at any or all of us.

"The briefing report provides an outline, void of specifics, but should allow all of us to know what each one of us might be charged to do, or at least have knowledge of. I do not think any of this is clandestine, but what has been brought to our attention needs to have a careful look."

Payne took the time to give a quick overview of the five-page brief. He then turned to Brumfield and Crockett to fill in some of the details.

"Matt and Spence, you have served in the legal field and certainly know the inner workings of our government, as we know it, can you give us your take on any of this and let us know what you need from us?"

Brumfield looked at Spence and with a nod, went first.

"What we have been dealt is a person named Ivanhoe who has a cache of information that they think is worthy of the public's right to know. We have had similar instances in our history where information has been leaked or simply thrown out for public consumption, but without much corroboration. There are conspiracy theorists from all parts of world history. This Ivanhoe person has the goods, from what we have be able to substantiate.

"The brief shows how this started, what is now termed the Ivanhoe letters. This involves all of us and many more people who have been given the responsibility the public trust. I think we all realize that this information not only implies government secrets, but shows outright cover-ups for whatever reason. From my point of view, this has not been an ideological plan, but one to subvert the truth, or simply not tell all of the truth for the public's good will.

"As we all are a part of the judicial system and believe in the rule of law and seek the truth, we are bound to get all information as right as possible. But what Ivanhoe has purported, and I might add has been proven to be true or more true than what we have been led to believe, gives us more to chew on. What is so confounding to me is so much of this information has been passed on through many years. While conspiracy theorists abound, now there appears to be concrete evidence that probably will lead to rewriting history. My sense of fairness and of curiosity push me forward.

"But that drive has its own baggage. Trust in our government is at stake. Our form of democracy, the best the world has seen, will be scrutinized. And we will be pushed and perhaps accused unjustly when elements of this inquiry get leaked to the public.

"What I see for us is to understand where this investigation might take us, be it the FBI, Archives or any one of a number of outlets. As we have talked individually and now as a group, I think internal communication becomes paramount, so we can keep a handle on power pushers who think they may have a stake in what we find. And eventually we probably will have to determine what is okay for the public. I think Justice Stewart saw that from the get-go. And if we face litigation or court decisions, we have to be ready for our own can of worms."

Cookson was well aware of her role in all of this and she added, "Matt, I think we have to start looking at the legal battles that appear to be in the offing. Randy and Curt, how far can any investigations go into redacted documents? From my point of view, redacted means a 'no-fly zone.'"

"That is the joker in the deck," Crockett said. "From what we have seen in the Ivanhoe letters, there is information that is available with no redactions. That is what has been perplexing about what we have found so far. Ivanhoe has documentation on any one of a number of subjects or events and has divulged reliable information for us to corroborate. I think you all know special agents Casey Kincaid and Jenny Warner who are working both the FBI files and documents in the Archives. They have met some stop signs, but they also have some of the Hoover files that are not redacted—just kept under lock and key at the Bureau."

"Curt and I are monitoring Casey and Jenny's work," interjected Payne. "They're documenting what they've found and have developed questions that come out of contradictions—FBI regular files versus the Hoover cache. The Hoover files are extraordinary, and I don't know of anyone who has ever looked through all, or even had access. But Ivanhoe certainly knows and is talking to us through letters."

"I believe the president has been briefed, so how do we keep the White House up to date?" asked Cookson, a McCade appointee now in her fifth year as the AG.

"I would expect that a 'keep in touch' would suffice, so if something sneaks into a media source, there is a certain level of deniability—at least until we have more concrete evidence," added Brumfield. "I suspect leaks will occur and we will have to deal with them, as media and conspiracy theorists love to catch people off guard. That feeds the frenzy, and ideologues will have their own read. What we have to stand on is the fact that the inquiry exists to search for additional facts that will help us understand the whats as well as whys of world history—with an emphasis on our own history."

Crockett was interested in the world view, as the world would want to know that extraterrestrials actually existed, that there were cures for cancer, and that there was alternative fuel source that would not only help solve carbon emissions, but lead to advanced technology.

"There is a lot of information to be learned or relearned," he said. "Ivanhoe has laid out a lot of information in the eleven letters sent to Justice Stewart. I suspect there will be more. And I, for one, am interested in knowing as much as I can, ever cognizant that some information, if divulged, may lead to chaos. We have enough chaos in the world now, so setting the world's history straight may have its own cloak of transparency."

"Let's keep in touch on this, communicate—even if it means need-to-know status for a select group," said Payne. "I think we've outlined our plan, so let's see where this leads us."

The five nodded in unison. The meeting would bear fruit, and not just the low-hanging type.

CHAPTER 45

Hailwood and Stewart Discussion

Hailwood, ever the confidant and protector, decided he needed to have a one-on-one with the student-turned- justice Bailey. He was concerned about her staying too close to the now-expanding deep dive into uncharted waters that would mean a feeding frenzy for those who meant to throw negativity at anything for whatever reason. She was too valuable to the court and the public good to be thrown into a maelstrom of misinterpretations, misdirections, deceptions, and outright lies.

Hailwood was a good mentor for Bailey, challenging her as a student and later as she grew into her role of a trusted and learned judge who rose to the pinnacle of the legal system as an associate justice of the United States Supreme Court. Yes, he was proud, almost like a second father. He was protective and quick to respond when someone even came close to penetrating his wall of her defense. She was strong, as he well knew, but with sinister people always lurking in the confines of DC, he was suspicious of anything that did not meet his standards of legality and fairness.

The loosely used saying in Washington, *lawyers run the government, and lobbyists and spies run lawyers*, left him with a skeptical eye about everything. The context of the Ivanhoe letters was disturbing enough, but the fact she was in the middle of it spurred him, for obvious reasons, to call for what he referred to as a "campfire"—a meeting they spent talking about sensitive issues as they applied to the court.

"I know we have some important legislation coming up, but this Ivanhoe thing has taken on a life of its own," began Hailwood. "Does that leave you with a possible conflict of interest? Should you even be in these meetings with your group?"

"I'm still wondering why I am the contact for Ivanhoe," she said, leaning back in her leather desk chair. "I'm good with getting information from whatever source, but this continues to be an unraveling of so many facts and contradictions to what we have known as facts over the years. Just the issues of alien visits, cancer cures, and assassinations are mind-boggling. I've come to respect Ivanhoe for supplying this information, but like you, I am wondering where the line in the sand is for me.

"I certainly can't be the one to contact members of the administration, Congress, or whatever agencies," she said. "If anyone asks, I risk having knowledge of continuing actions. The worst-case scenario is that I would have to recuse myself."

"You know how snoops work, good ones and evil ones, and it seems to me that someone will ask a question as to whether you have any knowledge of this, and you will have to say something."

"From a court standpoint, I don't have to answer, but from the public viewpoint, I would think I would have to offer something. This is where it gets sticky. I definitely do not want to be the center of attention. If someone were to ask me a question it would have to be off the bench, certainly not on the court's time. I suspect, though, someone will find an end-around and the four of us will be tagged relentlessly."

"That leads to the question of what you do if you are contacted by any governmental source, including other agencies known as black ops. There will be those who are protecting whatever power base they're standing on and will want to know what you knew and when you knew it. Just how far can we kick the can down the road?

"I assume Mike Manchester with the CIA and Dan Sweeney with the NSA have heard some rumblings. I would shy away from any direct meetings with anyone outside the Four. Hopefully Matt and Curt can be the point people on this, with you strictly being the conduit with Ivanhoe."

"As Ivanhoe has revealed more and more, it's only a matter of time before all of us are going to be in some sort of spotlight. At least I am not adjudicating a case. But the issue is what does the public have a right to know and what does the government owe in return? Lower courts can handle potential lawsuits that might lead to injunctions."

"But if Ivanhoe simply releases all of the information to the public, leaving all this raw information for all to see . . ."

"That could be a different matter, because I think you would see a swarm of lawsuits, injunctions, and denials all over the place. That could lead to chaos, as people would be left to draw their own conclusions. Like the Ellsberg, Snowden, and other information-dumping scenarios, loss of trust in the government, and in who knows what other entities and organizations, could throw the country into a tizzy. And that doesn't even count the politicians who would be grandstanding and calling for all kinds of investigations as to who did what to whom, and when, and for what reason. Ivanhoe has the information, and as long as we're careful, I think we're 'safe,' if that even comes close to the right word."

"Well, I am concerned for your personal well-being and your office, so if I need to deflect for you, if any of this information is getting to be a hot iron, let me know."

"Thanks, Alex. I don't want to get you any more involved, but I will keep you in the loop. When the four of us get together again, I will share our concerns and see how they want to handle any fallout. The last thing we need is a lot of finger pointing, especially from disruptors in Congress and the feeding frenzy of members of the Fourth Estate looking for a Pulitzer."

"Alex, maybe it's the skeptic in me, but I don't take the recent attempt on O'Driscoll's life as a mere coincidence," began Stewart, now fidgeting with her hands while holding a pen. "Jenny Warner had a home invasion. You know about the terror Zach and I felt at the lake when our boathouse blew up. Yates was nearly taken out, but investigators didn't find a bomb or anything else that might lead to further discovery, so the case was closed. Yates even called in a longtime undercover operative, Preston Doran, and between the two of them they couldn't find anything to lead them to another conclusion. All Yates told me was 'everything was handled.'

"Other odd things have happened that leave me a tad unsettled. Even Brumfield and Crockett have said some strange things have happened to them in the past few months."

"I wasn't aware of anything happening to Matt or Spence," Hailwood said. "What was going on there?"

"Matt got stuck in an elevator for over an hour when he was at the Archives building. Maybe two weeks later, Spence was walking down the street with some friends and a car jumped the curb, missing them by maybe twenty feet before careening into a fire hydrant and creating quite a blow. Both incidents were written off as coincidence."

“Didn’t something happen to you on your way home a few months ago?”

“That was scary,” said Bailey. “Luckily I had Yates there, and he basically ran those some-of-a-bitches off the road. Who knows what other ‘coincidences’ have followed any one of our extended team? This thing with Gordon has calcified my thinking about what Ivanhoe warned us about such trials. I’ve come to a point that maybe we should bring in the Bureau and Service.”

“Haven’t the agencies been in the loop of on all of this?” he asked. “What came of their investigations?”

“The car chase and the attack on Gordon for sure were investigated, but the other events would have been written off as coincidences,” she responded.

“Yates got his NSA and Secret Service friends involved after we nearly were slammed off the road. At the time he didn’t have any solid leads, but a couple of months later I asked whatever became of the investigation, and again, all he said was ‘it was handled.’ He seemed satisfied from the look on his face, so I felt content.

“As for the suspected poisoning of Gordon O’Driscoll, I’m not sure of the status of that investigation. It was alarming to me as well as others, showing our vulnerability wherever we go. No one at the restaurant was under deep investigation, so the case may still have some substance.

“The attempt on Jenny in her home was FBI stuff. One of the perpetrators was shot and killed on-site. Apparently there were two others, and that investigation is ongoing. My heart and mind tell me all of these happenings are connected, and while I put on a brave and responsible persona, I do feel as if I’m looking over my shoulder from time to time.

“I think we need to document anything from anyone,” she continued. “Maybe this is the time to have another meeting of the Four and ask if any strange things have befallen any of them or anyone on their extended team. Then, maybe the agencies need to start trying to connect any dots. I would surmise, as you do, that coincidences need to be taken seriously, and in this case, we must watch our backs. Ivanhoe has warned that sinister forces—both in and out of government circles—might have something to lose big time, and we’ve seen some mighty peculiar things happen in our lifetimes that have gone unexplained.”

“By the way, have you heard from Ivanhoe lately?” he inquired.

“No, and that’s just as interesting. But to that end, I haven’t posted anything in the paper, either. Granted, the team has been working in different directions and when we meet from time to time, we simply give updates and plan our course going forward.”

"When is your next meeting scheduled?"

"This weekend, as soon as Zach gets back from Minneapolis. His meetings were to wrap up this morning and he should be back here tonight. I really need his take on all of this."

"You want to schedule a follow-up on this for Monday?"

"We have a busy schedule with all these cases being proffered for the fall session, but let's at least set aside thirty minutes for a quick review."

"I'll set it up with Candy. Maybe sometime around the lunch break if the usual member session doesn't have a working lunch."

"We haven't gotten to that yet, but we're less than a month from the first Monday in October, and then all hell breaks loose with the cases drawn to be heard by the court.

"From what I hear, the solicitor general has been overwhelmed with briefs and is trying to whittle down the seven hundred or so cases we probably will be looking at. We both know there's going to be some pushing and shoving on what will be a priority, or at least should be, so I would think our private time will be harder to come by. But this Ivanhoe story isn't going away, and the more I see and hear, the more concerned I get as to what should be disseminated and what needs to have some form of redaction. I have to admit, I'm treating this with just as much seriousness as any case I've ever been involved with. Even with all of the distractions—including possible threats to any or all of us—I still am interested in seeing it through. And I think Ivanhoe has made it clear that they want that, too."

With nods, the justice sipped the last of her coffee, and Hailwood, more of a soda guy, finished his root beer. The time well spent, the two departed. Stewart was all too willing to share her thoughts with Yates on the forty-minute drive back to Fairfax. And he was all ears.

CHAPTER 46

Dilemma for the Court

Although six Supreme Court justices are required for a court quorum, seldom has that ever been an issue. However, the recent presumed attempt on O'Driscoll's life made Stewart even more wary, as she thought ahead to any possible court-case submission through Solicitor General Julia France that would be a part of what was becoming the Pandora's box of the Ivanhoe letters and subsequent investigations. Stewart was counting noses on this one, assuming more litigation would work its way through the lower courts and be handed off to the Supremes to make a final decision.

Similar petitions had made their way to the high court before but were denied for various reasons. Some resurfaced with a different point of view. Some took a slow journey, perhaps as long as six years, while others were fast-tracked in two years. The collection of similar cases that were bunched into the right-to-know grouping were beginning to pile up. Just as curious was the fact that some contradicted one another. The right-to-know vs. the right-to-not-know.

This, she now surmised, may pose a problem. Would she, Chief Justice Walter Gallien, and her colleagues Justices DeBarrow and Yost, in whom she had confided, have to recuse themselves? If O'Driscoll was not available, the number of justices to hear a case may fall under the minimum. And if that happened, the lower court decision would stand.

Another Ivanhoe letter was waiting for Bailey when she got home. Relaxed in her easy chair in her second-story home office, Bailey opened the 9 x 12 envelope, noted that there were five pages to be read, grasped at her glass of chardonnay, and began the latest chapter of the Ivanhoe saga.

Stopping from time to time to take it all in, using her analytical mind to sift through possibilities, she was as entranced as before by what Ivanhoe described. The chardonnay gone and her mind spinning, Bailey couldn't wait for Zach to get home.

CHAPTER 47

Crockett and Brumfield at Old Ebbitt Grill as Questions Arise

Crockett had been around the block a few times, and as a former general counsel and special prosecutor he had seen a lot of mysterious outcomes. Soft-spoken in general conversation, he was a leader when it was time to work, and people admired his style.

Per usual when he and Matt Brumfield walked in the door of the Old Ebbitt Grill and made their way to the back of the establishment to 'their' table, people hailed their names and gave a wave. The two were like showmen and accommodated all who reached out to shake hands or make eye contact. While they tried to shun the limelight, they knew others were watching their every move. Now in the confines of the coveted booth at the back of the restaurant for privacy, it was time to share some serious discussion.

"So, what's so serious that it couldn't wait until we got back to the estate?" said Brumfield, sipping his bourbon and seven.

"Well, we knew we were going to catch some heat eventually," replied Crockett, giving his vodka martini a hard swallow. Their usual lunch choices—filet mignon for Crockett and a Reuben for Brumfield—arrived.

"Got a call from Liz a few days ago, and rather than talk on the phone she suggested I come over to Justice for a quick chat," continued Crockett. "She's like us, wanting to connect the dots as soon as a new one appears. She follows her instincts; that's why I hired her when I was the AG. In a day and age when Washington has more rumors than any other city in the world, she is cautious about jumping to conclusions and definitely does not have a knee-jerk reaction to what she sees or hears.

"Her concern was that she saw an uptick in inquiries from not only congressional sources, but some in the intelligence community. Sometimes rumors are just a way of someone throwing a grenade at the other side, but she said that there was some cross-referencing here and that I—we—should be aware of the chatter."

"She wasn't talking about any court-ordered wiretapping or additional DOJ time, was she?"

"Not at all. Just the regular monitoring of independent sources. In that she is fully aware of what we are doing and the end game we have espoused, she thought we should be aware that there appeared to be roadblocks coming up. Let's face it, as much as we have tried to stay under the radar, there were going to be leaks as well as rumors. Washington is known for those scenarios. Goodness gracious, DC is a giant colander. Usually it's one side simply making wild accusations that prompt an investigation and committee meetings as well as a media circus. When special interests are involved, anything goes."

"Did Liz give you anything specific?"

"Yes, and she didn't feel it was anything classified, as the inquiries were directed to her office by those who apparently want to know what she knows. She isn't under any specified rules or implied protocols, so she was polite to them and said she would look into the matters. I'm not sure that would stop the hounds, and knowing DC, that won't stop at a mere inquiry. I would expect some legal maneuverings. As we well know, some people simply like making things up and starting rumors—truthful or not.

"This has an eerie feeling to me, one that trip-wired me to a case I handled as an SP when a group of lobbyists were tied to several congressional members for a conflict of interest. The congressional members skated, but three of the lobbyists were indicted. They all pled out and served some time for their misdeeds. The fact the members of Congress were implicated didn't sit well with them and I guess that allowed them to bad mouth our team. In that they didn't get indicted should have meant they would have been thrilled or at least sent us a fruit basket. But that is not what happened, from what I heard through my sources."

"So, who's the culprit here?" inquired Brumfield, finishing the last of his Reuben sandwich.

"According to Liz, she got an earful from Henry Glenn, a well-known oil industry lobbyist, and Murray Bloom, who has pharmaceutical industry ties, as well as House Speaker John Fishel, Congressmen Alan Troy and Les Slone, and Senator Jackie Hansen."

"Were they specific or just blowing off steam for their 'constituents'?"

"The inquiries from all sides were made to find out what the DOJ was looking into, but nothing outside of that, from what I understand."

"So, Liz did the cursory 'we'll check into it and get back to you with a response'?"

"That's my read. My concern is that the leaks already have occurred and probably came from someone who knew someone else or overheard chatter at a social gathering. Rumors are just that, but when there is some meat on the bones, then you get these snoops banging on doors or making insinuations. Liz has been in the loop all the way. In my team's drilling, we are looking at government documents that are not readily available to the general public. Or to government officials, for that matter.

"Casey and Jenny found the Hoover 'puzzle' file and reported it to Randy. Randy called me to alert me that certain information in that file could be damaging to certain people or industries, so we all have to be aware. I thought you and I should analyze this before we meet with Bailey and Zach. And I am concerned as to where Bailey should be, as we move forward.

"Like we talked about at our last meeting, Bailey could be caught in the crosshairs of a conflict of interest, given what I think these people are capable of doing to obstruct an inquiry or true investigation. I think it's more than a coincidence that people related to this inquiry have had near misses or accidents. To think Justice O'Driscoll had some sort of poison—that certainly got my attention.

"I think we all agree that there are some special interests that stand to lose a lot. Power in DC is everything. I saw that firsthand as a judge and SP. We also have to recognize that we have expanded our teams, and as much as we have admonished everyone to keep a lid on it, people share information, perhaps innocently, and sooner than later the story grows, and the rumors spread. The case against the congressmembers and lobbyists had a lot of hearsay evidence and I didn't see anything so concrete as to follow that road. The lobbyists, however, usually have memos, letters, and documents that lead to direct wants and needs. And once the accused see that there is a softer landing than decades in jail, they usually plead out and call it a day. We certainly had the hammer on them."

"So, what do you suggest you and I do now, before we meet with Bailey and Zach?"

"I think we need to take the lead and ask both of them what they want us to share with them. Sort of like the deniability quotient. Bailey has the connection with Ivanhoe and I suspect we will hear a lot more from that source. Zach will be there to support and protect Bailey, so we need to share with them what they want to know. Bailey already has been embedded in this, so she may well say we need to tell all. If there is a conflict down the road, she'll have to recuse herself anyway.

"What have you found through the Archives?"

"There is a wealth of information there, but there are a lot of redactions. I would think we could use any of the Archives sources to lead us back to the FBI and other secret files. For instance, if we saw something in one of the subjects in question—JFK and other assassinations or to do with the pharmaceutical companies in their ultimate quest to find a cure for cancer—something may lead us to look for something more specific elsewhere.

"Is Randy okay with us coming and going to the FBI files?"

"To my knowledge he is, but we'll stay within his parameters. After all, he is under the jurisdiction of the DOJ and ultimately the president."

"And President McCade is good on all of this as well?"

"According to Jim Fox, he has kept the president well apprised of what we're doing. If something comes up that he needs to know, we'll make that contact. The last thing we need to do is have the president be asked a question in a White House briefing where he has to deny or even defend what might be going on behind closed doors. I think we have been forthright on connecting with all of our extended family, but if Liz, Randy, Jim or any other government person in the know is questioned, we need to make sure we all are on the same page."

"So, we are good to go with our next meeting in Fairfax and we will bring Bailey and Zach up to date?"

"That would be my vote."

The two had spent the better part of two hours going over all they knew. By the time they finished, the Grill patronage had been cut to half of what it was in the busier time, but the two were still hailed as they left. Ah, such was life when people got along.

CHAPTER 48

The Four Meet at Longfellow Estate

Brumfield and Crockett drove caravan style to the Longfellow estate, chatting on their cell phones all the way. They were going their separate ways after the weekend meeting and thought it better to drive solo. As they approached the drawbridge, they simply were in awe at how Zach had made it so picturesque. It was late Friday evening, and other than having a couple of social drinks, there wasn't anything planned for the evening. The pool was available and they all enjoyed the pleasures of the inside pool and lounge chairs. Comfort without distractions.

The Saturday morning was meant to be the time to review all, and they had a lot to cover. With the usual display of breakfast buffet prepared by Annette, the visiting members of the Four felt like they were at some resort. The round table that comfortably sat four was set up in the family room, along with two large whiteboards that they had grown accustomed to using during their get-togethers. It allowed them to think freely and jot down facts and theories without much fanfare. The also decided to record their meetings to help refresh their recollection about possible options to consider.

Crockett took the opportunity to bring Bailey and Zach up to speed on what he and Brumley had discussed. Bailey and Zach listened intently, making notes as Crockett divulged some of his concerns. They all knew that going forward they would have to stay in closer touch and meet more often, if schedules allowed. Bailey had the most to coordinate, given that the court's fall session started on the first Monday of October.

"I appreciate your concern, and I know Zach is there for me," said Bailey. "Like all of you and the people who make up our collective teams, I'm ready for a fight because we know what has to be done. I will not be intimidated, or threatened or embarrassed by anyone, and that includes the likes of any elected official, lobbyist, or lawyer for that matter. I knew what we were getting into, and now that we've seen some rather serious coincidences and inquiries to the DOJ are ticking up, we need to be even more aggressive on corroborating Ivanhoe's information."

"Are we opting to simply release all that we know, or follow our own course?" asked Brumfield. "I would say that our fail-safe would be that we have the truth, the facts, if you will, and if anyone threatens any of us or our team, then all bets are off. From what I gather, Ivanhoe seems to have a tap on everything we're doing, and no doubt knows who would be throwing grenades in whatever direction."

"Bailey, from your standpoint, do you feel your being so involved would be a detriment to your position on the court?" asked Crockett.

"We've sort of talked around this before, but if this gets into the lower courts, then additional legal maneuvering may or may not let some of those cases reach the Supreme Court," said Bailey. "If anything gets there, I would have to consider recusing myself, of course. And that may lead to more problems, so, yes, I am concerned, but I'm committed to moving forward, even though some of these evildoers will do anything to stop us in our tracks."

"And that might include outright threats to any of us?" said Brumfield.

"Yes, I wouldn't put it past them, whoever they are. Mysterious deaths and foul deeds have littered not only this town, but the nation and the world itself when people in power or those who stood to lose something felt the air might have been slipping out of their balloons. As a member of the court, I have seen a lot of cases, legal mumbo jumbo, and seemingly absurd insinuations that led to unsatisfying or even disgraceful endings. Sometimes facts aren't there to substantiate a conviction. Some of the people who have argued their cases before the high court knew how to manipulate facts. Our job—all nine of us—is to interpret the law. And our job goes further, either sustaining a lower court order or making a determination that the Constitution agrees or not."

"And if we get into litigation from a lower court that should be heard by the high court, would all that be nullified because of your involvement?" asked Zach.

"That could be the case, but I have a feeling that Ivanhoe is waiting for any shenanigans. If anyone means to throw us under the bus or try to discredit any or all of us, then that may make for the biggest circus this town has ever seen. Truthfully, though, I would like to see our investigations continue on all fronts and then evaluate what the public has a right to know?"

"Let's draw up a new general outline and see where we can go with it," offered Brumfield. "We have stickies from our past meetings, so let's look at all we have and make some reasonable challenges. I agree, too, that we need to keep meeting more often, but we have to be respectful of Bailey's schedule first."

"I appreciate that, guys, but we have to set up some sort of secondary line of communication, now that the court session is upon me. I expect that I will be working the usual twelve-plus hours every day, and some of that work will be brought home. I also need to do my share for our group, so I'll figure out another line of communication."

It was time for Zach to speak up.

"Maybe that's where I come in," he offered. "I have a floating schedule, and aside from the seminars and meetings I go to from time to time, I should be able to move about without much detection. I also think Bailey should stick to exchanges from Ivanhoe and leave it to us to follow whatever leads and facts are divulged."

"Not a bad idea, Zach," said Crockett, already thinking about how he might make arrangements to meet with Zach at various places. "But I have to think that you are being followed, to some extent."

"Then we'll have to develop a labyrinth that will test any snooping," said Zach with an adventurous smile. "Maybe this isn't the best scenario, but at least we might be able to keep in contact about papers, documents, or strategies without actually meeting once a month. We love having you guys come over, but as we see an increase in inquiries, we need to be ready for any sinister threat. Also, as you said, Spence, we need to keep the partners—DOJ and, of course, the president—informed so there is deniability."

"I'm good to go and will pile another log on the fire at the Archives," said Brumfield. "From what Spence and I talked about and now know from the drill down in the Hoover files, there is a lot to be reviewed and then scrutinized by Randy at the Bureau."

"Bailey, perhaps you can contact Ivanhoe through your *Post* classifieds and ask if anything else in the Hoover files that would be forthcoming?" said Crockett. "I suspect that the recent find of the puzzle file will be opening many more files and lead to more inquiries at Justice."

"Consider it done," said Bailey with enthusiasm. "At least I can prompt some 'conversation' with Ivanhoe that will allow us to cut to the chase and stay ahead of the disruptors. Can't tell you how much I loathe disruptors. I would say hate, but my father once told me I shouldn't hate anyone, but I could despise or dislike someone or something. He even tried staying that course when he was the chief justice of the California Supreme Court."

Bailey learned a lot by listening. She listened to her compatriots and was just as determined as they to play her role and see this through—no matter the consequences. She was willing to take on a challenge or sift through whatever documentation necessary to reach a fair and just conclusion. She had taken an oath to preserve, protect, and defend the Constitution of the United States, as required at her swearing-in ceremony: *'do solemnly swear that I will administer justice without respect to persons, and do equal right to the poor and to the rich, and that I will faithfully and impartially discharge and perform all the duties incumbent upon me as a Supreme Court justice under the Constitution and laws of the United States.'*

The afternoon started to fade, and Bailey and Zach had planned another trip to the Army Navy Country Club. There was no resistance by Crockett and Brumfield. The meeting had been extremely productive, and now the Four had a clearer view of their immediate needs and they had to move swiftly as the waters of "Snoopy River" were rising.

CHAPTER 49

Ivanhoe Letter—12

Once again, the cryptic ad in the *Washington Post* resulted in a quick response from the mysterious Ivanhoe. As busy and consumed as Bailey Stewart was with the court's ceremonious first Monday in October, she was anxious to see and read what Ivanhoe had to offer.

Dear Justice Stewart:

If I am reading between the lines, I suspect you have found some information through your investigation of the FBI files—more specifically the J. Edgar collection of more than a million such files. As I have stated before, when Hoover was appointed the Bureau director in April 1924 by then President Calvin Coolidge, there was an inherent need to investigate who, what, when, where and how of every facet of American life. Yes, there were secrets well before Hoover came to the forefront, but he managed to collect data from a number of sources that date back centuries.

J. Edgar made the FBI. He molded it into an organization that was both respected and feared. He also had a personal stake, knowing he could gather information from any number of sources and investigate anything without reproach. He had the truth about people, places, and historical facts that made him untouchable. There were those who tried to get him out of the Bureau so as to retain their own power or simply to protect some of their own from being exposed. His longstanding feud with the Kennedy clan was well known, but there were deeper secrets that led to more clashes than the public ever would know.

As I have intimated before, Hoover knew everything about the Kennedy assassinations and the killings of Martin Luther King and Marilyn Monroe, among others. He simply kept quiet. But his files were not sparse, and the information in them was meant to protect him, not the public. Think about the missing files and what they could tell the American citizens about history, including their own government, or how the world would see mysterious happenings that only brushed the top of the real stories. Those in the media were anxiously waiting for details through leaks, only to be fed bits and pieces of all the facts presented.

Some of the information I now am privy to has to do with historical facts outside of the United States. They give credence to how some events interacted and may have changed the course of history, at leastthe historyt we have known.

As Hoover's inquiries and collections of information continued to grow from domestic sources, they also intertwined with people and events throughout the world. The evil of the Nazi empire was exposed by a number of sources from US and British intelligence, the Norwegian underground and people within Germany itself. The Nazis were working hard and fast on developing an atomic bomb as well as a jet plane. Had those two projects been completed, theoutcome of the war certainly would have been changed. The underground made sure the shipment of heavy water (H2O2), necessary for an atomic bomb and bound for Germany, sank into the depths of Norway's Lake Tinn.

German historian Rainier Karlsch found corroborating evidence that Erich Schumann, who served in Germany's weapons division, had hard facts on the development of a method of generating high temperatures (several million degrees Celsius) that would trigger nuclear fusion with conventional explosives. The Germans, of course, had other developments in medicine and genetic research that would have changed the face of civilization had they prevailed.

Hoover preserved his secrets by having all of his files digitalized, so whoever thought they were getting away with the dirtiest entries will face judgment day. Trust would become distrust. And would he be held in highest esteem or be written off as a fabricator? Having read all of his files that I believe were confiscated, I trust what is in there because it gets into details and connects the dots. Hypotheticals become focused into a giant jigsaw puzzle and the pieces fit.

So, perhaps Hoover is the key to it all. In FBI files are some that contain some unredacted documents that only the Bureau can and or will release. I suspect there will be some legal shenanigans to block some or all of that. Archives has documents that show redacted portions which lead to the many conspiracy theories. While I applaud those who have delved into any one of a number of historical facts, there is more to learn. The fact we have documentation in digital form and were privileged to happen upon such information has been breathtaking. Trust me, I have been overwhelmed by what I have seen. That drove me to your busy doorstep and I apologize for the overload, but as a citizen, I think some of this needs to see the bright light of the day.

You mentioned "The Puzzle." I knew that the thieves that took what they thought was the most damaging part of the Hoover files simply missed that file. While some of this information is in the files still under the Bureau care, Archives has some additional tidbits that will help fill in some of the missing pieces.

But be wary of those who will be coming after you or any of your team. I would suspect there have been some rumblings by now, but as I have said, I have a contingency plan that if anything happens to me, or you, or any member of your team, the whole story will be told. We are talking evil here, from individuals, organizations, businesses, even countries that would, for the purpose of retaining power and not ever being brought to justice, eliminate those who dare to implicate them in wrongdoing.

I've mentioned the Kennedy assassinations, cures for cancer, alien presence, alternative fuel sources and other areas of interest to me before. Have your team look into the Bilderberg Group, the Betz Sphere, the Whippoorwill Project, the Russian space disasters, the Ponce Directive, the Topaz Crystal, even the Vatican. Those areas all are under the radar and probably will help you solve the puzzle quicker.

As I have pored through volumes of materials—all digital, I might add—the files have become a library of facts, figures and historical treasures.

Do not let redactions stop you. Leads from the FBI or the Archives all may lead to further investigations. Eventually this all will play out and the end of the reality movie will provide a better understanding of what happened, along with the why's, where's and how's. I expect you are busy with your court duties, so I will end this letter with, good luck.

IVANHOE

Having read and reread the latest Ivanhoe script, Stewart simply was in awe. Ivanhoe really does have a lot to offer, and she didn't think whoever this person was had any intention of letting any investigation simply come to an end without the truth being told. While she had her own business to tend to, she couldn't wait to share the latest with Matt and Spencer. She did so under a newly devised secure line, developed by none other than her bodyguard/driver/confidant Francis Yates. He, too, was after the truth and the protection of those who knew it.

CHAPTER 50

McCade, Fox, Butterfield, Boyd, Wendt, McKenzie

As the clouds of secrecy started to wane like the haze of an early morning, it was only a matter of time until a swarm of bees—in the form of the media— would make their presence known. The bees, as they were sometimes referred to in private conversation, were the nuisance, if you will, of any president. And so it was with President McCade, universally liked by both sides of the aisle as a moderate. As the media were the bees, the members of Congress often were called vultures, and the lawyers and lobbyists had less favorable references. Put one hundred people in a room and someone would take umbrage, even if you announced a cure for cancer.

The president was pacing in the Oval Office, with Chief of Staff Jim Fox, Secretary of State Gil Butterfield, Senior Aide Bill Boyd, National Security Advisor Neal Robert Wendt, and White House Communications Director Carter McKenzie sitting on the two parallel couches.

"Okay, folks," he began, continuing his slow pace. "You all have been briefed about this ongoing investigation, inquiry, or whatever it's called, about government secrets. As expected, some people are asking questions, and while I am good with defending, I do not want us to get caught up in being defensive. From what Jim has told me, this investigation is not so much about the here and now, but about the before and what our government is responsible for. Taking that question seriously, we need to know the facts as they are being discovered and then determine our own course of action. I have asked Jim to be the point person in this, so if questions arrive or filter into your areas of responsibility, I ask that you let him know so we can keep ahead of what I expect may be a tidal wave. Jim, please take it from here."

As McCade sat in his leather chair next to the two couches, Fox rose to give his synopsis of what he knew.

"In our previous briefings, you were made aware of this series of inquiries. We expected some pushback and have started to see some, although we sense this will be turning into a three-ring circus quickly. As you know, a person named Ivanhoe has directed people to corroborate some rather interesting and perhaps controversial information about history, not only ours, but of the world.

"The information was sent to Justice Stewart, who we all know will seek the truth, but will be responsible and sensitive to what ultimately is divulged. Her team includes her husband, Dr. Zach Longfellow, a world-renowned cardiologist and one who knows many people of all walks of life. The team also includes two of our friends: Matt Brumfield, president of Harvard University, and Spencer Crockett, once a federal judge, deputy attorney general and special prosecutor. All four are well-respected, honest patriots.

"The whole story revolves around what Ivanhoe has purported in several letters to Justice Stewart. We have copies of all and will share those with you. We are not against any such inquiry, as it falls under the banner of the Freedom of Information Act. We are cognizant of what Ivanhoe has indicated and what might happen if any such facts became known—ones that might disturb our citizens and other countries. Apparently, Ivanhoe has the facts. Bear in mind, the Ivanhoe letters are not subject to redaction because of national security or information deemed top secret.

"What is just as potentially explosive is that Ivanhoe also has all the voluminous J. Edgar Hoover files, unredacted and, from what I understand, quite revealing."

There was a collective gasp from the people in the room. Fox continued.

"What we are faced with is trying to make sure we see whatever Ivanhoe is purporting, and that would include the Hoover files, before they are exposed. That, of course, could take weeks, months, perhaps years. From what we have learned, Matt Brumfield is looking at the Archives for pieces while Crockett is looking at FBI files under FOIA. While we trust their discretion, we are facing a lot of inquiries from the media, Congress, and other persons who have something to potentially lose if certain facts were to become known.

"The Kennedy assassinations, cures for cancer, alternative fuel sources, and even alien visits are part of the mix."

Again, a gasp with some serious looks from those gathered. The president then spoke.

"These issues are commonly discussed in conspiracy circles, but trust me, there are a thousand more that go along with Ivanhoe's letters—so far. While we are not the ones to sit in judgment on any of these, I think we all would like to know the truth as much as any other citizen. But to what extent must be the ultimate question.

"We all have press conferences or do interviews all the time, and this subject will pop up at some point. We need to have a collective voice," said the president. "I guess I'm the one who will get asked the most and most often, but I needed to let you know that we are going to be sharing all pertinent data once we hear from any of the Four, as they refer to themselves. If the facts bear out that the government had anything to do with the Kennedy assassinations, or with the demise of Dr. King, or had knowledge of cures for cancer, alternative fuels sources, aliens and who knows what, someone is going to pay, and it may well be our form of government.

"We can claim innocence because we weren't there, but if we knew and didn't share, were we complicit? What is right and what is wrong? What is fair and what is not fair? If we have known cancer cures, then why not make that public knowledge, saving lives and helping our health care system? Could the research industry suffer? Would that upset the world money cycle?

"Same could be true with alternative fuel options, saving our environment and being more efficient, only to have the oil companies get all but wiped out, to say nothing of those exporting oil across the globe. That could destroy many an economy. That also may force us to retool our machinery and infrastructure."

That brought a "yikes" from Wendt, a career operative who knew the world better than anyone else in the room.

"As surmised, the government—J. Edgar—knew exactly what happened in the assassinations, but stayed silent," continued the president. "This scenario says the Mafia set up the hit and the CIA helped make it happen. That should go over well with the public. And as for aliens, I would be thrilled to know when and where, but from what we've learned, there have been many visits and a lot of knowledge left behind. I was intrigued by why there were so many pyramids built on nearly every continent at different times. I just can't wrap arms around how they were constructed, although some theories proposed make for a startling scenario.

"I have asked Jim to have regular meetings with all of you as we try to sort out what we know and what we are going to find out from our compatriots through Ivanhoe. I, for one, am glad that Ivanhoe has given us an advantage of finding the true facts. It is for us to lead, not follow or get out of the way. I also ask that if you hear anything that is pertinent to this investigation that you contact Jim and he will brief me as we try to deal with every responsibility of running the greatest country the world has known. People from around the world know we mean business, so let's move on."

With that the group stood, now more interested and showing a willingness to explore on their own. A minute later, the president paced in the Oval Office, peering at the large blue rug that featured the Presidential Seal.

J. Edgar Hoover was a collector, from both his time and before he was around. His collection of information was meant to give him and his gatherers as much documentation of individuals, places, and events as needed to make any investigation legitimate. Some of those dirty little secrets literally would save his life and his job, as many people were after him for what he knew.

The Hoover files contained a wealth of information, now digitalized, and stored on a secret government server. No government official, including any president, had access to the secret storage place. But a savvy IT person, who worked in those circles, one day came across what was a perfect storm, where all such information was available at a unique moment in time. That person downloaded all of it. The download was sent to Ivanhoe in a microdot—on a postage stamp that depicted an eye of an eagle. Ivanhoe downloaded all of it. And the rest was about to be history, or a rewriting of history.

This was not about political leanings, just historical facts, that quite possibly would disrupt the political landscape or certainly upset the rolling apple cart. Ivanhoe's quest is for someone else to determine what was the public's right to know. Trust vs. distrust. Enlightenment or keep the facts of history alone? Some might call it revisionist history, others might say be careful what you wish for.

The search for Ivanhoe would intensify. Ivanhoe would remain a ghost.

CHAPTER 51

Justice Stewart Ponders Decisions to be Made

There were times when Judge Bailey Stewart didn't like her job, not to the point she hated it, but at times she felt pushed and shoved in her own mind as to what was right, with deep respect for the Constitution. As a court moderate, she was viewed as a swing vote, a position she relished. But to her consternation, the three liberals and three conservatives, as they were viewed by those in the know, left her and the other two moderates to decide an up or down on many issues that came before the court. She was good with her convictions, but found herself struggling with the interpretations of the Constitution.

Now she was consumed with the regular travails of the court in session, and that meant reviewing some seven hundred cases that needed to have some resolution. Her staff and the rest of the court's justices and staff shared similar compressed time. Free time was precious, so lunch was a time to catch a breath. With even more open investigations, based on the Ivanhoe revelations, the subsequent probing by those who may or may not have a vested interest was like piling another log on the fire. She was game but did not want to be played. She trusted her cohorts with her life and was determined to find the truth, no matter how long or how deep the inquirers drilled.

Her mind, distracted from the court's needs for a mere forty-five minutes for lunch, was back on track when she was part of the general justices' meeting at two o'clock. She was all eyes and ears, bent on doing the job she was appointed to do. She also wanted to follow through with the Four and looked forward to an evening in the comforts of home.

Now close to six thirty on what seemed like a long Thursday, Stewart had a planned meeting with trusted confidant Hailwood. She made sure she had wrapped her day's work so they could meet after the regular staff had left for the day. It was not uncommon for the justices to work later into the evening, but with court sessions and meetings, everyone knew there was a time to call it a day, get some rest and be ready for the next volley of the same in twelve hours.

Hailwood gave a quick knock on Stewart's door and entered. Their regular meetings were used to sort through priorities, and the Ivanhoe Project, as they had come to call it, was the main subject to be discussed. Their no-holds-barred campfire eclipsed protocol, and they talked like old friends without intrusions.

"You mentioned before that you thought members of the Four might be in jeopardy. Do you still hold that conviction?"

"Yes, I do. I'm vulnerable because I have specific information. The attack on Justice O'Driscoll and my blown-up boathouse proved that to me. Somebody is making a lot of effort to make sure certain roads are blocked."

"Is any of this about outing anyone in Congress, or the executive or judicial branches for anything personal? I think this town is well known for smears, accusations, innuendoes and outright lies, so anything goes."

"My read on this is tight. Ivanhoe is divulging government secrets—misinformation—but it seems like it has to do with history, not individuals who did something underhanded or perhaps illegal. Nothing I have read suggests there is finger pointing because of some payoff, sexual encounter, or tax evasion. If that was the target, then why not just turn it over to the FBI and launch an investigation?"

"Well, this has proved to be an investigation under the Freedom of Information Act, and that's sure to draw some attention."

"The FOIA requests have drawn out gazillions of snoops and conspiracy theorists for a variety of reasons. We can't keep them from producing even more theories. I'm not sure we have exposed ourselves to the media or public along those lines yet, but it's just a matter of time before one of those snoops starts to connect the dots."

"And that's where the president is really concerned, right?"

"That would be correct. JJ," as she referred to him in closed circles, "is well received by a lot of different people and ideologies, but like any other politician, he doesn't want to get blindsided."

"Can we connect with these snoops?"

"Not without disclosure. Questions would be asked, and answers would be warranted. For one person's 'you can trust me' stance, there's another's slip of the tongue or leak. You know how it is."

"If someone comes knocking on our door, what do we tell them?"

"That's what I want you to take a hack at. Think of how we can answer without saying 'no comment.'"

"And if that question comes from a hard-charging journalist, respected or not?"

"That's your homework, and I will follow with my group. We have to line up a defense, so we don't have to be defensive."

The darkened sky left them with a time to call it a day. They were determined to see this through together and they had each other's backs.

CHAPTER 52

The Dark Forces

The president and those around him knew there were dark forces around any administration. That same thought wasn't foreign to Spencer Crockett. Crockett always had his ear to the ground, and when the Four came together, he knew that the inquiries would spark a reaction, and the plans of those who hoped to stop all could morph into something sinister. Politicals wanted to retain power, at almost any cost. Those who were pushing an agenda had something to lose, meaning some people might be vulnerable.

Jim Fox had briefed Crockett about anyone who had made veiled inquiries to the president. Fox was there to protect the president; Crockett was there to watch the dark forces. Crockett would start an internal file and have his team develop background. In a digital age, this became routine, but demanding. The hounds were howling and team Crockett was all too willing to analyze what he had learned and move quickly forward. At the same time, Crockett kept a watchful eye on the efforts of Kincaid and Warner as they dove deeper into the FBI files, with an emphasis on the Hoover documents.

Crockett assembled his team at a close friend's business, away from the hustle of downtown DC. He understood he might be followed and took necessary precautions. The group of fifteen arrived at different times and easily could have been believed to be employees of the business.

The large oak table with stylish chairs of green made for an upscale presentation. The room had all the trappings of technology, from hidden screens and monitors to table screen upswings. Multiple LED screens adorned the wood-paneled walls. Even the beverage console was hidden until remotely activated.

"This is the first time we've all been together," Crockett began. "Welcome all of you to the team," in his usual smiling and confident tone. "I need to remind everyone that what we say here and what we do with this project is highly confidential. Everyone has signed off on this with an NDA, but my need to remind all is that we are going to be dealing with some outside forces and individuals, so our challenge is to remain in the background and as invisible as possible.

"Before you is a briefing book prepared by a trusted staff under the guise of an NDA. It outlines what our challenge is, how we intend to get all done, how to circumvent stop signs or twists in the road, so to speak. The general briefing does not divulge all that is being done on all fronts, for security's sake. There may be risks. I ask that if any of you sense danger, or something appears to be compromising, to contact me immediately. We will with those dangers immediately.

"Once you read and reread this book, a lot of our quest will become clearer. As of this date we have seen inquiries from four sources and we expect many more. For now, we have assigned each of you a section to tend to. For instance, we have had three inquiries about pharmaceuticals, one about the Kennedy assassinations, three about energy and even one about the FBI itself. These inquiries have come from elected officials such as members of Congress, lawyers, and lobbyists. Just know that there are a lot of prying eyes and ears. Electeds spend a lot to get elected. To stay there they must make compromises. That may include some worthy as well as some unscrupulous partners. It's all about power and how to hang on to it.

"As the AG and then SP, I saw so much compromising material and comments that it made my head spin. But my job then was to search for the facts and make those facts known and adjudicated. The justice system sometimes may seem unfair. It is the presentation of the facts to ensure that those who sit as judges, serve as counsel, and especially those wishing to prevail as plaintiffs or defendants, get a fair shake. Sometimes innocent people take a hit.

"We are here because a person known only as Ivanhoe has divulged some pretty startling information, facts that need to be treated with care, so we need to determine what is truly correct and what may be an abbreviation of the truth. Those who stand to be called into question will make every attempt to confuse us or create diversions or may even pose a threat. Why? Because of power and the endgame of keeping it.

"Ivanhoe has laid out a case regarding truths. Our quest is to corroborate or dispel what has been presented. For instance, Ivanhoe has stated we have known of cures for cancer for some time and that pharmaceutical companies and research institutes have been making enormous amounts of money by not allowing those cures to be known, costing lives in the process. So, does the public have a right to know?

"None of you were around when John and Bobby Kennedy were assassinated. Yet Ivanhoe has presented convincing evidence that, if true, will mean history books would have to be rewritten. Again, there are those who would stand to lose if the facts of Ivanhoe's information become public knowledge. So, again, what does the public have a right to know?

"One inquiry from three different sources challenged the compromising evidence that the government has known about alternative fuel sources for years. Ivanhoe has indicated there is information that should be brought forward, but would those who stand to lose a lot—the oil companies—ever want any of this brought to the light of day? Again, what does the public have a right to know?

"Consider, if you will, the disruption of the world economy if facts such as these were there for public consumption. And what would any of this do to sow the seeds of doubt about our own government and the entities that stand to lose the public trust? Ivanhoe has sent twelve letters with a plethora of information, damning facts, directions to find corroborating evidence and simply asks, what should the public know without compromising national security or any military secrets?

"So, in capsule form, our job is to research all these inquiries to see what any of these so-called 'interested parties' are up to and what they stand to lose. For the most part we can search the internet and get background checks, but there will be times when we must go outside of our own safety box and follow with inquiries on our own. That is where possible leaks and threats may come from. We must be careful and must, always, cover each other's backs.

"We have other people researching in the National Archives, the Library of Congress, the FBI. We are not cloak and dagger, but data collectors. I urge all of you to document what you are doing and for each pod to stay tight on its area. We will meet from time to time to analyze all our efforts. As I said, when new inquiries come up, you will be notified and perhaps assigned new territory. You all have been given encrypted laptops and passcodes. These are considered top of the line, including hacker barriers. If you encounter any potential hacks, report those immediately. Each of you has been given a code name and none of your real names ever will appear, should data be compromised."

The room was silent.

"Are there any questions?"

"How long do we have to finish any investigations?" asked one of the group.

"This is an open-ended project, as new inquiries certainly will be made by those who feel threatened about being found out."

"What about media leaks?" asked another.

"We can't control any of that, so if we see or hear them, we claim ignorance. I doubt we will be asked about anything anyway since we will be ghosts. The president may well be called out from time to time and he will have to figure if he can share or simply avoid really answering questions—something politicians are really good at."

One could see inquiring minds were formulating their own ideas and conclusions with a sense of cautious urgency. Crockett, who had been through numerous wars and struggles, was pleased with his assembled team. His smile was reassuring, and the would-be questers were relishing their work ahead.

"Well, then, let's take stock of what we have to do. Read the briefing book and let me know if you have any questions. I know this is a good team; let's show everyone just how good we are."

"According to Liz, she got an earful from Henry Glenn, oil industry lobbyist and Murray Bloom, who has pharmaceutical-industry ties, as well as House Speaker John Fishel, Congressmen Alan Troy and Les Slone, and Senator Jackie Hansen."

CHAPTER 53

Jim Fox and President McCade Assess Numerous Inquiries

As expected, the queries ramped up and the trickle became a stream. Liz Cookson got the bulk of the initial inquiries, but some spilled over to the White House. That was not what the president wanted with an already full plate. Senators, representatives, and even some lobbyists who felt they had privileges as donors to a political cause or campaign, were on the charge. Fox was able to deflect most of the snoops, but it was only a matter a time before he would have to meet with the president to plan another strategic course correction.

Their seven a.m. meeting was going to be filled with even more clutter, something they were used to when political decisions and strategies demanded they be on the same page. This was different because politics wasn't the issue, but rather power and trust in the government were front and center.

"John, Liz says she's being hammered by people from all over about some internal investigations," said Fox as the two were alone in the president's study off the Oval Office, away from the hustle of the goings-on outside. "People are hitting me too, and as we have said before, this probably will intensify scrutiny from the media pretty soon. Who is punching us from behind? I'm worried about others jumping on the bandwagon to get in front of cameras or see their names in print."

"I agree, Jim, and I know we have to have deniability to some extent. We need to know what is going on from the investigations, but not know all the details yet. Have you talked to Brumfield and Crockett? I think they are the ones leading the charge at Archives and the Bureau?"

"I have a meeting with Spence today, and Matt said he would be able to come down from Boston later this week. I like keeping in touch with some key people as the need arises. They want an audience with you. I have pushed them off as best I can. I suspect they will apply pressure on other outlets, so what we expected would happen appears to be a gathering storm."

"Well, we're just going to have to get some facts and see where the hell they are going with their demands," said the president somewhat grimly.

"How do we keep putting them off?" asked Fox. "Some of the verbal discord borders on disruptive behavior, something the country has seen enough of, given political differences. The fact you have a good relationship with both sides of the aisle probably has toned it down, but if some of these so-called friends in Congress start wanting answers that we have no intention of giving them, will we face enough hostility that the know-it-alls in the media will start a range war?"

"I guess we should plan for that," McCade said. "I would like to think we could take our allies into our confidence, but leaks are bound to happen, especially when you consider the information, and given the quest for power and retaining it. All bets could be off pretty soon. I do have a concern that Spence, Brumfield, Bailey and Zach may face backlash because some people will do anything to protect their interests or shield others."

"The Bureau as well as some of our other agencies have been informed, so wouldn't all of them be there to protect not only the Four, but their teams as well?"

"I would like to think so, but if any of these investigations start pointing fingers in any of the wrong directions, any agency might not be as protective as we would think. Look at it this way: if the Bureau had knowledge of what really happened in the Kennedy assassinations, the murder of Martin Luther King and other suspicious deaths, who would stand to lose if the facts were known? And the government would be blamed as well. Even those who are still alive that were a part of the Warren Commission or the people who did the autopsy on the president would be hounded, if not threatened. I understand the sanctity of secrecy and a nondisclosure or the more powerful confidential disclosure agreement, so we need to be aware of those kinds of documents.

"And that is what this Ivanhoe person has said all along," Fox said.

"From what I have read, Ivanhoe has the information, and Crockett and Brumfield have their teams digging while Bailey is the conduit with this Ivanhoe person. It would be good to actually meet Ivanhoe, but I suspect that never will happen, from what I gather. Bailey has been torn between her sitting as a Supreme and acting as a citizen wanting to do what is right and proper. How could any rational person not want to do the right thing?"

"But the bottom line, John, is that these inquiries aren't going to stop as more leaks come forward. I hate to think of this as a war, but there are a lot of risks to consider and I sincerely hope nothing of strategic importance surfaces that demonizes the government."

"Jim, these facts were suppressed long before we were here, so our best bet is to compartmentalize whatever is leaked and keep kicking the can down the road. The American people will understand if the truth helps settle some conspiracies and that we would all come together. Closure might heal a lot of wounds"

"But if the government willingly suppressed cures for cancer and other catastrophic diseases, or knew about alternatives to current fuel sources that meant millions to a select few and added to pollution, I think the public would be outraged. And we're the ones who will be called on the public carpet. The court of public opinion can be a dangerous one to gauge. Do you really expect we, as the captains of the good ship America, will be given a pass?"

The perplexed look on both men said it all.

"Are you going to address any such questions if they come up Thursday at your weekly briefing?"

"I guess yes, but it depends on who's asking the questions. There are some media types that will not want the can to be kicked down the road. I just imagine how something like this would be if we didn't have a high favorability rating and a somewhat trusting relationship with the media. From my point of view, we haven't lied about anything or even misled anyone, but I don't want to hit an iceberg either."

The Thursday morning White House press briefing began with the usual domestic and international questions, but then Charles Wingo from CNN raised his hand, got acknowledged and threw the first salvo.

"Mr. President, we've heard some rumors about inquiries into the FBI and National Archives about historical facts. Can you comment on that and where those inquiries are going?"

McCade was never shy about responding and was quick on his feet. Even the most stupid questions always got an answer. But it was the questioners that he internally seethed about, people either not knowing the facts or those making them up for grandstanding purposes. The media always could go through internal channels, like contacting Jim Fox, but it was the "look at me" attitude that McCade loathed inwardly. McCade got along with most of the media, but things didn't sit well with him and Wingo, a self-styled wannabe Pulitzer Prize nominee. While McCade addressed most of the media by first names, he didn't with Wingo.

"Mr. Wingo, we've heard the same rumors as maybe some of you have, but under FOIA, anyone can check records."

"But Mr. President, doesn't it concern you that someone might be digging where they shouldn't be? And can we talk to these people?"

"Mr. Wingo, the FOIA was established in 1966 for the express purpose of allowing any citizen to search for anything. That act protects citizens as well as the government, and some documents are redacted for that very reason. As for talking to those people searching for whatever, there have been and will be countless inquiries by people to explore as they wish. And those people are not under any order to answer any questions if they so choose."

Now somewhat put off, Wingo blurted out, "Isn't the White House somewhat curious as to what is being done in this case?"

"It's a free country, Mr. Wingo. Next question?"

Seeing none and with the room in near silence after the brief exchange with Wingo, the president simply said, "Thank you for being here, and have a pleasant day."

CHAPTER 54

Fox Meets with Stuart Bach

Stuart Bach, president and CEO of Orin Pharmaceuticals, was a fourth-generation administrator of the family's business. He, like his father and past patriarchs of the family, was well known in the pharma research arena and often stepped into the political parade with donations to certain candidates. He did speak his mind. With his connections, valuable information about congressional inquiries or other research was somewhat easily available, allowing him to plan a defense or divert what would be a train wreck elsewhere. Whereas his father Sterling simply made a phone call to get what he felt he needed, Stuart was on someone's doorstep and not always welcome.

As a rather large donor to the president's war chest over the years, Bach had access, but only through Jim Fox. They had gone to school together. While Fox had gone on to get his medical degree, Bach had chosen to follow the family business in pharmaceuticals, earning doctorates along the way. Fox was always amenable to taking Bach's calls and often made sure Bach was on the social list when the president entertained people at a White House function or elsewhere.

It came as little surprise that Fox's private line identified the caller as Stuart Bach. While time was short this day, Fox felt an obligation to at least get a whiff of what Bach had to say. He well knew it had to have something to do with the recent leaks about the pharmaceutical industry and its hold on cures for any one of a number of catastrophic diseases, cancer being at the top of the list. He was ready for what he hoped would be a short discussion, as meetings were scheduled the rest of the day and there was little time for chitchat. After the third blink and soft-toned beep, Fox opened the conversation with a phrase he had picked up from the president.

"Stu, what's going?"

"Foxy, need to meet, offline if possible."

"May I ask why, and why offline?"

"Better left for a private discussion."

"Well, not here, then. How about an out-of-the-way place, knowing someone probably would be tailing us. I certainly will have the Service with me and I suspect you might have a security person around you. Restaurant or public place?"

"Either works for me."

"How about the Archives building? We can get a private room after we meld into the general traffic. With our people watching our backs, they would see if there are any tails."

"Good. What's your schedule, since you always seem to be booked 24/7?"

"How about Saturday at 9:45? More people. The president is out of town until Monday at Camp David, so we can meet, disappear, and then reappear."

"See you Saturday."

Having mixed with the usual Saturday crowd at the Archives building, Fox had connected with Anita Wright at nine-thirty and was ready for a staff member to recognize Bach, who was wearing a Go Irish green button. The Notre Dame football team was playing Syracuse that day in Nationals Park. Fox, Bach, and their security people were ushered into Wright's personal conference room. Fox asked for the two security team members to wait in the outer reception area. Coffee and tea were available at the intimate table that normally would seat six.

"So, what's so important that we need to meet in a somewhat clandestine manner?" asked Fox, knowing full well what was going to be discussed.

"Jim, my intelligence people have informed me that the government is looking into the pharmaceutical industry for a variety of reasons, and I need to know what to expect."

"Stu, the industry has been under quasi-investigation for several years, mainly due to the high cost of drugs and whether the pharmaceutical companies have a monopoly on what is available."

"This has always been a case of supply and demand, but you well know research sucks up a lot of our dollars—government or privately funded. What

I have heard lately, though, is that someone is snooping into specific cures, cancer being number one on the hit parade."

"That would be a logical inquiry, but how does that affect the government and specifically the president?"

"My information goes further, that the government is looking into whether the industry has suppressed possible cures for cancer for the good of profits."

"Is that true, Stu?"

"I can say we have developed several cures for all sorts of diseases, including Ebola and influenzas. We have done a lot of research on cancer. I can say we feel we are on the verge of a more aggressive cure for almost all, but aside from getting FDA approval, we are simply playing a waiting game."

Fox pressed on. "Without going into detail here, we have come by some information from an outside source that purports that there has been a cure for cancer for years and that the industry has suppressed same. This information, if substantiated, says there is proof of several government secrets that have been held back for any one of several reasons. It's not only the pharmaceutical industry we are talking about here, Stu. This information digs into energy, assassinations, and facts that would question history as we know it."

Bach almost dropped his coffee cup, aghast at what Fox just told him. "How is anything like this believable?"

"Can you look me in the eye and tell me you do not have a cure for cancer and other diseases that could rid the world of early death and grief? Can you imagine if the informant's allegations are proved to be totally true? The pharmaceutical companies would be overrun by angry humans around the world."

"Perhaps you should ask your informant to prove it."

"Are you saying you do not have an absolute cure for cancer?"

"As I mentioned, we have helped in the treatment of many cancers. As new diseases come up, research kicks into high gear to see what works and what doesn't. Think of the chemo and radiation treatments, even stem cell applications, that have helped us make great strides. The industry is vast, and I can't speak for all. I just know that we are on the cusp of some great discoveries. But if other cures are available, then I don't know of them."

"So why this meeting, why the concern from your end?"

"If wrong or misinterpreted information gets out for public view, we could be ruined. Not only would that hit research, but it might cause even more deaths because people wouldn't trust what is available, even if experimental. R and D requires a lot of time and money."

"We all recognize the great work done in research, but where does the accounting for R and D start and stop?" Fox sighed. "Well, I can tell you, Stu, that this is not a government inquiry. The president knows of some people who are working under FOIA, and anyone is free to do so at any time when information reaches the unclassified threshold. As I said, these investigations deal with more than whether there is a cure for cancer.

"I can also say the president is concerned about what the public has a right to know. As we get more information, be it from the informant's hypothesis, suggestions, or perhaps just plain facts, are we to simply let it all hang out there for everyone to see? The president and others who know about the investigation are worried about how we would handle the newly discovered info on assassinations, energy sources, and whatever."

"I'm concerned about all of that as well," said Bach, now leaning forward. "But I am focused on my company and industry. To think it could be wiped out with unsubstantiated facts or misinformation, it's devastating to even consider."

"We haven't reached critical mass, but I suspect the inquiries are going to lead us to somewhere—and fast. I do not want the president to be caught unaware of whatever is being investigated through FOIA. I would hope that if your company has any information on research, either by you or others, that you could at least give us a summary, so we are not caught short."

"Will you let me know if my industry is about to get tarred and feathered?"

"Yes, I can keep you in the loop. But I need to know if there are land mines with some of your cohorts."

"I'm not sure how I can do that if I don't bring them into the conversation. How do you want to handle that?"

"You might make discreet inquiries to those who you know best and ask if they have heard anything about people looking for information through FOIA."

"And for those in far-away lands?"

"All bets are off there. I suspect they would play this closer to the vest because none of them are under our laws and confidences. They certainly wouldn't willingly give up what they feel is proprietary information. Especially if they also are on the cusp of a more concrete solution to eradicating something as deadly as cancer."

Glancing at his Fitbit watch with all the extras, Fox said he was on-the-go to a meeting with a cabinet member. The two met up with their security details and were off into the light of the overcast Saturday. Bach was looking forward to seeing the unbeaten Irish take on the once-beaten Orangemen of Syracuse.

CHAPTER 55

Stewart Contemplates Next Ivanhoe Letter

Three months had passed since Bailey Stewart had received an Ivanhoe letter, leading her to think the connection had been broken. Her work as part of the Four continued, but with so many tangents now a part of the mix, she was anxious to get some direction, or at least some clarification. Her last cryptic message simply said "Doubters Prevail." She would have to wait for a response.

Consumed with the court's docket and the time needed to balance her professional with her private time, Stewart made another plea to hear from Ivanhoe, this time stating "Proof Wins." She had invested way too much time to not see this through, and now with more people involved in the quest, she was determined to push herself to the limits. She, like the rest of her team, was getting not-so-subtle inquiries about what they were up to, but some of those suggestions were a bit more threatening. The president, kept advised through Jim Fox, had a stake as well.

Was Ivanhoe going to be the savior? She certainly hoped so. She not only enjoyed the Ivanhoe letters, but came to use them as a guide. Was there something else to know, more historical facts to be divulged and perhaps more disgruntled people out there who were not about to let any of those secrets destroy their financial or power positions?

Stewart was anxious to see the next chapter in what was becoming a best-selling book—figuratively, not literally.

Friday evening had arrived and a somewhat weary Justice Stewart slipped into her Lincoln Continental with Yates at the wheel. Seeing her sigh deeply when she settled into the back seat, he started a conversation.

"You seem exhausted or frustrated," said Yates, looking into the rearview mirror, eyeing her head resting against the seat. "Anything you want to chat about?"

"Yates, I've shared with you this Ivanhoe story of stories since it all began almost two and a half years ago. I was skeptical, but interested. The letters were intriguing for sure, but they wound up being a 'want to know more' exercise. That, coupled with the cases we have with the court, have drained me. My first obligation is to the court, so this 'project,' as I would call it, has seemingly sucked up all my energy and free time. About seven thousand cases are submitted to the court each year, and only eighty or so get to oral arguments. But the justices, or better yet our staffs, read maybe one hundred fifty cases a week. I don't want to get sidetracked here; if Ivanhoe were a case, I could allow the time to be attentive. It certainly appeals to me for a variety of reasons. But it's a distraction.

"My concern now, though, is that someone might force the fight, because the litigation quite possibly could reach SCOTUS. I'm trying not to be paranoid, but I haven't heard from this Ivanhoe person in over three months and now I wonder if there is anything more. I need to tend to my main responsibilities, yet follow my curiosity. And my need to know may well result in the need to make a decision on what I think the public's right to know should or could be. To make matters worse, we expect to get some inquiring minds leaning on any one if not all of us. There is a fire coming and I'm not sure where it might spread."

"Are you in any danger or fear that someone might take it out on you or any of the four of you?" asked Yates.

"That has crept into the conversation. I guess knowing more from Ivanhoe might help eliminate some of that angst. I'm not trying to be esoteric, but it's a matter of knowing the unknown. I've shared with you the factoids as presented by Ivanhoe. Some such facts seem to be a tad preposterous. The ones the general population might be most interested in—like the Kennedys, medical research, fuel sources, extraterrestrials—would make for some interesting conversations, but could also cause a gigantic uproar from a lot of people who might feel as if they had been had."

"So, you believe what Ivanhoe has said and you're willing to stand up and shout it to the world?"

"Not sure I would be the one to shout that out. But if someone asks the president about any of this, he is going to have to be ready with some quick responses. You can bet the media will make it a circus. Whether those in the shadows ever let this happen is an unknown.

"The court's business keeps me busy and I rely on my team to keep me on schedule, so maintaining the pace with other distractions has been the biggest challenge of my life. I guess I expect Ivanhoe to keep supplying more and more facts. But I haven't had any communication for quite a while and that has bothered me. I wonder if I should be concerned."

"Not if you get another letter. I understand not seeing an even flow of information, like you have with your court cases, but do you really think Ivanhoe has hung it up?"

"No, but I do wonder why the gap."

Now nearing eight o'clock and the drawbridge that led to the Longfellow estate, Yates understood Stewart's dilemma. He drove her to the walkway that led to the front of the estate, and there stood Zach. Yates helped Bailey out of the car and drove to his quarters on the side.

"You're back early from Zurich, everything go okay?" she said, her eyes showing some sparkle while her body looked weary.

"Wrapped up early and decided to get home for an entire weekend." The two moved to the family room and their two favorite chairs. "You look a little tired. How about a glass of your favorite?"

"You had me at 'you.'"

"Before you tell me about your week, I have something for you."

She suspected she was about to get a gift, like a necklace or something sparkly, but Zach returned with an envelope. The tiredness seemed to go away, and Bailey got her adrenaline fix.

CHAPTER 56

Ivanhoe Letter—13

Dear Justice Stewart:

Did you miss me?

Have to assume the gremlins are running and that people must be coming out of the woodwork because they feel a threat to their money and/or power base. I can assume they will become even more of a nuisance and distraction. My advice is to hold them off by whatever means necessary.

Some people stand to lose money, power, and trust. The assassinations and other dirty deeds are a part of the political fabric in DC and elsewhere. Some, like the assassinations, occurred more than fifty years. What did each of these killings do for the flow of money, power, and trust? Sure, history would—and will be—rewritten. The players of that day are gone or out of the way and there are new people on the scene. If the public becomes outraged that its own government had a hand—indirect or not—in eliminating someone, then someone is going to be held accountable. Consider the assassination of President Lincoln. Who pays for the real truth? The government.

I daresay that when the real facts are known about medical science there will be outrage against people of today, even though they did not start the process. They have kept the light hidden for many years. Fair? Hell no!

As for energy, I would guess the environmentalists would howl first, but how about the people who have been gouged with gas and oil prices all these years? And think, too, about how the world economy would be flipped if a lot of machinery suddenly became obsolete. Machinery now dependent on oil products would be run by clean and more efficient processes.

The fact aliens probably were here would freak out a lot of people. I, for one, welcome a personal visit because I am intrigued by out-of-our-world beings. Extraterrestrials already brought some things to the table that I guarantee most people wouldn't believe. In my wildest dreams I cannot believe the knowledge of our ancestors was so advanced that they were seemingly better off than we are today. I get the technology with computers and innovations, but you must admit that there is more than coincidence that history shows that ancient peoples were highly motivated and skilled. I don't think the pyramids were the thought of someone who conjured up how and where to build such masterpieces.

I am not for a new world order, just something that sets the record straight. I do not care about today's politicians spewing whatever ideology. This is about history and our chance to know how it all happened. With some of that we get to the why, rather than the how. Why did history record things that weren't true? Must be, presumably, money, power, and trust.

So, when these servants of "let's keep this to ourselves" come along, I would not be intimidated. That's easy for me to say, since you and your teams may well bear the brunt of threats or perhaps embarrassment. But as I have said, if any of the team gets such threats, I will release everything, and the fingers won't be pointed at you but at those who have something to lose.

And believe me, I'm watching.

When I get to it, hopefully soon, I'll lay some more interesting tidbits on you. You think you are interested now—wait until the new news about old facts.

Keep in touch. And stand your ground.

IVANHOE

After two readings and including Zach in each page, she gave a deep sigh and asked if he was up for a swim. The weather outside was cold, but their indoor pool was well heated. They shed their clothes and took a dip.

Ivanhoe Doubles Down—14

Dear Justice Stewart:

Got to thinking, after sending my last letter, that one of the most poignant questions that probably would be asked is "who cares?" If some or all of this factual information were out there for public consumption, would there be a demand for some sort of justice, followed by government hearings, or just shock and outrage? From those who lived through the country's personal tragedies to those who learned of them through history books, just how would we deal with it? Conspiracy theorists would be leading the charge, but to what end?

J. Edgar Hoover is the key to this whole collection of information. He had over a million files that went along several tangents, not only political. He gained information through a bevy of agents, connections, and informants. He liked being the person in the know and didn't particularly care if anyone else knew that. I even gave consideration to him being the one who came up with the term "need to know."

So, back to the original premise of this letter. Just how many people really care? Some individuals who still play in the game probably would be threatened. Companies that have fleeced humanity over whatever number of years might be concerned. Historians probably would rush to rewrite some aspects of history. Conspiracy folks would let loose with all the "told you so's" and go on TV, radio, social media and the lecture circuit and ramp up the drumbeat about government lying, cheating, and misuse of the truth.

While the public is always consumed with the here and now and an explanation of how, why, and what just happened, time marches on and facts gets distorted and interest wanes. When I got all of this information I was overwhelmed. I'm still overwhelmed. These "I'm in it for myself" people will stop at nothing to preserve their position. They simply want all of us to let it all go away. Why besmirch individuals, organizations, even our own government?

What I would suggest is for you to talk to someone in the energy field who would give you the straight skinny on what they know about the trends in industry, and if they know of innovations that have filtered through research but have been held from public view. At least you would have some background when these hypocrites come knocking at your team's collective doors.

Call this another industrial revolution—and that would be our fourth. The internet certainly changed the way we do business. The oil companies are faced with not being included in the next true wave of transportation or machinery, for that matter. Fission, fusion, electricity through solar means will rule the world in the not too distant future. Think OPEC is worried? World monetary systems would change and the oil producing nations would become sand. And as I mentioned before, with oil products, machinery would have to be retooled to accommodate the new processes.

This brings me to other considerations. Will we even have cars in the future? That should help car manufacturers. I doubt movie theaters will be in vogue much longer as people stream apps and movies on their future iPhone upgrades. That should do well for the distribution companies that rake in about 50 percent of the revenue from movies.

Where does that lead us? Back to who would care? The general population would consume and pay whatever price"

Hoover, for all of his idiosyncrasies and paranoia, was smart and covered his tracks. I daresay he knew about all of this because of his connections. He was smart enough to have all of his files digitalized, and my source was at the right place at the right time to take the handoff and then make another handoff to me. Am I fortunate? Perhaps. But I do not want someone chasing me either.

The world has been moving at a quickened pace. Some people are willing to take an aggressive leap without knowing they may be jumping into quicksand. Look before you leap?

Think, too, of medical science as the world population expands because of research and discoveries. I contend that we have been held back. Hopefully we watch our population and expect to live longer. For those who have eradicated populations through mysterious diseases, get ready for your own doomsday. The Hoover files have it and you're about to get it.

I guess I've said enough. But I am one who does and will care. So be ready for some more of what we know and should have known—a long time ago.

Sincerely,

IVANHOE

CHAPTER 57

The Plot Thickens

It wasn't unusual for the senate majority leader or the speaker of the house to go to the White House to meet with the president. It was highly unusual when the two came at the same time to meet with the chief of staff. But there they were—Majority Leader Bob French and Speaker John Fishel—arriving for a planned three p.m. meeting with Jim Fox. President McCade had a commitment to speak at the Naval Academy and asked the two leaders if Fox could sit in for him. They shared a trust that all would be heard.

Retiring to the Cabinet Room and out of the way of prying eyes, the three helped themselves to their favorite beverages and settled into three chairs at the end of the long table. Fox, being polite and hospitable, started the conversation with, "What is this rush to meet, even if the president isn't here?"

"Jim, we wouldn't have pushed this if we didn't need to get out in front of what could be a real mess," said Fishel, a thirty-year congressman from New York who had been that body's leader for the past twelve. "Bob and I have been getting some rather intriguing if not puzzling inquiries from some pretty high-end constituents about government inquiries that may well threaten some valuable companies.

"All of this goes with the territory, and not only do constituents feel they have easy access, but donors and those who think they rule the world lay into us all the time. However, when we cannot have an open conversation with all of these people or their concerns, we feel it is our responsibility to find out what is going on. It's not like we're faced with an alien invasion. So, this is a conversation about whether there is something we need to know, even if it's off the record, so we can be ready for what may come—hopefully not a train wreck."

"We've been getting our own share of taps," offered Fox. "We are listening, but these inquiries are not our doing, so I don't know where we can go with this. The president, like you, has a lot on his plate with domestic and international issues. But believe me, this is not a government push."

French countered with media attention, more recently from the likes of CNN's Charles Wingo, who was by far the biggest nonelected grandstander in DC. "We need to know what is going on, Jim, and if the president doesn't know, then who does?"

"I didn't say that," said Fox. "The president is aware of some rumors and knows there are people following their own leads under FOIA. If a media frenzy erupts, people like Wingo will be on a soapbox and making it tough sledding for all of us."

"From what we've heard, these inquiries could shed some bad light on, even cripple or eliminate important companies," said Fishel. "If those inquiries continue, could we stop them through legislation?"

"I daresay that FOIA would stop any pushback from an overly watchful government," said Fox. "What are you wishing for?"

"Bob and I have talked about this and it seems that someone is digging into energy and medical fields and those are two of the biggest industries this country has," Fishel replied. "I guess our immediate concern would be for our country's industries. We already face a jobs issue. What would our country and economy look like if automation and industry transformations land a sucker punch on all of us?

"If we lose one major industry, we stand a chance of catastrophe. We aren't naïve enough to think industries won't adjust to technology, but it is inconceivable that major ones like energy and medical would be tossed to the side of the road."

Fox, trying to keep a positive outlook, responded with, "The president is aware of our challenges, both foreign and domestic, and legislation that facilitates our core values for the immediate if not near future has to be pushed. The same problematic concerns are front and center—health care, taxes, immigration, mental health, national debt, and welfare. The country seems ready to take care of people, and we don't want to implode. These inquiries into facts of the past may well disturb enough people to say they lack trust in the government.

"The fact you are both with the majority party in government, along with the president, probably helps. Knowing the president has always sought middle ground and a chance to find reasonable solutions to all of our problems is at least comforting."

"Is there anything you can tell us about these inquiries, anything that would give us some basis for doing our own investigations?" said Senate Majority Leader French. "The House has a more direct connection to its constituents, and when money, power and trust are concerned, we, the electeds, are going to get blamed for everything."

"We all are on the block when blame is distributed," said Fox. "Unfortunately, not everyone knows the backstories, and politically, that is a matter of leverage. Throw in the media and we are all going to get tapped."

"That brings up a good question," said French. "How do we respond to media inquiries? 'No comment' only goes so far. If we are open with our friends on the other side of the aisle, leaks are bound to happen. Look what's happened here with our first wave of inquiries. We have a good working relationship with our colleagues, but when there's a chance to gain an edge, the loyal opposition may well look for a political advantage."

"So, where does that leave us, gentlemen?" said Fox. "I guess we need to see what the president feels would be best and if we need to expand our list of confidants. Leaks are bound to happen, so we need to be aware of what answers we are willing to provide. That includes dealing with the media and any conspiracy theorists."

"Will you convey our concerns and let the president know we have kept him in our loop?" said Fishel.

"That I will do. I will brief the president on our conversation and then plan on periodic updates with at least the two of you."

"Thanks, Jim," said Fishel. "We need to stay ahead of this or all hell will break loose, and we stand to lose a lot—all of us."

Handshakes all around, and the two congressional leaders left the White House grounds. Their limos were at the gates, and there was Charles Wingo waiting with his film crew, along with other news outlets, sniffing a story, perhaps a Pulitzer Prize.

CHAPTER 58

President and Fox Morning Meeting

Their jobs were anything but boring or uneventful. "Normal" was not a word they used. General sighs, rolling of the eyes, and brief signs of temper were commonplace. Perfection was not attainable, but excellence and satisfaction were.

President John McCade and his trusted chief of staff Jim Fox were great listeners, able to control knee-jerk reactions and be civil even with those they privately loathed. In political circles, there always were those who thought they knew better. Opposing ideologies had their place. Conversations were to be a give and take. Add in the lawyers and lobbyists and special interest groups and you had a quagmire known as Washington, DC. It was a city where deals often were made for the benefit of relatively few.

McCade surmised he had friendly ears and eyes from nearly all who came to the seat of world government, at least from the political side. The United Nations was considered a collection of countries gathered to talk and perhaps to listen once in a while, and everyone held their collective breaths that the countries of the world would abide by general rules of trade, health, and mutual understanding.

McCade and Fox were braced for another early-morning meeting before each were off to a number of carefully planned meetings and appearances.

"Jim, I know you briefed me on your meeting with Fishel and French, but I just got wind of Mike Manchester at CIA and Dan Sweeney at NSA wanting a word," said McCade. "Are there that many leaks that people from all sides suddenly want to have some audience to see what we're doing? I thought Fishel and French would handle all of that. Did you tell them this isn't our doing?"

"I assured them the inquiries were coming from other sources and were well within FOIA," said Fox. "I think they got it. I told them if we learned something that was particularly important, we would let them know."

"But now the CIA and NSA are getting their hair messed and we just don't have time to monitor all of this," countered McCade. "I'm trying to get this e-waste legislation passed, to say nothing of the bipartisan bill for the parameters for the pharmaceutical industry. Just how many other distractions can we handle right now?"

"This isn't going away, and while we both know it has important implications for a lot of individuals as well as companies and industries, we need show some good faith with those in the need-to-know category," responded Fox.

"I really do not want to get into daily briefings with Mike and Dan, although they're good friends and have the best of intentions," said McCade, with a sigh. "I expect they'll be relentless now that they feel they have some skin in the game."

"I don't think they'll stop with just me meeting with them. You want me to set up a meeting?"

"I suppose so, but I am not inclined to open up to them," said McCade, shaking his head.

"Speaking of pending legislation, how is that e-waste proposal going? From the original white paper, it sounded pretty promising."

"I advised Fishel and French on the basic elements and now Frenchy said he has met with some concerns. I am going to push this, and Fishel and French said they would take the lead."

"What's the pushback?"

"We presented the facts. The world produces over forty-five million tons of e-waste every year. Some of that is recycled, some goes into landfill. The losers in this are the developing nations where most of the e-waste is dumped. While it isn't illegal to export used items like refrigerators, radios, TVs and such to wherever, sending some forms of e-waste is. But the conniving people who work the system and cut corners and don't give a damn about harming people and the land. Scavengers break down those components and make money by mining precious metals such as gold, silver, and copper from them.

"What this legislation proposes is that we keep those e-waste discards here, protect those who break down the components, pay them a living wage AND allow them to get a piece of the captured materials in the form of a bonus or profit sharing. The scenario would mean more jobs, a good work environment, less true waste into our landfills, and a chance for developing nations to save their lands."

"So, what's the argument against?"

"Potential carcinogens and other health issues for any workers, and of course, more crap thrown into our landfills."

"So those people are all for the developing countries facing a losing scenario when we have the technology and ability to eliminate some world pollution? I'm all for the elimination of pollution to our rivers, streams, and land. I know scientists are close to eliminating unwanted pollution with new technology.

"We have some of this technology in place now and we are close to minimizing a lot of our public waste, even regular trash. This is a world problem and maybe this country needs to take the lead. Will new technology cost our country jobs or create new ones through retraining?"

"That brings us back to the main issue with what Bailey Stewart and her team started and we now are a part of—what does the public have a right to know?" said McCade.

"Stewart has been a proponent in letting the public know, but when someone stands to lose something big time, then you get a beehive humming.

"I am not sure people will be as excited about industrial waste, since we all put out our trash every week and it just goes away," Fox said, knowing the president was hell bent on passing the e-waste legislation. "I agree with you that if something like e-waste was targeted and we stepped up the pace to do it on our own, I think the world would notice."

"That's why I am pushing this legislation, so that people will take notice and offer other options that might work as well."

The informative hour had passed and the two were destined for more intrigue. That meant more listening, controlled dialogue, and a chance to see what those with opposing views might have to offer.

CHAPTER 59

The Hoover File Memo

In Hoover's time, it was a common practice for executives, doctors, scientists, and other people involved in a lot of projects to write file memos to clarify recollections before the maze of everyday happenings piled on. The human mind stores a lot of information, but tapping into specific details at a moment's notice tended to be frustrating. So file memos, enhanced through technology and internet, had become the norm.

J. Edgar Hoover, a collector, if you will, was perhaps the greatest hoarder of information. He had his sources and then he had those who simply wanted to gift him knowledge. As an old timer he stuck to the written accounts, but later he was savvy enough to have it all digitalized and saved from prying eyes. He even had all of it encrypted.

Casey and Jenny were doing their due diligence with the Hoover files. The work was painstaking, as a lot of the information they were referencing was about people, places, and things they never heard of. Like the reference to Viktor Karimkosky or even Russian clandestine efforts to eliminate certain portions of its own and other populations.

But with hand on head and reaching the end of the day, Jenny stumbled onto a file that was labeled simply "file memos." How quaint, she thought. Sifting through perhaps twenty-five or so pages, there was one that jumped out at her. It appeared to be a letter to the director *from* the director. She called Casey over, and they both read the single-spaced letter.

Dear Self:

I feel like I need to tell someone about what has become of a mass of collected information. I never intended to be a collector of so much material. As time marched on, information just flowed. I never thought of myself as a writer or historian. But when I was put in my position so long ago, I felt I needed to be inquisitive and back up things with facts. I do not intend to write a book or have someone write a book about me.

The two turned to each other simultaneously and shared inquisitive looks. Was this the Rosetta stone of what Hoover had wordcrafted into a world almanac about people, places, organizations, causes—whenever, wherever, whatever? The first paragraph felt like the prelude to opening a time capsule. Now really hooked, the two dove back into reading.

Maybe it was the old-school in me or what I was taught by my father, but I always took notes and then followed with a file memo as I recollected meetings or conversations. In my early days, writing was common. That gave way to recorders and eventually the modern age. I was reluctant to trust new technology, but as my cache of information grew and grew, I felt the need to back up everything I had. I trusted an inner circle of five individuals, but none of those people had full access; each had just 20 percent of all the files. I felt a need for secrecy, and I had come to be challenged from what seemed to be all sides. I actually felt someone might try to confiscate all that I had, or even have me eliminated—literally and figuratively. Yes, I probably pissed off some people along the way, but a man must protect himself both personally and professionally.

Am I ashamed of anything I have done, or collected or saved? Hell no. Those who outwardly called for my resignation or tried to defame me with insults, innuendoes and falsehoods, all will have to face up to the facts at some time. I trust those who have helped me back up my written files. I am not in this to threaten anyone or establish myself as someone who I am not. I took this job to uphold the law and I feel I have done that.

For those who might delve into all of my files, be aware that some things just don't pass the test for public consumption. That's my opinion, and the job of the FBI is to collect information, not judge people or whatever cause they represent. That is a job for the Department of Justice. As some of these files may well be incriminating, it becomes a process to verify. Have to admit, some of this stuff is startling and may well confuse some, but if Justice does its job, then the truth would be told.

When my team finished its work I think we determined there were well more than a million files. That surprised me. But imagine nearly fifty or even more years of documents, stories, pieces of evidence piling up. At one time I had all of my files in my office, but that became storage issue. A great deal of the files had to be stored off-site. I've kept the most secret of my information locked up here at the FBI headquarters. Not many people know that, and no one can get to those files except me.

I have information that has been part of the National Archives, CIA, NSA and any one of a number of government organizations, on or off the books. That includes a "Need to Know" section, and I had that because I needed to know, and every administration felt that was reasonable because we were in charge, as far as national boundary security.

I can't say I shared that information with anyone else on my staff through the years, but there may have been an occasion when a subject blared out at us that needed background, and I had it. So, for conversational purposes, I was in the know.

Few people know about all of the secret locations used by the government to store vital records, but like what I have, think about organizations you know and multiply that by twenty. Archives has at least seven locations that are tightly secured all over the United States. Technology has saved many of these documents through a backup system, so I welcomed myself to the new age.

File memos are a saving grace for me. I get to write what I want, when I want. No editing. Just notes. I was an anxious note taker in college and used that skill to organize important documents for future reference, if not simply for historical purposes.

I do not put myself above the law, and I believe everyone should be accountable for their actions. Have I made mistakes? Hell yes. Am I vindictive guy? Hell no. Do others want me out of the way? I don't think that perception is out of bounds. Search for the truth. Make rational judgments. I did, and I hope history will treat me and others fairly.

I have summarized some of the more mysterious documents. Some people will interpret some of these documents and have a different conclusion. It is okay for them to make their own judgments.

As if in a trance, Casey and Jenny were ready for more. The Hoover file memo went on to discuss some of the more recent transgressions, reminding them that more information would be divulged. Even answers to ancient history's unsolved mysteries that have haunted humankind for centuries might well be in the offing. They were not disappointed.

Ivanhoe's information had been corroborated. J. Edgar and his cache of files were real. The fact that a quarter of those written files had mysteriously disappeared after his untimely death started a chain reaction. Enter Ivanhoe, who had all of the Hoover information, saved for posterity through the forward thinking of using digital technology. That and the transfer of all of the files and the rest of the supposed government secrets from a perfect-storm data collection point to some unknown person, to Ivanhoe then to the Four, had perpetuated a thread that was to become a rope that could not be broken.

The two intrigued FBI agents drew back in their chairs, probably needing a drink. Their weeks and months of probing had paid great dividends. Early evening now upon them, they retired to the Benjamin Bar & Lounge inside the Luxe Hotel for some time to unwind. The jigsaw puzzle was about fitting the pieces, and they were on it. They could hardly wait to share their find and conclusions. The question was, to whom first?

CHAPTER 60

Disorder in the Court

As stated in the general job description for the solicitor general for the United States, it was Julia France's responsibility to review the more than seventy-five hundred or so petitions submitted and determine the legal position the United States might take, if any. In addition to supervising and conducting cases in which the government is a party, the office of the solicitor general also files amicus curiae briefs in cases in which the federal government has a significant interest.

In the federal courts of appeal, the office reviews cases decided against the United States and determines whether the government will seek review in the Supreme Court. The solicitor general's office also reviews cases decided against the United States in the federal district courts and approves every case in which the government files an appeal.

The somewhat overwhelming and perhaps intimidating responsibility of the office includes whittling down the original petitions to a mere seventy-five to one hundred twenty-five that are granted an endorsement of a petition for certiorari, and then are subject to review, oral or otherwise, by the nine justices. As might be expected, there are always issues that gain the public's eye and passion. While the office of the SG frequently has been referred to as the tenth justice, it is the work of the nine that counts.

France anticipated more than one petition from a lower court ruling for the now-growing cases involving government secrets. Individuals, special interest groups, even government agencies all had any "skin in the game." France may well have been in the crosshairs to determine who might object.

Reviewing the merits of seventeen such cases that had been submitted under the guise of "the right to know," she had summarized all, read her staff into each, and then made her formal recommendations to the court. A daunting task for sure, and possible repercussions awaited. She knew the law so she had to put her personal feelings aside as always, much like what is asked of the Supremes.

Bound by legal constraints, France had about six weeks to decide which cases moved forward. A petition seeking review of the final judgment by the court of last resort must be filed within ninety days of the entry of that judgment. So the appeal process becomes a fast-moving train, especially for those who have something to gain or lose.

The SG is treated like a judge and is expected to maintain legal standards. While some people have summarized Supreme Court decisions as being too conservative or liberal, it became a matter of one's own convictions that were expected of those sitting in judgment, either as individuals or part of a panel.

The term "ex parte" refers to a judge talking with an interested party about a particular case, and it is not allowed unless all parties are present and agree that it can take place. It does not matter whether or not one is a party to a case or a member of the public who has an interest in a particular case. That does not mean that no one can talk to a judge. But when it is under the guise of a personal relationship or the disclaimer of off-the-record comments, the ethical line becomes thin. Having prior or subsequent knowledge of a case and its elements would force a judge to recuse himself or herself, in the interests of justice.

Julia France felt cornered. Now faced with seventeen cases that all warranted further consideration and were interconnected, the decision to package all had to be an option. Her dilemma was that she could not seek outside counsel, not talk even casually with a member of the court. Yes, she had been contacted by outside sources, although they were friends and acquaintances, but she had to beg off discussing anything related to court matters because that would breach her ethical code of conduct. It was her decision to forward the cases deemed most worthy of final approval by the court. Of the initial applications, perhaps 10 percent made the final cut.

Her staff of four deputy solicitors general and seventeen assistants were ready for their Monday-morning briefing, one which would outline her take on which cases warranted further review. That list of nearly two hundred would be pared down after reasonable discussion by the group. France would have the final say, but the law remained the line in the sand.

The final list had been reduced to a reasonable one hundred five, less the seventeen that she felt needed careful consideration and should be packaged as one. Her own convictions aside, she had waited until the end of the preliminary discussion to focus squarely on what appeared to be a tug-of-war waiting to happen.

CHAPTER 61

An Old Friend Reaches Out to Judge Stewart

Daniel Paddington was a longtime friend of the family, as the Stewarts and Paddingtons had deep roots in Concord, California. Bailey and Dan both excelled in academics and gained full college scholarships. While Bailey chose her course to Harvard, Dan became a Georgetown man, bent on criminal defense. Both became attorneys and quickly were gobbled up by challenging law firms.

They stayed in touch over the years, exchanging Christmas cards, and their paths crossed at legal symposiums as well as some charitable events. Having shared study halls and commiserated from time to time as they experienced their high school, it was easy for them to communicate and share thoughts, feelings and even legal interpretations. They admired each other for their chosen specialties, and when Bailey went on to become a member of the land's highest court, Paddington was duly impressed.

It came as somewhat of a surprise when Paddington called her office. The message was delivered, and Bailey would return the call later in the day when there would be time to chat. To be sure, the life of any judge was hectic, but in the case of the Supreme Court, any staff was somewhat overwhelmed when messages simply got in the way of the daily routine. It was part of the puzzle, and it took a lot of coordination.

Now nearing five thirty, when normal business hours waned—although the court frequently saw those hours extend well past seven—Bailey seized the moment and figured she could catch Dan at his law firm working his own extended hours.

A familiar buzz and the caller ID let Dan Paddington know his lifelong friend Bailey Stewart actually had time to call him back. His "Well, good evening Your Honor" was followed with her "And you as well, Counselor. You left a message and I wanted to get back to you as soon as possible, since sometimes possible is impossible. What's up on your side of the swamp?"

"Thought we might get together for lunch. Know you always are busy, but I have something I want to discuss off-site, if possible."

"Anything we handle with a phone conversation or do we need to stay away from prying eyes and ears?"

"There are more prying eyes and ears in Washington than any other city in the land, perhaps the world. I'd like to have lunch to catch up on what is going on in our lives, but I do need your counsel, so you tell me the time and place and I will be there."

"Let me check with Alex and I'll get back to you as soon as possible. Things are starting to ramp up here, so time is measured in minutes."

Leonard's Backyard Bistro was a frequent lunch spot for those who weren't looking for the constant hustle and bustle of Old Ebbitt Grill. It catered to the who's who in Washington who had time for a quick lunch, not one that would last two hours. The two had met there a few times before, and management made sure there were some somewhat discreet places for two, three, or four people to meet with some semblance of quiet. Now settled in a booth in a windowless side of the bistro, Bailey checked her Fitbit, channeled her attention to Dan, and began the conversation.

"Your request sounded somewhat urgent, so I am intrigued. What's up?"

"We've known each other a long time and I certainly understand barriers, protocol and all that stuff," he said. "I've enjoyed my career and its challenges, but I feel like I am at a crossroads."

"How so, Dan? You've built a strong reputation with your work. How can you be at any crossroads? You're certainly not thinking of retiring?"

"No, this has to do with ethics." Her brow furrowed, but she quickly leaned back with her hands raised; no prejudgement intended.

"I'm all ears," she said.

"The legal profession certainly has its barriers and secrets, even if it means prosecuting or defending people you think are on the wrong side of the law or issue. Even the attorney–client privilege provision strikes a sensitive balance about what is right and wrong. My job—my mandate—is to provide the best defense for my clients, and I can truthfully say I have done so with honor over the years.

"What I am struggling with here has to do with litigation regarding the energy industry that has worked its way through the courts. While I don't have a direct connection, I anticipate I might have at some time. And, being aware of ex parte communication, I feel a need for my own clarity.

"One of my clients has strong ties to the automobile industry. I understand technology as it relates to this industry with electric, hybrid, solar, even hydrogen cars. Advancing technology makes it even more compelling to look ahead and be mindful of where to step. For that, I owe it to any client to provide the best possible advice. If innovative technology gets compromised because of litigation, will that directly affect some portions of the industry?

"Using those parameters, I'm in a quandary, looking out for my client as well as myself."

Fully attentive, Bailey weighed in. "Well, we both recognize our positions; ex parte guidelines prevail. However, it's not news to say the American public is waiting for an interpretation of whether there is a right to know. I can say the principles of the right-to-know decision will be monumental."

"Bailey, my client is afraid of being outed for having what may well be a truly innovative energy source that would affect how cars work. That could affect a lot of others in the automobile industry. The client could wait it out and see where litigation offers a acceptable solution or sell the patent. I'm of a mind to withdraw, sensing that I may face my own conflict of interest."

"I'm not sure what I can tell you to say to your client. To say someone in a particular industry is wrong might cost them the public trust and may lead to some disastrous consequences—maybe litigation or even industrial oblivion."

"I haven't read all of the lower court decisions and I would guess there is a lot of crossover—some for and some against—but this isn't just about money, although that is the major issue here. Luckily, I've been able to support and represent my clients, so I am torn between doing everything I can now to finish my intended responsibility."

"Trust me, Dan, being a judge has its potholes as well. As one of nine justices, we agree, we disagree, and we agree to disagree. This has become a perplexing problem with these seventeen cases that have been bunched together."

"So, what might you recommend, friend?"

"My best advice would be to sit down with your client and be open about it. It appears they have two choices—be forthcoming or wade through litigation. A crapshoot, for sure."

"How are you holding up?"

"A work in progress. We haven't gotten to a point of measuring the whole as the sum of its parts. We all know there is no appeal, so this becomes the precedent of precedents."

The hour and some minutes passed quickly, but the two friends felt comfortable discussing things that didn't need a collection of people who had a multitude of opinions. Theirs were the only ones that counted.

Yates was waiting to take Stewart back to the court for what promised to be a longer end of the day. Paddington had his driver ready to take him back to what he hoped were the friendly confines of Dickson, Strong & Paddington in the heart of the DC madhouse.

Each justice has law clerks that do research, including reading petitions of certiorari that have been divided amongst the participating justices. Clerks provide a brief memorandum and make recommendations as to whether a particular case merits further review. The nine review all recommendations during the Justices' Conference.

CHAPTER 62

The Bridge to Nowhere

As if the daily windmill of turmoil in Washington DC wasn't enough, the multitude of lawsuits staggered even the sanest in the legal field. But it was the bevy of pro and con petitions to the high court regarding what was perceived to the public's right to know that drew the strongest spotlight. The nine justices on the court had what may well have been the most important dilemma in recent times on their hands.

While most members of Congress were all too consumed with answering to their constituents and maintaining power in their own circles, the president as well as the court played a key role in seeing this hand played out. To some, trust in the government was held in the balance. Outrage to some was transparency to others. It was right versus fair.

From the original petitions first viewed by the solicitor general, reduced to what most people would consider reasonable at seventy-five, seventeen were segregated and held as one. The litigation process from the first petition had taken nearly two and a half years, and the other sixteen all pertained to the same subject—namely, what the public has a right to know. Petitions from any person or group that had a stake in what was deliverable had something to gain or lose. This was big time on the big stage. Ruling for or against affected them all, so the seventeen cases were hinging on the court's decision.

There weren't enough plumbers in DC to close off the leaks that came in abundance. Throw in some unfounded rumors, the media, some well-placed attorneys and special interest groups and lobbyists and you had chaos, which was Washington's answer to a bridge to nowhere. This was front and center to all.

Rarely were there any indications of what the court might decide, so speculation about the possible decision was left to the pundits and those who understood what might sway a ruling, based on the Constitution and legal precedent. Without knowing for sure, those pundits were sure there would be disorder in the court. And yet, when that final decision was rendered, those on the outside would have nowhere to turn. There was a lot of sweating going on from all sides.

The president was sitting in his study, sipping his coffee and looking out at the grounds of the White House on what was the beginning of a warm and beautiful day. A knock at the door was followed by permission to enter, and in walked Chief of Staff Jim Fox.

"What's going?" said McCade, knowing that there were a multitude of subjects they could and would talk about each day, depending on the calamity inside the nation's borders and in the rest of the world.

Fox cut to the chase. "John, the scuttlebutt from the court is that there may be a problem on the right-to-know case."

"And what would be the problem?" McCade quizzed.

"There are those who think there could be marches and possibly riots against any one of our government sectors, no matter what the decision. There have been many circulated rumors that have riled up many folks."

"I can't think of any precedent that would allow members of the three branches of government to meet and discuss, out of fear of collusion or someone calling it obstruction. Hell, everything is obstruction and collusion these days. Perhaps we can meet with the congressional leaders and at least show a sense of solidarity. But if there are pushbacks along political lines, then all bets are off."

"As we are about four months away from the release of the court's decisions, we have to play a waiting game. I think we need to alert DOJ and the FBI as to our concerns, though," said Fox.

"Agreed. Handle it."

"I don't know about you, but I'm not sure where the upcoming court decisions will take us," said House Speaker John Fishel as he and Senator Majority Leader Bob French shared a coffee in the Speaker's office. "We're going to get called on the carpet no matter what."

"My colleagues share the same concerns," offered French. "We only know bits and pieces, based on what was advanced by petition, so wherever that goes is anyone's guess. And some of that language in the petitions is so vague we don't know what to think about it. I've been hounded by my own sources for protection against whatever, and I presume you are too, so here we are trying to placate our friends, donors and even our constituents without much room to wiggle.

"My guess," continued French, "is that the court will have to weigh in on the entirety of the petitions it's reviewing and come up with one decision. I wouldn't want to be in their collective shoes. The lower courts have pushed all of this up the ladder, and yes, this promises to be a quagmire. The fact some petitions contradict others is a mess."

"Have you received any strong-armed pushbacks from anyone in the senate?"

"Yes, and there isn't much I can say, as this is not a congressional decision. You?"

"Same. There have been some very interested people who have pushed for us to step in, and all I've said is this is in the hands of the court and well beyond anything we can say or do."

"Have you talked with the president?"

"No, other than what Fox told us early on. McCade doesn't want to muddy the waters any more than we do, and Fox related that McCade's reflections about collusion and obstruction are well founded."

"Should we inquire or just stay on the sidelines?"

"I'm of the opinion that we need to stay on the sidelines, unless the president feels it necessary to have a joint meeting."

"At least we all appear to be on the same page on this one."

"That's right; it is beyond politics and ideology."

The clock was ticking, and four months would seem like a long time.

CHAPTER 63

The Court of Public Opinion

Polls, like the weather, change with the winds. Any survey can be manipulated by the questions asked, and if there is an ulterior motive to reach a conclusion, people use their own analysis to be enlightened.

The right-to-know question was the main topic, surrounded by the usual what-ifs, who do you trust, even who should be punished and how do you rewrite history. While the facts of the right-to-know case were out there for the public to rummage through, the skeptics played their fair comment and privilege cards. The public was all for a game and the pundits were all too willing to put their own spin on their surveys.

For all of the players who wanted to have their say, public opinion played a role. The polls analyzed convictions of people from all walks of life. Results varied and were dissected. Whereas one poll, written to be antagonizing, asked respondents "should all secrets be revealed?" and received a sixty-eight percent "no" response, another poll's "no" responses were close to fifty percent simply because of the way the question was asked.

One thing for sure was that people weren't afraid to share their opinions. The court of public opinion led to even more questions. The biggest question was, when it came to corrections of what had been historical facts, would people be accepting or rejecting?

So, it was for juries and decisions from lower courts to start the process. In the public's view, all streams of justice should flow evenly. But everyone knows there have been times when the innocent are judged guilty and the guilty are given a pass. And the public remembered those injustices perhaps more than the final outcomes that seemed honest, consistent and fair.

As much as the lower courts had rendered what they thought were decisions based on the law, the final opinion was that of the Supreme Court and its nine justices. Yes, there was precedent to stand on. Yes, the nine were charged with interpreting the Constitution. Yes, the individuals sitting in judgment were human and were bombarded by outside forces, including the public. But how so? Integrity, deciphering what was fair and right, not rewriting history, all were on the line. And the nine who sat in final judgment knew it.

CHAPTER 64

Department of Yikes!

In any household there is chaos, with varying schedules mixed in with chores, leaving precious little time to actually sit down and discuss daily happenings. It was no different in the Bailey/Zach household. With their demanding responsibilities, they made every effort to slink into their protective cocoon whenever possible. While they enjoyed watching some TV or listening to music, they found most comfort in skinny dipping in the indoor pool or simply sitting in the confines of their family room and enjoying a favorite drink and getting caught up.

They loved sharing stories, especially ones that seemed hilarious or simply the result of someone's misguided opinions. While Zach only had heart surgeries and technology to share from his travels, Bailey was in the middle of civilization, as they thought of it. The court weighed in on a multitude of issues and was constantly bombarded by people trying to sway a decision through published and voiced opinions in a number of mediums. That, in and of itself, was a continuing nightmare.

Zach had just returned from another seminar, this one in Toronto. As one of the keynote speakers he was well prepared, but as it was for anyone who has had to fill such a role, it was an exhausting experience. Getting home to friendly confines was his goal. He also remained aware of the stress members of the court had to feel in dealing with legal issues that punctuated American culture. It wasn't a case of "hell to pay," but the heat was on, nonetheless.

"During our phone conversations, you sounded rather stressed," he offered. "I think I know you well enough to know you would never back down from a fight. So, what's going on?"

"I'm ready if there is a fight, but we have some decisions to make," she began. "I'm not so sure the court might be compromised. The odd thing is that it isn't about political ideology. My sense is that we will be stuck in neutral."

"What do you mean neutral?"

"The four of us knew from the get-go that we would be facing opposition from outside sources and I think we were—and continue to be—in it for the long run. Let me give you the thumbnail version. We have seventeen cases that are interlocked from a pro and con aspect. I'm not sure we can separate or collectively agree on everything."

"Is this something discussed behind closed doors, in one of your conferences?"

"Some, but not all. Imagine having seventeen differing opinions and then having nine people deciding what is right or wrong, acceptable or not, weighing in on the block of seventeen. There are good arguments for all briefs that made it to the final round after the lower courts ruled and kicked the can down the road. I love the judicial system, but this is the most bizarre collection of decisions I've ever come across."

"Do you have a legal stand or are you stuck on what you think is right or wrong?"

"For us being on the inside, I think we get it. The question is whether any of those petitioners agree or conflict with one another, perhaps compromising our judgment."

"Compromised in what way?"

"As you can imagine, one person wants a 'yes' the other wants a 'no.' I get the enormity of making a legal decision. I didn't step into this job not realizing someone isn't going to agree with the majority. Hell, there have been times when we've had an 8–1 court and one would have to wonder why one person would be a lone holdout. Times have changed and justices over the years have brought their own interpretations to the court. Sometimes it seems like it is a liberal or conservative view. Pundits and legal scholars have argued that modern-day interpretations weren't what the framers had in mind.

"The Constitution was written by some pretty smart people, who in their day framed a document that has withstood many challenges through interpretation. They even came up with a Bill of Rights, and the country has approved amendments along the way. I'm still awed by all of this and I've been on the court for eighteen years."

"But this one bothers you?"

"Zach, when Ivanhoe sent the first letter and the others that followed, there was an element of skepticism. We've seen them and have been awestruck by their information. I had my doubts at first, but one letter after another, containing valuable information about a variety of questions, all point to what may be a right to know. I have been blown away. I feel like I'm reading a book or watching a movie that is unfolding.

"We've all done our homework, you included, and I think Matt and Spence would offer the same conclusion. I think it would be wise if we met before the final court decision is made and well before it's handed down," Bailey said.

"When is that supposed to be?"

"June, and I have a feeling this will be a split decision. Our meetings have not offered a true yea or nay. There is a perception that the court is neutral along ideological lines thanks to McCade, but I just don't think that matters in this collective case."

"Where to from here?"

"The four of us certainly have maneuvered around these mine fields before and I think our collective minds might give us a good roadmap going forward."

"Want me to call Matt and Spence to see if they can meet us this weekend, since your court plate is full these days?"

"I think we need to do it, not only for our own satisfaction, but to realize what we will be supporting."

"I agree. I'll call them this morning. Should the president and any members of Congress be alerted?"

"I wouldn't go there yet. I'm sure they are as perplexed as we are. Something has to give, and I hope all hell doesn't bust loose and we become the center of attention."

Little did they know how the court would be compromised.

CHAPTER 65

The Hounds Were Howling

Whenever there are two differing opinions and each side is fully entrenched in their belief, the argument can get down to name calling, inuendo, and vile behavior. The United States was built on freedom of speech and due process. Even so, when court decisions were handed down, naysayers were ready to make their comments, and that often resulted in a one-word summary: conspiracy.

The Supreme Court, in all its glory and by its direction derived from the Constitution, was the last bastion for such decisions. Through the power of democracy in a country that was a republic, the decisions handed down stood. No appeal. Maybe another cache of litigation framed with different words would overcome it, but precedent was precedent.

During the past year there had been a spike in the number of petitions to the court, but none were more riveting in the legal arena and the public's eye than the ones now referred to as the right-to-know cases.

There was a lot to win. There was a lot to lose. There have been justices who were referred to as visionaries and still others who had nary a vision. There was no shortage of either.

The hounds were howling. People who were steadfastly sure of their beliefs were glued to their convictions. The decision of the court's nine justices would come soon enough, and aside from the usual pundits who argued for or against, there wasn't a leak to be found from people in the know. The court took a dim view of leaks and those who were close to anyone in that esteemed branch of the government respected that ban. But that didn't stop pretentious people from all walks of life from showing their impatience. The waiting game was one of patience.

Who Let the Dogs Out

The president had his own pack of restless hounds. Congressional leaders were making some semblance of drafting bipartisan legislation, but the usual detractors always tried to change the narrative and focus on the negative. That got media play. It's one thing to wave the flag for all the good that goes on when people listen and come to a reasonable compromise. But it was a negative here and there that got the public's attention.

The president, Fox, and Speaker Fishel were enjoying their morning coffee in the president's study when Secretary of State Gil Butterfield was announced and joined them.

"Gil, thanks for making it," said McCade, offering him a seat on the couch and a cup of coffee. "We've all talked enough about this upcoming right-to-know decision, but what have any of you heard outside of normal circles?"

"Mr. President," offered Butterfield, "I was late because I just talked to one of our operatives in England, and the scuttlebutt is that there would be a danger if what happened to push us into World War II got out."

"How so?" asked the president. "There's always been speculation about what Churchill did or didn't do and what he withheld or conveniently didn't disclose."

"The facts as they are known could be altered if the real truth actually gets out there," Butterfield said. "There would be a distrust with the British government as much as there would be here."

"But we weren't the ones making those decisions," said McCade. "We've privately discussed all of these scenarios and it's anyone's guess as to how the court will decide. Is this just a waiting game or a ticking time bomb?

"And how does this factor into our dealings with the rest of the world, Gil? What about Germany, Asia, allies or not?"

"The Germans don't have much to say, except those who stand to be called out re the oil industry, perhaps medical science," said Butterfield. "The Axis powers of World War II have reinvented themselves as collective good citizens. We all know the United States is the centerpoint of power and influence. Russia and China, relegated to contributing partners in the world's defeat of evil in the Second World War, have become the new adversaries, if you will."

"So, would we be the only country really weakened, or would England feel the heat and the rest of the countries simply trust us less?" asked the president.

Fox was quick to point out that being open about any exposed information about historical facts or untruths would be the safest way to go. "If the court says there is a fundamental right for our people—perhaps the people of the world—to know real facts, then getting out in front of this would allow us to be a part of any establishment or reestablishment of trust in the government."

"Do we know the real facts, at least from what this mysterious person has divulged?" asked McCade. "We are betting on this to be true, but as we well know, the conspiracy theorists will ring our bell no matter what.

"Dang, I hate not having a clue as to what is going on at the court. But we certainly can't compromise what those folks have to do. And I'm not sure we could ask any of them for any insight, for fear of being called obstructionists—though I'm sure none would tell us anything anyway.

"Mr. Speaker, what's your read on Capitol Hill?"

"Like all of you, we've been buttonholed by way too many lobbyists, lawyers and those who think they have something to gain or lose with whatever decision is rendered. And that's from both parties. Perhaps the good thing here is that we have good communication from our friends across the aisle. But how this would play out when the decision comes down the road, I don't know."

McCade drew in a deep breath, looking at his watch to see that he was three minutes away from meeting with the prime minister of Ecuador.

"Gotta go, but I think the next three months are going to be hairy, so I think we better arrange to meet at least once a week to see which direction the storm is coming from."

The Mayflower Hotel

Matt Brumfield had taken a couple of days to meet with Spencer Crockett, traveling down to Washington. Aside from having their trusted security people, they met alone in the presidential suite of the historic Mayflower Hotel.

Crockett was a frequent visitor to the Mayflower, both during his days as a special prosecutor and during his time as part of the Four. "Matt, I'm not sure we can find much more than what Casey and Jenny have found at the FBI. They've put in untold hours and uncovered valuable documents."

"We've all seen the documents and relied on the information we've collected to corroborate what Ivanhoe has given us," said Brumfield. "I get the feeling we are close to some resolution, and it appears it will be left to the court to decide.

"Because there are seventeen bundled cases, the court could decide it could be all or nothing, parts of, exclusions, I don't really know. What my gut tells me is that Bailey is struggling with this, and in deference to her, I have not tried to sway her one way or another. She hasn't intimated where the court is going with this.

"What I do suspect, though, is that the court faces a dilemma because some petitions contradict one another. This isn't about Ivanhoe, but facts as we have known them that may need some scrutiny. All of us, including our separate teams, have corroborated so much that there is bound to be controversy. Can the court justify releasing all? The common thread appears to be FOIA and whether anyone has the right to dig as far as they can. To me, this becomes a department of yikes."

"Where does that leave us?" asked Crockett. "At some point I would think the four of us would be listed in some way. I guess my first concern would be where that would leave Bailey. I'm not so sure someone wouldn't want to know how we came by such information."

"My concern there, Spence, is that Ivanhoe made it quite clear that if any of us, or all of us for that matter, were harmed, threatened, or called out, there would be hell to pay. I'm not sure if I'm scared or glad to be enlightened. After all, Ivanhoe's facts certainly have been borne out by our corroborations. I'm sure there is more in the Archives that is yet to be found and I think others will follow."

"We will be ahead of them," said Crockett. "Now the theorists can bake their own cake with whatever number of layers. I know Casey and Jenny have put their extra time into this and when they found the Hoover file memo, that cinched it for them. They were like two racehorses ramping it up to get to the finish line. They are as sharp as they come, and it has been a true delight to have them on my team."

"I share your enthusiasm for the work of our teams," said Brumfield, beaming. "They have done a remarkable job. So where does that leave us? The court could simply deny the right to know. Is it all or nothing? And we all know there is no appeal."

"Bailey has to be busy with all of the cases before the court," surmised Crockett. "Zach suggested we need at least one more meeting before we slide down snowy mountain."

"Good idea," said Brumfield with a smile. "Should we call her now to see what works?"

"Why not now?"

The cell phone buzzed in Bailey Stewart's car. Seeing the number ID, Bailey punched the accept button, listened to the caller, and merely said, 'Yes, I agree.'

CHAPTER 66

The Final Four

The Longfellows felt honored to be members of the Army Navy Country Club, which had all the amenities, including three golf courses, thirty-two tennis courts, and six swimming pools. The dining facilities were top notch.

In what probably was the last meeting of the Four before the court decision was reached, they sat comfortably in exquisite leather chairs in front of a fireplace, sipping their drinks of choice. Away from unwelcome ears, they spoke as if they were all alone.

This had been a well-planned and memorable consortium. They all knew each other from different circles, but when it came to combining skills, logical thinking, and a quest to find a reasonable conclusion, this foursome was ready to wrap it up.

After the usual clinking of the glasses and "cheers" around, Brumfield sipped his martini with two olives. Ever the teacher, he started the conversation after the brief pleasantries and small talk.

"I guess this does it before your court makes a decision," he said, with a nod toward Bailey. "Spence and I met the other day and thought we had not necessarily exhausted our team efforts to support what Ivanhoe has offered, but certainly had stirred the pot that has led to petitions to your court for review."

"I'm not sure if we created a porcupine or if this is something we simply needed to see through," she said. "We have all seen what Ivanhoe has proffered, but through our collective team effort, we have found some startling coincidences and corroboration. With every letter I was more amazed that one person has been privy to all of these facts, but like Ivanhoe said, it was a perfect storm. Someone lucked into it and saved it for posterity."

"We all realize that the inner sanctum of the court is a state of secrecy, but do you have anything you can share, if only for the four of us, that would give us an inkling of what is going to happen with all of this?"

"I wish I could, Spence, but I can't," she stated. "The discussions continue, and I really do not know what the others are thinking. The media, the pundits, the conspiracy theorists have all gained attention through their print and electronic means.

"When this is out in the open, someone will be asking questions, and I, for one, do not want to be the center of attention."

"Have we done our job, pursued what we felt was a logical avenue as Ivanhoe suggested we do?" asked Brumfield.

"Believe me, Matt, I have racked my brain trying to figure out who Ivanhoe is," she said.

Brumfield said, "From what I have read of these letters, Ivanhoe simply wants others to know, and to pass such information on, as a way to make sure that collection of facts doesn't get lost. There certainly will be some whose reputations and more would be in jeopardy if the real facts are released. And I daresay the public is always clamoring for more, even if it's just conjecture. In today's culture and through the use of technology, one person's facts won't necessarily match with another's narrative, truth be damned.

"As Spence and I were discussing the other day, Ivanhoe made it quite clear that if anything happened to any of us, the release of that information may well do more than Wikileaks did."

"So, are we good to stay silent until the final court decision?" asked Crockett.

"At this point I would say yes. We could review our notes to see if we missed anything, but I think the four of us, and our teams, have covered all we need, up to this point," she said. "How's this for an oxymoron? The next two short months will seem like a long time."

The Four retired to dinner in an elevated private alcove, overlooking the grandness of the soft-lighted terrace. The conversation turned away from the serious to what was going on in each other's worlds. Laughter abounding, this final meeting of the Four was memorable.

CHAPTER 67

Justice Stewart Stands at the Crossroads

Like anyone else who experienced encountering a fork in the road, Bailey Stewart had reached a crossroads. She felt the pangs of the dilemma and would have to balance personal and professional decisions and hope that her well-thought-out analysis would not lead to any regrets.

She was sitting in her comfortable easy chair reviewing the Ivanhoe letters that numbered fifteen and covered more than forty-five single-spaced sheets of paper. If nothing else, she thought, Ivanhoe wasn't afraid to take the time to pass on valuable information on a wide range of subjects. Aside from the fact these were more than casual conversations in letter form, they dealt with subjects that harbored some prime time in American and world history. You bet she was interested.

So, engrossed in her reading, she didn't notice Zach standing in the doorway with their favorite wines in hand.

"Why so serious?" he asked, walking into the study and handing her a glass of wine before making himself comfortable on the small sofa. "I presume this has to do with Ivanhoe or at least something to do with the court."

"Little of both," she said with a sigh. "You and I certainly have talked about all of this, but it's coming to some sort of conclusion, and I have to admit I'm perplexed."

"You, perplexed? I find that hard to believe. You have always been a quick study, shown a knack for being fair and consistent, and, I might add, been right almost every time when you've been called on to make a decision. I cannot imagine how tough it is to be a judge, just hearing you evaluate pros and cons.

I certainly have heard your arguments, even with this right-to-know thing with Ivanhoe. Where is this going? Is that what this is all about—that you don't know what to do?"

"My dilemma, if I really have one, deals with a set of facts delivered by an unknown person that seem to bear out fruitful changes to some well-known historical facts, compared to what anyone has to gain by disturbing old bones. I really believe Ivanhoe wants to share. I guess I want to meet Ivanhoe and learn as much as possible, but do I do that as a citizen or as a justice of the Supreme Court of the United States?"

"Does meeting Ivanhoe mean that much and would it make a difference in how you judge what you have come to know? Seems to me that there have been facts given to us in various forms over the decades, and now some of those so-called facts are being called into question."

"That's basically it, Zach. But what if some of those facts turn people against each other, add fuel to the existing distrust in governments, and run economies into a tailspin because of now-known advances in technology? My God, I guess as a human being I would like to know if there really is a cure for cancer. I do think of such cures, and had technology been shared, a lot of people would have survived and saved those who have endured a lot of pain."

"You've discussed this with your colleagues, so how is that going?"

"The battle lines are being drawn, but there is a difference with this subject as it is not based on ideology. And no one has found any research to refer to, so this is monumental. A yes or no could trigger any one of a number of reactions.

"I say we take a dip."

"You're on."

With that they strolled down the hall to their indoor pool, shed their clothes, and jumped in feet first.

CHAPTER 68

Ivanhoe's Last Call—15

The words "Right or Privilege?" appeared in the *Washington Post* classified section, another call to Ivanhoe for perhaps the last time. Time indeed was running out for Justice Bailey Stewart and the rest of her colleagues. She was all too aware of what was going to be perceived either as a fundamental right, born out of two and a half centuries of Constitutional law, or an ongoing line in the sand that only certain people could cross.

In some ways, Bailey Stewart felt Ivanhoe was a kindred spirit, someone who held out for truth, justice, and freedom. Although she was skeptical in the beginning, she had come to like this Ivanhoe person and wondered where they had come from—and if that person was close by. Just as intriguing was whether that person knew her. Part of that was scary, but another part of it was a desire to actually meet and to catch up on everything known or not known in the entire history of the world.

Was there anything else she needed from Ivanhoe before she finalized her own conclusions and let the right-to-know decision be determined? She had talked with Zach, as well as her two court justices and did her own sort of soul searching before making one last grasp at anything from her mysterious source. She had been picked for a reason and she had accepted that call.

Her cryptic line in the newspaper was answered with a three-page response. Seeing her mail included a large envelope on her desk, her anticipation of reading the contents was like opening a package at Christmas.

Dear Justice Stewart:

To believe or not believe? There is no right or wrong here, just what is right and who would believe. I trust you have made up your mind and will follow your gut. I know I followed mine when I contacted you because I studied you as a person and as a jurist. So, to answer the primary question here, yes, there is a right to know—national security excepted. There should be no privilege.

So, as you said way back, state your case. I stand by every word I have offered. Every fact that contradicts something that we have been led to believe needs to be substantiated. I trust you and whoever has been working with you have made the proper inquiries. I have read the litigation that came through the court systems and some of it is simply appalling. My cache of information is verifiable and even the skeptics will have to understand the real truth.

I do not envy you and your job. I do not envy any governmental agency that will have to answer for distortions or perpetuating any hoax. I do not envy any group that was either hired for or acted in its own way to change history. I do not envy those who wrote about or reported on happenings that they knew were farfetched, but did so anyway. I do not envy anyone who profited on withholding information or research that could have prevented world chaos through disease, terrorism, mistreatments—all for the power of wealth and world status.

To wit:

Do we know there has been a true cure for cancer and it has been sequestered for decades? Yes. Do we know who really killed John Kennedy, Martin Luther King, Bobby Kennedy and a multitude of others over the years? Yes. Do we know there is an energy source that would almost eliminate fossil fuels? Yes. Do we know when and where aliens have visited the earth? Yes. There is more. The list is endless.

Do I have something to gain by divulging any of this? No. Do I expect to be found? No. Do I want the world to explode? No. Do I expect those who have perpetuated some of these myths to come forward and own up to it? No. Do I think new technology is the answer to all of our worries? No.

My wish is for you and your colleagues to make all of this information available in some way or fashion. I would guess there will be the dissenters out there who will swarm all over the place and raise doubts. That seems to be the way of the world we live in these days.

Perhaps this will be our last communiqué, given that the court may well set a precedent. I sincerely hope your discussion with your court colleagues gives full measure to what is at stake. I am a good patriot.

With that said, I beg my leave.

IVANHOE

Stewart sighed, considering everything Ivanhoe had just related. It made her ponder yet some more. This was as good a final argument as she could have expected. Thank heavens Zach would return from his trip west in two days.

Her next conversation would be with Chief Justice Walter Gallien.

CHAPTER 69

Stewart Meets with Chief Justice Walter Gallien

It was not uncommon for one of the justices to meet with the chief, or for any mix and match of the nine who were asked to choose a side of preference and write opinions.

Bailey Stewart had asked for a meeting with Chief Justice Gallien, during a break in the usual court day, to spend some valuable time discussing her pertinent views on the right-to-know issue. She was also mindful that the court had many other decisions it needed to make. While many of those edicts were handed out throughout the court's term, it was the end of the term that most people waited for, as the sticky issues lingered.

Now sitting in the chief's nicely appointed office, the two were in leather chairs, each with a side table for their coffee. In closed meetings they referred to each other by their first names.

"Walter, we have kicked this right-to-know issue around the block several times and I know our colleagues have bounced in and out of majority and minority groups. I find myself struggling with whether I belong in either."

"How so, Bailey? Of all of us, you have served as the most levelheaded person, always throwing people a lifeline with objective views and a finely tuned sense of compromise. I think our group has relied on your reads. Why the question in your mind now?"

"I shared with you some time ago that I had received information from a person only known as Ivanhoe."

"I remember, and you said you were anxious to see where all of it led."

"It's not like we haven't been busy with all of the regular business of the day," she said. "I've remained involved in all of the other cases and have signed on one way or another. But this bundle of petitions has consumed my attention. I've received sixteen Ivanhoe letters, each detailing much more information than I have been able to share with any of our members, and to be honest, summarizing what Ivanhoe has purported is and has been overwhelming."

"Do you feel confident enough to weigh in on one side or the other?"

"I really do not know, and I don't know if there is a clear-cut majority on either side or if there is a chance the bundle could be split."

"From what I have gathered from the rest of the group, it's up in the air, but someone has to write for the majority or minority, and I don't know yet who that will be."

"What if there isn't a majority or minority ruling?" she asked.

"That has happened, but I think the litigants and the public at large are expecting a yea or nay decision."

"How much time do I have to take a side?"

"Well, we're less than two months before the end of this session. I guess we need to find out where the rest of our colleagues stand to see if there is a possible hiccup."

"I don't want to sound like I'm indecisive, Walter, but I think I know too much about this case—or cases—and that is part of my struggle. Now knowing what I have found out from Ivanhoe, I'm not sure how objective I can be."

"Do you want to share any of this with our colleagues at tomorrow's meeting?"

"The question would be to share what—what I have learned from the Ivanhoe letters and the investigations and research to corroborate? I certainly do not want to poison the well of reason."

"And you think divulging what you know might compromise our efforts?"

"My gut says yes. My mind is on the fence."

"Want to keep this under wraps for now? We can talk about this from time to time as we near a final group decision as to yea or nay."

"I guess that is the best course to follow. It's not like we can push this to a higher court. Time is not going to be an ally because we have other decisions to render and people are going to hound us about this one."

The two nodded, and she was on her way to have a fireside chat with her trusted executive consultant, Alex Hailwood.

CHAPTER 70

The Domino Effect

The "domino effect" phrase became a popular in the 1950s, when analysts believed that geopolitical upheavals throughout the world would set off a chain of similar events, much like falling dominoes. Now used almost daily for any one of a number of scenarios, it certainly has been applied in the financial world, as well as in politics and business.

Given the enormity of FOIA, critics of any one of a number of events, the media, ideologists, and those who have sought to protect themselves or their industries from the loss of structure and power, jeopardy was quickly identified. But was any one person, organization, or industry above it all, protected by a veil of secrecy and immunity?

The right-to-know decision soon to be released by the Supreme Court of the United States might well change the public's trust. The government wasn't on trial, but elements of the government were. The White House and Congress were besieged on an almost-daily basis. The lower courts had made decisions that got pushed upstairs. The court personnel were on the hook to ask for additional information to overrule or sustain all lower court decisions.

As for the media, pundits changed their minds and opinions almost daily. Factual or not, it was good theater. It sold newspapers and glued people to TV sets and social media platforms. The case before, and what was to be decided by, the high court set up a giant domino effect. At odds with some who stood to gain or lose, and who made it a point to get their voices heard by ears that mattered, was that if their industry failed, then the rest of the world, as we know it, might crumble as well. Not known to the general public: what the right-to-know decision was really about.

The people in the government were well aware of the consequences and had to develop plans for the decision, no matter which way it went. The White House continued to deny total knowledge and asked for the media types to wait and see. Members of Congress were getting grilled by their constituents to tell them what the hell was going on. And the rest of the interested parties simply wanted this all to go away. From their collective standpoint, what the public didn't know, wouldn't hurt them.

This was not a game of dominoes with a winner and a loser. This was a game of dominoes where if one domino fell, all the world's dominoes might come tumbling down. A potential catastrophe or a new awakening for not only the citizens of the United States, but the rest of the world as well.

CHAPTER 71

Hear Ye. Hear Ye. Hear Ye.

At precisely ten a.m. each day the Supreme Court of the United States is in session and after the sound of the gavel, those present and able arise and remain standing until the nine robed justices are seated. Then come the familiar and distinct words: *The Honorable, the Chief Justice and the Associate Justices of the Supreme Court of the United States. Oyez! Oyez! Oyez! All persons having business before the Honorable, the Supreme Court of the United States, are admonished to draw near and give their attention, for the Court is now sitting. God save the United States and this Honorable Court!* The words are recited by Johnson Vold, the marshal of the court, whose baritone voice and distinctive cadence has been a part of this ritual for the past twenty-four years.

Oyez descends from the Anglo-Norman oyez, the plural imperative form of oyer, from French ouïr—'to hear.' Thus, oyez means "hear ye" and was used as a call for silence. It would have been common in medieval England and France. Like many symbolic words, phrases, and traditions in the United States, the resonance alone is and was stirring.

This June 17 was judgment day, one some were anticipating while others were dreading. All other cases before the court this term had been decided and announced; there was but one left to be made public. Known only as the right-to-know decision, it covered seventeen cases that had been intertwined and subsequently packaged. The justices knew of the impending cheers and jeers, as the media had hyped this date ad nauseum. Because of the complexity of the decision, the justices had made a point to announce this decision separately from other business. No other distractions, just a decision. A final one.

There are one hundred seventy-five seats in the gallery of the Supreme Court, some usually taken by attending attorneys and perhaps one hundred for the public, some of whom had to stand in line for hours to catch a glimpse of the proceedings. In that there were no oral arguments this day, it was catch-as-catch-can for those who wanted to brave the elements, security checks, and polite pushing and shoving to get into the building. Cameras, cell phones, and recorders were prohibited, so the security checks were thorough.

The nine justices having been seated, Chief Justice Walter Gallien started the proceedings with a serious yet assuring face. He was well liked by his peers and he was a unanimous choice by the senate to serve as chief.

"Ladies and gentlemen, and all citizens of these United States, my colleagues and I have been given the monumental task to render decisions that at times strain our very collective cores. We are bound by a resolute Constitution from the 1780s, and through the years we have seen amendments to the document that have helped us to be more encompassing of our changing times.

"We sit before you today with perhaps the most compelling decision that has confronted this court. This right-to-know decision has been much discussed among us and has drawn interesting views. At this time, I would like to call on each of our members of the bench to relate their discussion points, so those who hear these words will understand the complexities of what we present to everyone today."

With that, Gallien asked each justice to offer their opinions, beginning with his own. The opinions varied in terms of duration, but with one justice left to be heard, the final declaration came down to Justice Bailey Stewart, and the vote was tied at four.

"Thank you, Chief Gallien,'" she began. "Like the rest of my colleagues, I struggled with the pros and cons of this petition that became a bundle of petitions. We walked ourselves through every petition and gave credence to the merits of each. There were reasonable arguments on both sides, and while we never are asked to write any laws, just interpret them, I feel confident in what are the requirements of this body.

"While I have personal feelings about this bundle and all of its elements, I admit that I have been privy to some underlying documents and investigations. I considered such additional information and factual notations that may have prejudiced my opinions, which is contrary to my sworn duty to be a keeper of the sanctity of the Constitution.

"It is my decision to recuse myself, Mr. Chief Justice."

With her final word, the room was silent for a few moments. That silence was broken by Gallien, who knew her stance and accepted the outcome without further conversation among the justices. "In that we do not present a majority, the decisions of the lower courts on each of the individual cases stands."

The stunned audience seemed bewildered. Gallien waited and then offered, "Seeing no other matters before this court, we stand adjourned." The gavel rapped the bench and many in attendance simply gulped.

The marshal of the court then announced, "All rise." The justices stood and left the bench. Then the gallery departed with hushed tones.

Outside, a bevy of electronic and print media personnel had encircled the prestigious court building, and reporters were clamoring for comments. The noise level increased and the circus was in town. The public that was held back behind barriers, far from the building's entrance, was outspoken as was predicted. The non-decision simply continued the uncertainty and would leave the pundits to make up their own scenarios.

As a member of the gallery, chief of staff Jim Fox was just as befuddled as everyone else. His first call was to the president, who was sitting in his office with Speaker Fishel and Senate Majority Leader French. The words "What?" and "You have got to be kidding!" couldn't come out fast enough.

"Where does that leave us now?" continued McCade. "Jim, get back here immediately. We're going to have to plan a strategy."

Executive Conference Room, Second Floor, Supreme Court Building

The nine justices sat in their conference room, fully aware they had kicked the can down the road to nowhere. They were all aware in advance that their differences of opinion were slight and the scale could have tipped either way at any time. They also knew Stewart remained on the proverbial fence and that she had not signed on for or against, making the majority and minority even, unless someone else changed their minds at the last minute. There was a solemnness to their sitting in their conference room, knowing full well there were going to more questions and fewer answers in short order.

There were many instances when the court refuses to render a decision that supersedes a lower court's order, either by the high court's pass or a deadlock with the panel of nine. But few, if anyone, saw this coming. There had been an electric feeling in the air, a for or against to be debated. Now there was nothing. The decision of the highest court of appeals for each case would stand. So chaos reigned.

"I think I speak for you all, that this was a difficult and no-win decision," said Gallien. "This was not an ordinary case where one argument tipped the scales. I am not sure where this goes other than more litigation and a return to our doorstep sometime soon. I'm also not sure there is any additional information that would help us see all of this differently. Perhaps our minds might change as time passes. Bailey, maybe you want to give us some of your thoughts?"

"I realize we've all put in a lot of time during this term to discuss what we feel is a fair and just position," she began. "This case, or the bundle as we have called it, had enough twists and turns to test my mettle. We have shared our personal feelings and relied on our interpretations to lead us through this maze. But although I have shared with some of you certain inside information, I haven't said everything, out of fear of compromising the basic question—the right to know. I struggle with that very concept.

"My perception of that right was challenged by what I was given in the Ivanhoe letters. Why this Ivanhoe person picked me remains a mystery—at least to me. What has been purported in those letters has shaken me to the core, because our very framework of due process begs for facts, corroborated and argued before those sitting in judgment.

"That is what we are here for, and while I lead the challenge to know, I also respect the reasoning for those who don't want to know, or even those who find it too damaging to make it revisionist history.

"I also think we realize this is not about delving into national security or political ideologies or what anyone said. I have been of a mind and still feel that Ivanhoe is speaking the truth about these facts presented. Being privy to all of those thoughts I think drove me to recuse myself. Do those facts deserve to be thrown into the court of public opinion? Maybe that was what we were to decide. I'm am not trying to be a fence sitter, but I do offer an apology to my esteemed colleagues, if this has caused any of you, or this honored court, any grief."

Gallien sensed the justices were spent and thanked them for their due diligence. As was their custom at the end of a court term, they would gather for a social time within the next two weeks and before the Fourth of July. They wished each other well, retired to their cloakrooms, and left the court through their private underground garage, away from the media and other onlookers.

CHAPTER 72

And Finally…

As the dawn of the new day started and rays of sunshine splashed against high wispy clouds, Zach was settled in his customary kitchen nook chair, sipping his usual hot chocolate with marshmallows. He rarely missed his morning hot chocolate, even when away from home. If he wasn't sifting through the sports pages, he was surfing the internet for whatever he could find that related to sports. As an early riser, this quiet time suited his pregame atmosphere, as he called it, to the adventures of the day.

He had a serene air of contentment about him as he listened to the morning news that featured a breaking report that a journal had been found, one that exposed a bevy of government secrets. As the newscaster excitedly related,

> *"The journal, if substantiated, would bring many mysteries and unfinished theories out into the open. It is unknown at this time where the journal came from or who has been involved in seeing that these so-called secrets were revealed. The White House, Congress, the Department of Justice, the FBI, the NSA, even the CIA, have a proprietary interest in the dissemination of any of the journal's contents. So, it's safe to say everyone is looking at one another with a skeptical eye. To say who's in charge also raises an interesting question, as excerpts of the journal have been conveniently leaked to each entity. Suffice to say, there won't be enough pointing fingers to go around.*

"At this time, saying 'stay tuned' is a mild understatement. We will follow this story with great interest as the players become more defined."

Being a Saturday meant Annette, the family cook for the better part of twenty years, had the weekend off. It also meant a casual day for the Longfellows.

As the six o'clock chime rang on the grandfather clock, Bailey wandered into the kitchen and reached for the coffee pot that Zach had turned on some time ago. Earlier he had slipped out to Baxter's Donut House to make some selections for the two of them to enjoy.

Ever the curious one, Bailey followed her "Good morning" with "What was that I heard on the news?"

"They were talking about the journal that was surprisingly found, but happily they left your name out of it. I would expect someone will be asking some pointed questions sometime soon."

He was talking over his sports page and lowered it as she walked further into the room.

"I'm not sure how we can evade the gazillion questions that will be asked," she said, sipping her coffee and taking a bite out of her chocolate donut, her favorite. She would have a second one, too. "I'm still curious as to how this all came about, like why me, why us, why now?"

Zach again lowered his page and looked at her again. "Stuff like this has to come out at some time, don't you think?"

"Perhaps some, but going back a thousand, two thousand, or three thousand or more years is a tad farfetched, isn't it?"

"Someone had a story to tell or felt that others had the same interests in finding out what really happened at some point in history. We have more of an interest in the recent stuff than going back to when the Vikings traveled up Hudson Bay and through the back waters of Lake Superior and Michigan's Upper Peninsula. The Great Lakes, especially Superior, produced vast amounts of copper and iron that were mined and taken away. Whether the Polynesians and Minoans settled in South America and Mexico has been debated over time. And the Greeks saved a vast amount of material from the Library of Alexandria before it was burned to the ground. All this well before Columbus. Talk about hand-me-downs. Columbus was the beneficiary of the struggles and efforts of others.

"My question is why would the government, our own government, hide some of these precious artifacts from us?"

The daylight brightened the sky. Bailey glanced out the windows and saw the sunlight work its way through the trees that ringed the pond. Her mind clicked. He knew. He knew. She had solved the puzzle.

She looked back at Zach with a Cheshire smile, gently lowered his newspaper, and said, “Hello, Ivanhoe!”

Fade Out....

About The Author

Aside from his successes in Major League Baseball and the communications industry, **Ed Munson** has maintained his love as a free-lance writer, including a movie screenplay, "treatments" for 30 would-be novels (*The Letter*, *No Man's Land*, *On Target*, *Threshold*, *Full Count*, *Last Chance*, *The Fountain of Youth*, *The Antique Collector*, *The Wish*, *Crossroads*, *K 23*, *The Link*, *Crossbow*, *The Crystal*, *The Whippoorwill Project*, *The Compass*, *Command Decision*, *Countermeasures*, *The Big Casino*, *The Domino Effect*, *A Game of Inches*, *Instincts*, *Enough*, *The Kilgore Manifesto*, *The Code Breaker*; *The Topaz Crystal*, *Heaven on Earth*, *The Poseidon Triangle*, *Silenced* and *The Equations*) and various essays, poems, 'words of wisdom', newsletters, brochures, media releases, features, magazine and event program features as well as scripts.

His MLB career includes serving as an Official Scorer for the past 42 seasons for games in Anaheim and Los Angeles. His communications exploits have included serving as board chairman and president of companies, organizations and clubs as well as an executive producer for events and programs. Athletically he lettered in football, basketball, baseball and track in his younger days. He also earned his Eagle Scout badge at age 13.

Cover Design By: Joe Felipe